He felt his heart begin to race, even as he reached for her

She didn't resist as he took her into his arms. His lips touched hers, gently at first. So gently that he felt both unsatisfied and tantalized by the sweet and seductive taste of Holly. With a soft moan of frustration, he pulled her closer. Tightly against him. Deepened the kiss. Waited for her to resist, to pull away, tell him to get lost.

But she didn't. Instead, he heard a soft sound of surrender and need as she pressed herself against him.

His tongue delved into her mouth, tasting her. Wanting to taste her more, all over.

Gabe pressed against her, felt her respond by a low moan that made him even crazier. She didn't pull away and didn't seem to want to.

Did that mean she desired him as much as he desired her?

Dear Harlequin Intrigue Reader,

We've got what you need to start the holiday season with a *bang*. Starting things off is RITA® Award-winning author Gayle Wilson. Gayle returns to Harlequin Intrigue with a spin-off of her hugely popular MEN OF MYSTERY series. Same sexy heroes, same drama and danger...but with a new name! Look for *Rafe Sinclair's Revenge* under the PHOENIX BROTHERHOOD banner.

You can return to the royal kingdom of Vashmira in *Royal Ransom* by Susan Kearney, which is the second book in her trilogy THE CROWN AFFAIR. This time an American goes undercover to protect the princess. But will his heart be exposed in the process?

B.J. Daniels takes you to Montana to encounter one very tough lady who's about to meet her match in a mate. Only thing...can he avoid the deadly fate of her previous beaux? Find out in *Premeditated Marriage*.

Winding up the complete package, we have a dramatic story about a widow and her child who become targets of a killer, and only the top cop can keep them out of harm's way. Linda O. Johnston pens an emotionally charged story of crime and compassion in *Tommy's Mom*.

Make sure you pick up all four, and please let us know what you think of our brand of breathtaking romantic suspense.

Enjoy!

Sincerely,

Denise O'Sullivan
Associate Senior Editor
Harlequin Intrigue

TOMMY'S MOM
LINDA O. JOHNSTON

HARLEQUIN®

TORONTO • NEW YORK • LONDON
AMSTERDAM • PARIS • SYDNEY • HAMBURG
STOCKHOLM • ATHENS • TOKYO • MILAN • MADRID
PRAGUE • WARSAW • BUDAPEST • AUCKLAND

ISBN 0-373-22688-8

TOMMY'S MOM

ABOUT THE AUTHOR

Linda O. Johnston's first published fiction appeared in *Ellery Queen's Mystery Magazine* and won the Robert L. Fish Memorial Award for Best First Mystery Short Story of the Year. Now, several published short stories and novels later, Linda is recognized for her outstanding work in the romance genre.

A practicing attorney, Linda juggles her busy schedule between mornings of writing briefs, contracts and other legalese, and afternoons of creating memorable tales of paranormal, time travel, mystery, contemporary and romantic suspense. Armed with an undergraduate degree in journalism with an advertising emphasis from Pennsylvania State University, Linda began her versatile writing career running a small newspaper, then working in advertising and public relations, and later obtained her J.D. degree from Duquesne University School of Law in Pittsburgh.

Linda belongs to Sisters in Crime and is actively involved with Romance Writers of America, participating in the Los Angeles, Orange County and western Pennsylvania chapters. She lives near Universal Studios, Hollywood, with her husband, two sons and two cavalier King Charles spaniels.

Books by Linda O. Johnston

HARLEQUIN INTRIGUE
592—ALIAS MOMMY
624—MARRIAGE: CLASSIFIED
655—OPERATION: REUNITED
688—TOMMY'S MOM

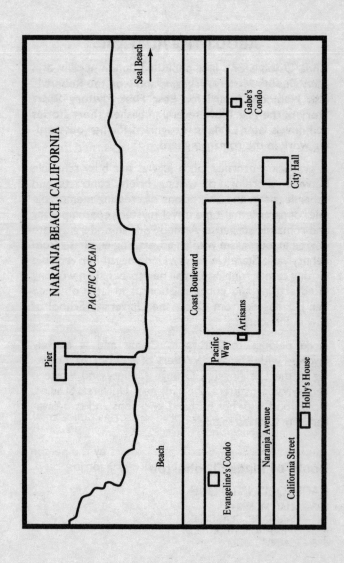

NARANJA BEACH, CALIFORNIA

Seal Beach

PACIFIC OCEAN

Pier

Beach

Gabe's Condo

City Hall

Coast Boulevard

Artisans

Pacific Way

Evangeline's Condo

Naranja Avenue

California Street

Holly's House

CAST OF CHARACTERS

Holly Poston—Daughter of one cop and widow of another, she will do anything to keep her young son safe, while vowing never to get involved with another law enforcement officer.

Gabe McLaren—The newly hired chief of police has a covert reason for taking the job. He learned the hard way that the relatives of all cops should be treated like family.

Tommy Poston—Holly's four-year-old son was in the next room when his daddy was killed. Why won't he speak about what happened?

Thomas Poston—Holly's murdered husband was a good cop...wasn't he?

Al Sharp—Thomas Poston's partner will do whatever it takes to solve his partner's murder, as long as it doesn't harm him.

Edie Bryerly—Holly's best friend and chief baby-sitter.

Mayor Evangeline Sevvers—Her family raised Gabe, and now she wants him to pay them back—maybe even at the expense of his own integrity.

Mal Kensington—Gabe's predecessor as police chief died of an *apparent* heart attack....

Sheldon Sperling—Beaten and robbed by the person who killed Thomas Poston, he is looking for justice.

To Evelyn and Robert Johnston,
in love and gratitude, especially for Fred.

Prologue

The yelling made Tommy Poston look up, but only for a second. He knew big people yelled at each other. His mommy and daddy did sometimes. Mostly they didn't. And they both loved him. They'd told him so.

He was a big boy. That was why Daddy had said he could stay in this room all by himself and sit here at this table and color his pretty pictures.

Tommy liked to use crayons. Bright colors were his favorite. Lots of bright colors. Today, he colored some flowers, red and purple and yellow with great, big, pretty green leaves.

Daddy was still yelling in the next room. So was someone else. How many big people were there yelling? Tommy couldn't tell. He didn't like so much yelling. He picked up an orange crayon and drew a sad face with it. But sad faces shouldn't be with flowers, so he crossed it out. He took a red crayon and tried to make another flower.

Then there was a loud sound like when he dropped something, two loud sounds, and no more yelling. That was better.

Except that after another minute, Tommy didn't like being by himself in here anymore. He didn't hear talking, either. Did Daddy and Mr. Sperling go away? Did they leave him alone?

"Daddy?" Tommy called.

But Daddy didn't answer.

"Daddy?" His lower lip trembling, Tommy pushed his big chair away from the table and jumped down. Just like his mommy taught him, he reached way up high to the table and packed his crayons back into their box. He put them with his papers and other stuff into his pretty red bag and put the bag away.

"Daddy?" he called again. But Daddy didn't come. And Tommy still didn't hear him in the next room.

Daddy didn't say he couldn't come see him, so Tommy went to the door and pulled it open.

Mr. Sperling's shop had lots of shelves and cabinets, tall ones that Tommy couldn't see over, with lots and lots of things on them and in them. Tommy stopped and looked around. He didn't see Daddy or Mr. Sperling. He walked farther into the room.

He didn't want to cry. He was a big boy. But he wanted his daddy or his mommy. "Daddy?" He tried just to whisper, but it came out loud.

He saw a movement and turned toward his daddy. Only it wasn't his daddy. It was a monster! It had come to life!

Its face was great big, green and ugly, with a red tongue, giant teeth and a mean frown. And it came toward him. Its arms were raised and it reached its claws toward Tommy.

"Grrrr!" It was growling at him. "Go away, little boy," it shouted. "Get out of here! Now!"

"Nooo!" Tommy cried out as he ran toward the door of the shop. Only there was a big counter in the way. As he got near it, he tripped. He looked down. And screamed, "Daddy!"

But Daddy was asleep. There was bright red all over him. Blood, like when Tommy fell down and cut his knee.

And the monster came closer.

"I said get out of here, little boy. And if you ever talk, if you ever tell anyone what you saw, I'll come and get you."

Gasping to breathe, Tommy ran around Daddy and toward the glass front door. It was a big door. A heavy door. But he pushed and pushed. And then he got it open.

Tommy ran outside and down the sidewalk, screaming and crying and very, very scared.

Chapter One

"Oh, Holly, you poor thing. I want you to know, the whole town is nearly as devastated as you about Thomas's death." Evangeline Sevvers breezed into the funeral parlor's small anteroom off the front of the chapel.

Evangeline would be aware of what the whole town felt, Holly Poston thought wryly. In addition to owning a boutique down the pedestrian mall from Sheldon Sperling's arts and crafts gallery, she was mayor of Naranja Beach, California.

Holly had been waiting in the small room for the memorial service for her husband to begin. Sad, numb, scared—those were emotions she applied to herself for the loss of Thomas and the turmoil from the circumstances surrounding his death.

Devastated…not really. Not yet, at least.

She glanced down toward her son Tommy, at her feet. He looked at Evangeline, but quickly resumed playing with a toy car on the floor.

His hair, as dark a brown as Holly's, had been neatly parted and combed to the side a few minutes ago, but now it was mussed. She would undoubtedly have to brush dirt off his black dress pants, maybe off his white shirt, too, but Holly was thankful that Tommy was acting like a normal child...almost.

He hadn't said a word for the past four days.

"Wait until you see how many people are here to pay their respects to Thomas." Evangeline's enthusiasm sparkled in her eyes.

"That's great," Holly replied, a lot less excited.

Evangeline, ever the politician, would be pleased for a throng anyplace she happened to be. Evangeline was also a good friend. A consummate professional woman, she almost always wore a suit—at least while not in costume, for she was a driving force and starring actress at the Naranja Community Theater. Today, she wore a tailored deep cranberry suit that should have clashed with the dyed shade of her red hair but somehow didn't.

"You'll see for yourself soon," Evangeline continued. "Right now, though, I want to introduce you to someone."

Oh, lord, Holly thought. Not yet. She'd brought Tommy here early, before anyone else arrived, to protect him from the polite verbal poking and prodding of other mourners. And the not-so-polite intrusion of the media. As a result, she had avoided them, too. She would have to face them eventually. Probably soon. But she had to prepare herself.

Before she could object, a man entered the room behind Evangeline.

"Holly, this is the new police chief of Naranja Beach, Gabe McLaren. Gabe told me he hadn't met you yet."

No wonder Evangeline wanted to introduce them personally, Holly thought, as a very tall man entered behind the mayor, practically filling the small room by himself. He was a relative of Evangeline's, or so Holly had heard.

Chief McLaren wore a navy blue suit and a conservative tie. Could his shoulders and chest be as vast as indicated by his clothing, or had he worn body armor to a funeral?

He had a wide forehead, and his thick brown hair was cut short in a military style, parted on the side and combed off his face. His jaw was an expanse of steel, his mouth an earnest line beneath a strong and even nose.

"I'm sorry about your loss, Mrs. Poston," he said, holding out his hand.

I should say the same to you, Holly's thoughts rang sardonically. She knew from long and sorry experience that cops only cared about other cops, and their duty.

This man had lost one of his officers in a crime still unsolved. He was in charge of a police force with a blemish on its record, at least so far—an unenviable position for a police chief.

She accepted his proffered handshake and said, "Thank you." She knew she wasn't being fair. Sometimes crimes were solved quickly, sometimes they took a while. But a cop had been downed. The Naranja Beach Police Department wouldn't rest until they knew exactly what had happened that misty morning in Sheldon Sperling's shop.

And if, along the way, they learned who beat Sheldon unconscious and traumatized her small son so much that he wouldn't speak, that would be an added benefit to them.

To her, it was a prerequisite for getting on with her life.

Chief McLaren was still holding her hand. She wanted to pull it away but found this stranger's grip oddly comforting.

Never mind that what she knew about him wasn't favorable. She had heard Thomas and his partner Al Sharp discuss the new chief hired three months ago after the sudden death of the former chief, Mal Kensington, from an unexpected heart attack. Nepotism, Thomas and Al had complained, since McLaren was a distant relation of the mayor's. Sure, he had police administration experience, but he was too young to be seasoned. He had an attitude, made it clear he would run things his own way, never mind that things had run just fine under old Mal Kensington.

Chief McLaren continued to grip her hand, and his green eyes, beneath thick, unruly brows, bored into hers.

"Mrs. Poston," he said, "I want you to know—"

"Hi, Tommy, my lad. And Holly. Chief McLaren, Mayor Sevvers... May I come in?"

Holly moved so she could see the anteroom's doorway. Sheldon Sperling stood there.

Sheldon was one of Holly's oldest friends. The pallor of his face nearly matched the whiteness of the sling he wore to support his right arm. He was only sixty-one years old, but the wrinkles around his eyes and the hollows in his soft cheeks had deepened over the past four days, making him appear a decade or more older. He had gone through a lot, poor man.

"Sure, come in, Sheldon," Holly said uncertainly. She wasn't sure where he would fit.

"I'll talk to you later, Mrs. Poston," Chief McLaren told her, releasing her hand. It felt suddenly empty.

Watch it! she admonished herself. She wasn't going to be one of those widows who clutched at anyone and anything to avoid feeling alone. And certainly not a stranger.

"I'll go with you, Gabe," Evangeline said. "See you in a bit, Holly."

As they left, Sheldon squeezed by them into the anteroom. He moved slowly, easing himself down on an upholstered chair facing the floral print sofa where Holly sat. He looked gaunt in his black suit.

She hadn't much black in her own wardrobe, but she had put on the next best thing: a short charcoal skirt with a lace-trimmed blouse several shades lighter. She'd had to belt the outfit tightly at the waist. She had lost weight in the past few days. She hadn't been able to eat.

"How are you feeling now, Sheldon?" Holly asked softly.

"Much better. The headaches are almost gone, and I can move my wrist a little now. And you? How are you two getting along?"

Terribly! Holly wanted to shout, but of course she couldn't. Not with Tommy there. "Tommy has been a very good, very brave boy," she said. "And he has been a real comfort to me."

At least that wasn't a lie. She wasn't sure what she would have done without her son to keep her going. For despite all that had happened between Thomas and her, all the anger and bitterness and even indifference, she had never anticipated—had refused to anticipate, despite his being a cop—that she would finally lose him this way.

And that it would hurt so much.

"I'm sure Tommy has been a big help," Sheldon agreed. "He certainly helped me."

Holly shot a warning look toward Sheldon. She didn't want to remind Tommy of that terrible morning any more than she had to, not right now.

Holly wasn't sure how much Tommy had seen, and that frightened her even more. He hadn't told her. He had been taken to the hospital that morning and examined, then released. Physically, he was fine. But after consulting with a child psychologist, she hadn't allowed the police to interrogate him. Not yet. She had, however, permitted her husband's partner Al, whom Tommy knew, to visit while off duty and ask a few simple questions. Tommy hadn't answered.

Soon she would do everything necessary to get him to talk about what happened, for only then would her small son begin to heal. But for now, they had to get through Thomas's funeral.

Sheldon nodded his understanding, just as the door opened once more. It was Evangeline. "I hate to bother you again, Holly, but there are so many people here who want to express condolences in person. I know it's usually done after the service, but would you mind coming out for a little while?" Evangeline was engaging in her primary role in life: organizing, making certain things ran smoothly.

Holly hesitated. Maybe it would be better to get it over with. Yet if she greeted them now... She glanced down at Tommy.

Evangeline obviously got the message. "Do you know what?" she said brightly. "Edie's out here, and she really wants to go for a walk. Do you think Tommy might want to keep her company? She doesn't want to go by herself."

"What do you think, Tommy?" Holly asked. "Can Aunt Edie take you for a walk?"

Edie Bryerly was Holly's closest friend. A couple of years younger than Holly, she was the ultimate bohemian in this seaside town full of individualists, notwithstanding her mundane job at City Hall as a secretary in the Planning Department. She often baby-sat for Tommy.

Tommy turned on the floor and looked toward Holly, small brow furrowed as if he considered this request carefully—the fear caused by his terrible experience obviously outweighing everything else, even his love for Edie. When her son finally rose, Holly had her answer.

Evangeline ducked out of the small room, and in a minute Edie came in. She was very tall and very curvaceous. Today, she was clad conservatively, for her, in a leotard top and abbreviated green skirt. Though the short pixie style of her platinum hair emphasized that her nose was too large for the rest of her features, it somehow made her appear stunning.

"I hear I've got some good company in here ready to come for a walk with me," Edie said. "Is it…Mr. Sperling?"

Tommy shook his head in the negative.

"Is it…Mommy?"

Again her son shook his head, and Holly smiled.

"Well, then, it must be Tommy!"

This time he nodded and smiled. But he still didn't speak.

It'll come in time, Holly told herself. She hoped.

"Please keep him in the garden," she told Edie. The funeral home had a secluded garden for the family of the bereaved. Their privacy was maintained by high, thick hedges. No one would bother them there.

After Edie and Tommy went through the exit into the garden, Evangeline, at the doorway to the chapel, motioned to Holly.

She felt a hand on her shoulder. "You don't have to do this just because Evangeline told you to," Sheldon whispered into her ear. "It's not normal protocol. People will understand." He probably hadn't spoken aloud out of fear he'd be royally reprimanded by Her Honor, the Mayor.

But he had managed to contradict her nonetheless, and Holly smiled at him fondly. "It's okay. I'll be fine. But thanks." She felt the warmth and comfort of having friends around in this very difficult time. She appreciated them all. A lot.

Thomas's parents had died years ago in a car accident. Her own family hadn't come to the funeral. They lived a thousand miles away in Chicago. Her mother, recuperating from pneumonia, was too ill to travel. Her father had made appropriate noises about needing to stay home to take care of his ailing wife. Holly knew better. What her mother said—and didn't say—made it clear her father, a long-time detective with the Chicago Police Department, hadn't made time to come. He was on yet another big case. Holly wasn't surprised by his absence, but it still hurt.

Holly figured she should muster her courage, square her shoulders and march into the chapel like a brave trooper. After all, most of the people out there who waited to greet her *were* troopers. Cops. As Thomas had been. As her father was.

But *she* wasn't. Still, letting her overwrought emotions hang out like freshly washed underwear on a towel rack would only embarrass her in the long run. She was expected to take it.

For now, she would do what she could to meet those expectations.

After all, she was the widow of a cop.

"I CAN'T TELL YOU how sorry I am, Holly," said Al Sharp. He was dressed in his blue uniform. Al was about forty years old, and he had an extra chin despite how lean his body remained. His hairline had receded, and what was left was cut into a stubble. He had delivered the news about Thomas's death, for he had been his partner. He had also come to see her the next evening and talk to Tommy.

"I know, Al," she said. She stood at the front of the large, high-ceilinged chapel, near where Thomas's closed casket lay on a bower surrounded by huge flower arrangements. The luscious, vibrant aroma of once-living blossoms whose lives had been cut short to mourn her husband's death wrapped around Holly and choked her. She wondered vaguely if she would ever be able to work in her own garden again.

Behind Al, other cops lined up to pay their respects to her. Lots of cops—men and women. Maybe hundreds, certainly more than the entire Naranja Beach force. Some stood in the chapel's center aisle and others at the sides before the stained glass windows. She recognized a few, but most she didn't. Some were in different uniforms, indicating they had come from other jurisdictions to salute a fallen comrade. Some wore suits, signifying they were detectives, not patrol officers.

No cameras, at least none that she could see. Maybe the reporters who had hounded her since Thomas's death were somehow intimidated by such a large showing of law enforcement, but she doubted it. Wouldn't it instead act as a magnet to them?

She swallowed hard. Could she take this? There were so many people. And despite her resolve to show only courage, she wasn't certain she could continue....

Chief Gabe McLaren joined them. "Mrs. Poston." He took her hand once more and shook it, as if in greeting. But he had shaken her hand before. "May I talk with you for just a second? I need to tell you what I started to say earlier."

She had the impression that what he intended to communicate was private, yet they were in the midst of a flood of people. Shouldn't he wait until later? But he obviously didn't want to delay it.

He was the chief of police. He had been her husband's superior. Courtesy dictated that she not brush him off. And he clearly wasn't about to leave her alone until he'd had his say.

She looked up at him, waiting for him to speak.

"I want you to know something, Mrs. Poston."

"What's that?" She didn't exactly feel comfortable held in his unyielding grip, the subject of his frank stare, but she didn't pull away.

"I've instructed the entire Naranja Beach Police Force

to do two things. First, to find out exactly what happened to Officer Thomas Poston and bring his killer to justice.''

That was no less than what she had expected. Another stanza of the same old song she had heard sung throughout her life, first as the daughter of a police officer, then as the wife of one: cops take care of their own.

He continued, "Second, everyone on the force is your family, and they're to treat you as such. Myself included. Every need of the wife and son of a fallen officer will be taken care of, I promise. Anything you want, anything bothering you, just let me know. House or car repairs, gardening, you name it.''

Sure, Holly had heard that was supposed to happen. Other cops' wives had told her so. The spouses even had a coalition to share mutual concerns. She'd gone to some of their meetings. A bunch were here to show support— including, she'd been told, representatives of a national group for widows of fallen law enforcement officers.

Plus, a collection might be taken up for her. She would want to refuse their check, no matter how kindly it was meant, but she wouldn't because of Tommy. Thomas had left insurance and sales of her artwork would help, so she wouldn't need to get a job at least until Tommy was in school. Still, she wanted to start a college fund for Tommy.

But in her experience, anything more—anything requiring more than a check and an occasional visit from the cops themselves—was just another unsubstantiated urban legend, which was fine with her.

Yet Chief McLaren's gaze was so straightforward that it shouted of sincerity. He meant every word he said. Didn't he? And if so…

She had sudden disquieting visions of cops everywhere, well-meaning but underfoot, not allowing Tommy and her to get on with their lives.

And that, she was certain, would include Chief Gabe McLaren—perhaps the most disquieting of them all.

HE WASN'T her family. He didn't even know her. But to emphasize his words, the show of support he'd offered, Gabe took his place beside Holly Poston in the makeshift receiving line.

He caught her sideways, questioning glance—like, who was he to hang around her?

"I know there're a lot of people here, Mrs. Poston," he said. "They all want to say how sorry they are for your loss. If you don't feel like talking to any of them, you don't have to. I'll thank them for you. Or you can wait till later, after the service. Just let me know. We've already excluded the media from the chapel."

She faced him directly, her expression surprised and, if he read it right, outraged at his audacity. But then it softened. She even managed a small, tight smile. "Thanks, Chief McLaren."

"Call me Gabe," he said. She nodded in acknowledgment.

Sure, it was damned presumptuous for him to stand here with her, but his presence emphasized a message he'd already communicated to his own officers: we're all members of the same family, and families stick together.

Holly Poston appeared exhausted, with dark circles beneath her stunningly doelike brown eyes. She was most definitely a beautiful brunette. Her hair was a shade of brown he'd describe as deepest, darkest chocolate. It was cut unevenly in a becoming style, longer in back, swept away slightly to show her ears, and fringed along her forehead. Her eyebrows were an even darker shade, arched but not plucked thin the way so many women did. Her mouth was full and lush, moist-looking despite the fact she wore no lipstick. Her cheekbones—well, he'd never really noticed cheekbones much, but he noticed hers. They helped to add definition to the oval shape of her face.

All in all, she was a stunningly beautiful lady despite the pain so obvious in her eyes.

Thomas Poston had been a lucky man—until someone had stabbed him to death four days ago.

Poston was the first police officer lost during Gabe's tenure as chief, though he wasn't the only one whose death had been suspicious lately. Gabe hoped Poston would be the last, but he, of all people, knew exactly how dangerous being a cop could be. Even in an area as laid back as Naranja Beach.

He didn't know whether Poston had been murdered because he was a cop, but Gabe sure as hell would find out.

REVEREND MILLER had appeared. It was time for the funeral service to begin.

"Excuse me," Holly said. "I have to get my son." A small sense of relief passed through her at this perfectly logical reason to flee not only the continuing parade of well-wishers but also the presence of this intense and disturbing man.

This man who wasn't merely a cop, but a leader of cops.

Who had made it clear he intended to inflict more cops on her, in the name of helping her.

The kind of help she really needed required that she never again, for the rest of her life, see a policeman.

"Of course," he replied. "I'll come with you."

"That's all right," she said quickly. "I can—" But he took her elbow and began politely bulldozing a path through the crowd toward the door from which she had previously emerged.

She should despise his take-charge attitude. And yet, for

this moment, at least, it felt good to have someone deal with the crowd on her behalf.

She'd been handling ninety percent of the things in her life and Tommy's by herself for quite a while now. There was time enough for her to learn to deal with the other ten percent alone.

But perhaps she should just let Tommy stay outside during the memorial service. She knew Edie would continue to watch him, for her friend was like a second mother to her son. He was so young, after all. The funeral wouldn't bring any closure to someone so unknowledgeable about what it was supposed to mean. And although Holly had checked with the child psychologist and been given the go-ahead, she wondered if it was a good idea to have him here after what he'd gone through.

Still, whatever he experienced here might allow him in the future to deal with his father's death better. Thomas was about to be given a hero's sendoff. That might help little Tommy remember his daddy. Whatever else Thomas had been, he had been a good cop.

Chief Gabe McLaren's vast shoulders appeared to shrink the size of the already small waiting room once more as he led her through it and outside the door to the adjoining garden. There, Edie was pointing to something on a flower. As Holly drew closer, she saw it was a butterfly.

Tommy was laughing, and Holly felt herself smile in response. It was the first laughter she had heard from her son since that awful morning four days earlier. She soaked it in as if *she* was the butterfly, and the sound was the nectar from the loveliest of blossoms.

Edie looked toward her, and their eyes met. "It's time," Holly mouthed. Edie's nod didn't dislodge one hair in her short pixie hairdo, and she stood.

Even as tall as her friend was, she still seemed almost

petite compared with Gabe McLaren. Edie clearly noticed, for she smiled up at the chief from beneath flirtatiously lowered lashes and held out her hand. "Hi," she said, and introduced herself.

"Hi," Chief McLaren said in return. He extracted his hand from Edie's and extended it to Tommy. "I saw you before, but we didn't get a chance to talk. You're Tommy, aren't you? I'm Chief McLaren. Your dad and I worked together."

Tommy's smile faded. He regarded the large man with huge, solemn eyes. He held out his small hand that was dwarfed by Gabe McLaren's much greater one and received the polite handshake in an adult manner that nearly made Holly cry.

Holly couldn't help liking the way Gabe hadn't diminished Thomas in his son's eyes by stating the truth: that his daddy had worked for him.

"It's time to go inside, Tommy," Gabe said. "Is that all right with you?"

Tommy nodded, still not speaking, not even to another man. But of course this man was a stranger. Holly took her son's hand and together they walked toward the chapel. She didn't look to see if anyone followed. She knew Edie would, and most likely Gabe McLaren would, too. Maybe she shouldn't leave the flirtatious Edie behind. She certainly didn't want her best friend to wind up involved with a cop.

What was she thinking? This wasn't a singles bar. Edie and the chief weren't here to make small talk to one another. This was a funeral. Thomas's funeral. And Chief McLaren was probably already married.

Holly felt sorry for his wife…didn't she?

They went through the door from the small waiting room into the chapel. The minister stood at the front of the room at the pulpit overlooking the closed casket and its surrounding garden of aromatic, dying flowers.

Holly took a deep breath as a thick lump formed in her throat. She somehow had to get through this.

The seats right beside the door where they entered were all occupied by police officers. As Tommy and she entered, everyone stood. A sea of uniforms surrounded them.

And suddenly, unexpectedly, Tommy began to scream.

Chapter Two

Holly quickly knelt before her son, held his small, shaking body against hers as he continued to sob and shriek wordlessly. "What is it, honey? Tell Mommy. Please, Tommy, it'll be all right." Her own voice cracked with all the emotions evoked by Tommy's terrified screams. The loud, heart-rending noise resounded in her ear, pulsed through her brain like a siren that was the herald of an indescribable disaster.

But even her tight hug, the attempt to soothe her panicky son with quiet, loving words, didn't calm him.

"What's wrong?" Edie stood beside them, her hand lightly on Tommy's head. Tears filled her wide eyes as she caught Holly's gaze. "What can I do to help?"

Holly didn't know. She noticed Sheldon and Evangeline hovering about, too. Evangeline turned and began talking to Reverend Miller, taking charge of the situation, as usual.

But still Tommy screamed.

"Tommy?" Holly said. "Tommy, please hush, honey. I can't help you while you're crying so loud. I need to understand what's wrong."

She *knew* what was wrong. His daddy was dead. Tommy had probably seen Thomas's bleeding body. There was even the possibility that he had seen his father being murdered, though Al Sharp and the others had reassured Holly it was unlikely. Someone with as little compunction about killing as the fiend who'd stabbed Thomas would probably have had no scruples against killing any eyewitnesses—even one as young as Tommy.

Scant comfort, but Holly had understood its logic. And it had given her hope that whoever it was would not, after the fact, harm her son.

But what had triggered Tommy's agonized reaction now? Had the sight of the coffin upset him so much? Did a four-year-old even understand the significance of a coffin?

"Hey, sport." Gabe McLaren knelt beside them, talking softly despite the likelihood that Tommy could not completely hear him over his own screams. "Know what? You're right. This place sucks. I noticed you were in that garden outside. I liked it, too. And those butterflies? Awesome. Would you like to see if they're still there? I'm not from this area. Are there monarch butterflies around here? They're those pretty, bright-colored ones, oranges and browns and yellows."

That had been the exact right thing to say to distract Tommy, though Holly doubted that Gabe realized it. Her son liked nothing in this world more than colors, the brighter the better.

Tommy's screams subsided into sobs that indicated he was gasping for breath. He seemed near hyperventilation.

"Slowly," Gabe said. He reached over and gently took Tommy from her. He held his shoulders. "I was taught in police school how to breathe when I'm upset."

Holly doubted it, but this wasn't the time to call him on his veracity. Unless maybe he had paramedic training, too. She looked around. No paper bags here. Wasn't that what was needed when a person hyperventilated, to breathe into a bag?

Tommy regarded Gabe with wide, frightened eyes that asked a question.

"Here. Like this." Gabe took an exaggeratedly deep breath, and let it out very slowly. And then another. "You try it."

Tommy coughed, then stilled his panting long enough to studiously inhale, then exhale.

"Hey, that's great! It took me a lot of practice to get it right, and here you're doing it first thing."

Tommy smiled as he breathed the same embellished way once more. His respiration grew more regular.

"Good deal," Gabe said. "Now, are you ready to see if we can find some of those butterflies?"

Tommy gave one decisive nod.

"Do you remember their names, the kind I told you about?"

Again, Tommy nodded.

"And what is it?"

Tommy stopped smiling. He blinked.

He obviously wasn't ready to talk yet.

"You can tell us later, okay?" Holly said.

He nodded and held out his hand. She took it and rose to her feet, then glanced around. Edie still stood beside them. Reverend Miller, on the pulpit, regarded her questioningly, with Evangeline standing beside him. Sheldon had taken a seat nearby.

Holly knew the eyes of all the hundreds of funeral attendees were on Tommy and her. She couldn't exactly take Tommy out into the garden for a lesson in entomology right now. But she couldn't abandon him, either.

Gabe apparently understood her ambivalence. "Tell you what, sport," he said to Tommy. "I think your mom needs to stay in here for now. Grown-up rules and all. But for the moment they don't apply to me, so just you and I will go outside, okay?''

Tommy looked at her, appeal in his gaze. He obviously wanted to go with this man. Speaking of ambivalence— was Holly ready to let her frightened son out of her sight? Especially now?

But he couldn't be in any safer hands than those of the chief of police, could he? And this man, this stranger, had somehow known exactly what to say to calm her son.

''That's a good idea,'' she said, her words stronger than her conviction.

''Great. Come on, Tommy. I guess this isn't a good place for a race, so we can't see who can get out there fastest. Maybe once we're outside we can play a game. Okay?''

Tommy grinned and nodded yet again.

Gabe McLaren had to be married and have a houseful of kids, Holly thought as she watched Tommy tuck one small hand into Gabe's huge one. How else could he know how to deal with a terrified child that way?

And why did the thought of his active marital status send a pang of disappointment through her?

The very large man and the very small child walked hand-in-hand out of the crowded chapel. As they reached the door, she saw Tommy turn back and glance not toward her, but toward the crowd. His sweet face screwed up again as if he was going to cry once more.

Gabe apparently noticed, for in a moment he swept Tommy into his arms as if he were as light as meringue, and they disappeared through the door.

NINE O'CLOCK in the evening was too late to come to the Poston house. Gabe knew it, even as he pulled his blue

Mustang up to the house with the number he'd been searching for. He could see by the streetlight that it was an attractive pale blue stucco home with white trim. As with the rest of the eclectic residential neighborhood a couple of miles inland from the beach, the Poston house resembled none of its neighbors. Gabe had to drive around the block, looking for a parking space.

A few media vans still lurked here on California Street, but their occupants appeared to be packing up. Gabe had designated an information specialist from his department to deal with reporters. She was to act cooperative while saying as little as possible about the Poston case.

He had meant to arrive earlier, but time had gotten away from him after Thomas Poston's funeral. There were several administrative matters he'd had to take care of that day, and the memorial service had messed up his schedule.

More importantly, he'd delved further into the investigation of Poston's murder. Even though the detective in charge was the best, Gabe wasn't happy about the progress so far.

Especially not when it might relate to the undercover matter that brought him here in the first place.

And so, he'd decided to insinuate himself right, smack into the middle of this one. In fact, he was going to work on it here and now. Tonight. Assuming he found a parking space.

Not that he was about to try to twist Tommy Poston's arm. Poor little tiger. He was the closest thing to an eyewitness they had. Gabe didn't completely subscribe to the theory popular around the N.B.P.D. that, if he had witnessed the killing, Tommy would have been dead right alongside his daddy. Maybe it was so. Maybe it wasn't. In any event, Gabe wouldn't risk the boy's life on it. He'd warn Holly Poston not to let Tommy out of her sight unless he was with someone completely trustworthy.

He finally found a parking spot and pulled in. Deciding to leave his holster and 9mm Smith & Wesson in the car, he unlocked the glove compartment and swapped them for a smaller pistol. Carrying a weapon was standard procedure, no matter which police force he'd worked on. Here, because of his undercover investigation, it was imperative. He stuffed the pistol in his pants pocket and put his suit jacket back on, his cell phone in an inside pocket.

His thoughts still swirled as he walked the two blocks along the dimly lighted residential streets to the Postons' house.

Gabe suspected Tommy had seen *something,* even if it wasn't the actual murder. That could be why the kid wasn't talking.

Poor Tommy obviously missed his daddy already. He'd latched onto Gabe in the garden as if he were starved for a man's attention, hanging onto his hand, listening to everything he said, pointing out all the flowers and butterflies and birds.

He hadn't spoken at all. That was another thing Gabe needed to talk to Holly about. He'd learned, from the perfunctory report filed by Al Sharp after visiting the boy, that this silence was probably a result of the trauma of losing his father. It wasn't normal for Tommy Poston. But was Tommy talking to his mother? If so, maybe Gabe could coax him, over time, to describe what he'd seen. Or maybe he'd already told Holly.

Now, Gabe heard the hubbub of voices as he strode up the short, yucca-lined walkway to the Postons' front door. It might not be too late after all. He'd assumed that neighbors and friends would continue to rally around widow and son after the funeral service, bringing food and whatever cheer they could. He just figured most would be gone long before now.

Maybe that had, in fact, factored into his non-decision to come late. If there were too many people around, he wouldn't be able to speak much with Holly about Tommy.

Gabe also wanted to know what he and his officers could do to help her, to make sure her chores got done, repairs made, expenses met—everything her fallen husband had done. Except the most important things, of course—companionship, love, sex…

He scoffed at himself even as he rang the bell. Sure, Holly was one of the most beautiful women he'd ever seen, despite the sorrow that shadowed her face. But to think of sex right now in relation to this poor lady—this lovely, provocative, sensuous lady—who'd just lost the man most important in her life… "Pervert," he whispered aloud to himself.

"Excuse me?" The front door had opened. Holly stood there looking at him. She had changed clothes and now wore brown slacks and a short-sleeved yellow sweater that hugged her slender curves.

He felt his face redden. "Er—Mrs. Poston. Holly. I hope it isn't too late, but I've come to pay my respects."

There was a wry look of amusement on her face. Damn! She must have heard what he'd said. He only prayed she hadn't figured out why. "No, it's not too late. I've still got a lot of visitors. Come in." She stood back to let him walk inside.

Very carefully, he skirted past her. He didn't want to brush her accidentally. He didn't want to touch her at all. She might get the wrong idea. *He* might get the wrong idea.

Of all the women in the world, this one was the farthest

off-limits to him, assuming he even wanted a woman. Which he didn't.

Holly Poston was a new widow. And on top of that, she was the widow of a cop.

Even if she were ready to entertain the idea of a man's company again so soon, which was highly unlikely, that man wouldn't be Gabe. He'd been a rebound lover once. That was one time too many.

He stopped inside the door. The entryway to the two-story home was compact, and it was filled with people. Most women had purses slung over their shoulders.

"You're just in time to say good-night, Chief," said Al Sharp. "We were just leaving."

Good. With this crowd gone, just maybe Gabe would be able to get Holly Poston to himself. For conversation. *Only* for conversation.

"I SHOULD STAY the night," Edie Bryerly insisted. She was at the rear of the group of cops and others filing out from Holly's entryway. "Don't you want some company?"

"No, but thanks for asking. I need to be alone." Holly was exhausted. She doubted she'd sleep, but she was ready to curl up with a cup of herbal tea in front of an old movie on television and just rest.

She'd done that many nights when Thomas had come home late. She was used to it.

"Okay, then. You call me if there's anything you need." Edie's eyes, surrounded by a wide swath of liner and mascara, regarded her sympathetically.

"I will. Thanks."

Holly wondered how Edie could look so stunningly alert and pixielike this late at night, after working her butt off. She had bustled everywhere, helping Holly keep coffee brewing and guests' plates full of the casseroles and desserts people had brought to the get-together at the Poston home that had begun a couple of hours after the memorial.

"We'll get together soon, okay?" Edie persisted. "Tomorrow if you'd like. After work."

"We'll see," Holly said. "In any event, I'll be in touch."

Edie stooped to press their cheeks together, and then she followed the horde outside.

Even though it was a summer evening, this residential area was only two miles from the Pacific Ocean, and the air was cool. Holly shut the door behind the group as soon as she was able.

Was she alone at last? She had put an exhausted Tommy to bed hours ago. Maybe it was finally her turn to relax.

But as she approached the door to her living room, she heard low voices. As she entered, she saw Sheldon engaged in a conversation with Gabe McLaren. They stood in the corner near the front picture window, with its draperies drawn tightly shut for privacy. Their heads were together, and they each held a glass—Sheldon's in the hand of the arm that wasn't in a sling. Both were still dressed in the suits they had worn to Thomas's memorial service. They were so engrossed in what they were saying that neither looked up as she approached.

"Can I get you anything else to eat or drink, gentlemen?" Holly asked brightly. Playing perfect hostess at this hour might give them the hint that they were about to overstay their welcome.

"No thanks, Holly." Sheldon was the first to glance at her. Awkwardly, he moved his glass around so he could look at his watch. "It's late. I'm heading home now."

"All right," Holly said, noting that Gabe didn't echo the sentiment. Instead, he watched her with narrowed eyes.

They were green, weren't they? She couldn't tell in the room's dim light, but she had noticed before.

She walked Sheldon to the front door, hoping that Gabe would follow. To her relief, he did.

To her dismay, he didn't follow Sheldon out.

Inhaling the fresh, ocean-chilled air, she watched Sheldon limp down the front walk. Poor man wasn't recuperating from his injuries very quickly. His age might be a factor. Sixty-one wasn't that old, but he certainly had begun to look and act older this week. Plus, he had a heart condition that he kept under control with medication. She would have to help him every way she could. He had been very kind to her, selling her stitchery creations in his shop, promoting them to tourists....

"Can you spare me a few minutes, Holly?" Gabe asked. He still stood behind her at the door.

She turned, wanting to tell him "no" but assuming he had something to discuss with her. Something about Thomas's death. Why else would he want to talk to her?

Of course she had heard his strange comment as she'd opened the door to let him in: "Pervert." She'd gathered he was chastising himself for some reason. It had struck her as funny, at a time when her sense of humor had gone on an extended vacation. She'd appreciated it.

"All right," she responded. She didn't look at him but regarded the chipped pink nail polish on her right index finger critically. She didn't suggest further refreshments to Gabe. She hoped he wouldn't stay long...didn't she? "Would you like to come back into the living room?" she asked him.

She didn't wait for his reply but headed there. At least she could be comfortable, in this room she had decorated to feel homey, with its thick russet-colored plush carpeting. She took a seat on the fluffy beige sofa, pushing some of the gold and green throw pillows aside. She slid her shoes off and slipped her feet onto the low coffee table. Knowing she was going to have company, she'd removed the small stack of magazines that she kept on it, piling them in the closet. Usually, she rested her feet right on top of the periodicals. Thomas hadn't liked that habit. He'd told her so often.

At first, she'd made an effort to comply. Over time, it hadn't mattered.

Gabe removed his suit jacket and folded it carefully over the back of the reclining leather chair beside the sofa.

Then he sat on that chair. It had been Thomas's chair. Exclusively.

But Thomas wouldn't mind now.

Did she? This man was making himself right at home.

Thomas had worked out a lot. He'd been five-eleven and muscular. But the substantial chair that had once belonged only to him now seemed a lot smaller with Gabe occupying it.

She caught the glint of amusement in Gabe's eyes as he glanced at her bare toes, with their bright red polish, then back up at her face.

So what if she didn't take as much care with her fingernails as she did with her toes? She couldn't reach her toenails as easily to pick off the polish when she was upset or nervous.

But she felt discomfited by Gabe's stare. She curled around so her feet were tucked up under her. "So, Chief McLaren, I gather you have something on your mind," she said. *Besides my toes,* she wanted to add but didn't.

"Gabe," he corrected. "Yes, I do. A few things. First, I know some of my officers have been in touch with you, but I wanted to let you know personally how the investigation into Thomas's death is progressing."

A chill passed through Holly that had nothing to do with this house's proximity to the Pacific, and everything to do with her fear about what Gabe would say…and what he might not say.

"Have you caught his killer?" she asked softly. She doubted it. Al would have told her right away, if he'd known.

Gabe shook his head. There was a grim tightness about his lips that had told her his answer already. In fact, he looked angry. "No," he said. "Not yet. But we will. You can bet on it." He spoke with so much intensity that Holly believed him. He'd get the killer. And soon.

She was uncertain how much she really wanted to hear, but she asked anyway, "Do you know exactly what happened that morning? How Thomas was killed and Sheldon hurt?"

"We've pieced it together, though we're not sure how accurate we are so far. But before I tell you, I have to ask a few questions. I know you've already talked to Al Sharp. Since he was your husband's partner, the guys doing the footwork on the investigation thought that would be easier on you."

She nodded.

"But I'm handling the investigation now. Personally. I want you to know that. And I have some questions that Al wasn't able to answer. Okay?"

He leaned forward. He had unbuttoned the top buttons of his shirt and loosened his dark blue tie. The combination of formal clothing and the casual way he wore it seemed boyishly charming.

And yet there was nothing immature about this man who seemed to take charge, no matter where he was. Even in her living room.

His large hands were clasped between his knees as he

watched her with compassion. She had a feeling that, if she told him she just couldn't talk about it, he would understand.

But there was an intensity in his stare as well. A fervor that told her that if she didn't cooperate, if she couldn't cooperate, he'd simply bulldoze around or through her to get the information that she could most easily impart.

She liked that, somehow. Even if it made her uneasy, she felt that Gabe McLaren's zeal and dedication ensured the fact that someday soon, somehow, this cop would fulfill his duty. They would know exactly who killed Thomas, and why.

And then maybe her son would talk again, once the bad guy was in jail.

"All right," she said. "What would you like to know?" She'd tell him what she could, as long as it wasn't personal. There were a lot of things about Thomas, and about Thomas and her, that were not relevant to the investigation but would hurt her, and Tommy, if people learned about them.

"First of all, what was Thomas doing at Sheldon Sperling's at that hour of the morning? And with little Tommy, too. Thomas was already in uniform, but he wasn't on duty yet."

Holly nodded. She could talk about this. "It was part of our daily routine. I tend to work late and sleep in. Thomas woke early even if he went to bed late. To let me rest, he'd get ready for work and take out Tommy, who's an early bird, too. Sheldon has been a close friend for a long time. He even sells my work. He's an early riser, like Thomas, and they'd often meet at the shop, then either just walk along the beach or the pier, or stop in for breakfast at one of the restaurants on Pacific Way near Sheldon's."

"I see. Then it wasn't unusual for Thomas to be there that early, in uniform, with Tommy?"

"No."

"What's your work, and how does Sheldon sell it?"

Holly blinked and looked at Gabe. He smiled, so winsomely that she couldn't help a tentative grin back.

"I know that doesn't have anything to do with the investigation," he said. "I'm just curious."

"I'm an artist of sorts," she told him. "I create quilts and wall hangings and other pieces out of fabrics—mostly impractical, but intended to be attractive. Fortunately, some people seem to think so. They sell well, mostly to tourists. Sheldon carries most of them in his shop for me, and he gets a percentage of everything he sells."

"I'd like to see your work," Gabe said. He glanced around the living room, but no pieces hung there.

It had been a sore point between Thomas and her—one of many. Thomas had considered what she did frivolous and resented the large amounts of money she made when any of her pieces sold—even though he didn't mind her spending it on things he liked but couldn't afford.

Like his reclining chair.

So as not to provoke additional arguments, Holly kept everything in her private workroom, an extra bedroom upstairs beside Tommy's room.

Now, though, she would be able to display her work in her own home. Enjoy it herself...

She sighed. She could simply have divorced Thomas, if she'd wanted him fully out of her life. But she hadn't, for there really wasn't anything *simple* about it.

Gabe must have misinterpreted her sigh. "I'm sorry. I'm keeping you up late. I can ask most of my questions another time. But as far as the investigation goes, we believe what happened was an armed robbery."

Holly couldn't help asking, "Really? With a uniformed police officer there?"

Gabe shrugged. "It could have been an addict desperate for money for a fix. Or maybe the killer didn't see Thomas until it was too late to back off. We were hoping to get more from Sheldon, but he apparently doesn't remember much. I didn't talk to him for long here so I haven't confirmed it yet, but according to the police report he said that Thomas and he were having a heated little argument about the merits of the Dodgers over the Angels and weren't watching the door. He doesn't recall anything after that, but says he'd put some change into his register to prepare for the day. His cash drawer was empty when the crime scene investigation team checked it."

"I see." Holly looked down at her lap. Poor Sheldon. It had only been four days, and his injuries were still really bothering him.

"Holly, there are things we need to discuss about Tommy."

She looked up with a start. Gabe had risen from the chair and stood beside it now. He looked huge and intimidating.

"What about Tommy?" she asked in a hesitant whisper.

He sat again, this time beside her on the sofa. His presence so near was even more disturbing. She swallowed.

"Al told me he stopped talking after the incident. Before, I gather he was like most four-year-olds I know who babble a blue streak."

"Your own kids?" she blurted, then wondered why she'd said it.

He laughed. "No, I'm not married, never was and never had any kids. But I'm an uncle several times over—sort of. It's a little complicated."

He obviously didn't want her to ask how, so she didn't.

But she felt ridiculously relieved that he appeared to have no closer ties than unclehood.

"Yes," she replied to his question. "Tommy talked a lot until the…incident, as you call it. He hasn't said a word since."

"He hasn't told even *you* what he saw?"

Hoarsely, she said, "No. But Al…I was assured that Tommy couldn't have seen the murder, or someone as horrible as the murderer would have…hurt him, too."

Gabe nodded. "Could be. But it also might *not* be."

Holly stared at him. She had to look up, even though he was sitting beside her, to see into his unflinching eyes.

He was right, of course. But she had wanted so much to believe what Al had said….

"We need to get him to talk," Gabe said, "just in case."

"I agree," Holly replied shakily. "Whatever he did or didn't see, he won't be able to start healing from losing Thomas unless he can talk about it."

And if, incidentally, what Tommy said led to Thomas's killer… No! Despite Holly's inclinations to get involved, to help, that was police business. She, and most particularly her son, would stay out of it. *Far* out of it.

"Also, just in case…" Gabe moved closer to her on the sofa and took her hand. His was warm, and it dwarfed hers. But because of the nature of their conversation, it was anything but comforting. "I'd suggest you keep a close watch on Tommy. Don't leave him with anyone unless you have to, and if you do, make sure it's someone you trust. Without knowing for certain the motive for Thomas's murder and the battery on Sheldon, we can't be sure—"

"You don't really think someone we know did this." Holly made her words a statement, though she knew they were untrue. Her feet were on the floor now, and her back was stiff and straight. She looked toward the closed draperies, and not at the man beside her who, although gentle, did not allow her to pull her hand away. "No one we know is so hard up they'd kill for a few dollars from a cash register. They'd know they could come to us for a loan, and—"

"That's assuming the money wasn't just taken to make us think robbery was the motive."

"Oh."

Gabe squeezed her hand. "I'm sorry, Holly. For everything."

He really sounded sorry, though he had done nothing to cause any of her pain. She appreciated that. She appreciated how kind this man seemed to be, and how he had been so disclosing about the investigation, despite not knowing much yet.

So gentle in warning her to protect her son.

"We'll catch the murderer," he continued. "But in the meantime…"

His voice trailed off, and she looked at him.

He was watching her. She felt unnerved. She wanted to rise and recapture her hand and tell him it was time to leave.

But she didn't.

"In the meantime?" she asked, her voice low and hoarse. She watched his face. It was a strong and masculine face. Angular in all the right places, and very handsome.

Very intense. Too intense. Too sexy. But still she didn't look away.

"In the meantime," he said softly, his gaze unwavering, "I want you to tell me anything you need. Anything."

He blinked then, obviously hearing what he had said and realizing how suggestively it could be interpreted.

He released her hand and cleared his throat. He stood and looked over her shoulder, not directly at her. ''What I mean,'' he said, ''is what I told you before. I've directed everyone on the force to make sure you're treated like a member of the family. You just tell one of us whatever you need. Like I said earlier, chores, repairs, we'll do them. I promise.''

''Thank you,'' she said, not even attempting to repress the giggle in her voice now that the intensity of the moment had ended. That had undoubtedly been all he had meant all along. She had just read him wrong, hadn't she?

She considered saying something light and teasing, to ease them over the moment. But before she could, she saw a movement out of the corner of her eye.

Tommy stood silently at the door to the living room, watching them. Tears were running down his face.

Chapter Three

"Hey, sport." Gabe's heart went out to the quietly crying child. "Did you have a bad dream?"

He nodded solemnly, one small hand clenched into a fist at his side and the other rubbing his eyes. He wore a baggy yellow pajama top and matching shorts that revealed his thin legs. His feet were bare.

"Oh, Tommy." Holly headed across the room toward her son. She lifted him into her arms, nuzzling him.

For an instant, Gabe envied the little boy.

He joined them by the door and looked down at Tommy, who'd laid his head on his mother's shoulder. There was a vague clean scent around him, like baby powder or soap.

It blended well with the fragrance hinting sweetly of luscious fruit that wafted gently about his mother.

Tommy's dark hair was about the same shade as Holly's. Gabe had thought so, but he hadn't seen their hair so close together before. Tommy's was mussed from sleep.

Holly's was skillfully mussed, thanks to the artful look of her sexy hairstyle.

"Would you like to tell me about your dream?" Gabe asked, putting two fingers on Tommy's damp cheek. "Sometimes it feels better if you talk about it."

But Tommy didn't move, except to close his eyes. Tears still streamed down his face. Holly rocked him gently.

"Okay, I've a better idea," Gabe said. "How about if I read you a story?"

The small head rose, and Tommy smiled through his tears.

"That's not necessary," Holly said. "It's late, and I'm sure you're tired."

"I'll sleep better myself after a story," Gabe said firmly. He wasn't about to explain to Holly in front of Tommy, but he had begun his campaign to get the child to talk.

"Well…all right."

Gabe got the message. She wanted him to leave. There could be a million reasons why, not the least of which was that he made her uncomfortable. He understood that. He'd felt uncomfortable, too, in those last minutes before Tommy appeared in the living room. Still did. Right down in his crotch. This woman was damn sexy without even trying.

She was also hands-off.

He intended to help her, whether she wanted help or not. He'd spend a little male quality time with her son, for starters. That was something she couldn't do herself.

And if he got Tommy to reveal exactly what he'd seen the morning his daddy died, well, all the better.

HOLLY SAT on a small blue chair near the desk in Tommy's room, watching her son's enthralled expression as Chief Gabe McLaren read him a bedtime story.

Gabe had let Tommy choose the storybook. It was one of Tommy's favorites, full of brightly colored pictures of wild animals, real and imaginary.

Gabe kept a muscular arm around the small boy in the pale yellow pajamas. Tommy's head rested against Gabe's broad chest. She saw it move up and down with the vibration when Gabe laughed at something in the story. Which was often.

It was a wonderfully moving sight—man and boy together in sweet companionship.

The problem was that the man was a virtual stranger.

Thomas had seldom read a bedtime story to Tommy. That was a mother's role, he'd said. So was feeding the boy, bathing him and taking care of him when he was ill. Throwing a ball to him—well, that had been a father's job, except that Thomas had gotten bored with it easily, particularly when Tommy hadn't always been able to catch what he tossed.

Holly had been pleased and surprised that father and son had at least gotten into the habit of spending quality time together on the mornings she slept in. Or at least she assumed their time together went well. Thomas always shrugged at her questions, and Tommy had just beamed.

"Uh-oh," Gabe was saying as Holly's attention returned to the tableau on the bed. "You know what? I've forgotten what this animal says, and I'm too tired to read it. Do you know?" He looked at Tommy, who nodded.

"Good. That'll help. The animal is a bird, isn't it?"

Again, Tommy nodded.

"It's a funny-looking one. I've never seen a big blue owl before, have you?"

This time, Tommy shook his head.

"Right here, it says the owl made a noise like owls do. But the letters are too fuzzy for my tired eyes. Can you read them?"

Tommy shook his head again.

"Well, do you suppose you could tell me what an owl says? If not, I'm afraid we won't be able to finish the book. What do you think this owl said?"

Tommy looked distressed. Worried for him, Holly was about to join them and finish reading the darned book, when Tommy said, almost too softly for her to hear it, "Hooo."

"That's it!" Gabe gave Tommy a big hug. "That's exactly what it says. I'm awake now. Let's finish this book." Over Tommy's head, he caught Holly's eye and gave her a big, conspiratorial wink.

It was all Holly could do to prevent herself from hurrying across the room to hug them both.

"I CAN'T THANK YOU ENOUGH," Holly said at the front door awhile later. Tommy was tucked once more into bed, sound asleep.

Gabe had gotten him to talk!

And, very patiently, he hadn't pressed Tommy to say any more, not that night. But at least that one, tiny "Hooo" had been a start.

"You're very welcome, Holly." He was grinning, a very masculine, proud smile. He obviously recognized the significance of his accomplishment.

"So you're a police chief and a child psychologist. What else do you do?" Holly couldn't help teasing despite her exhaustion…and the fact that she was aware that, once he left, she was going to be very much alone in this house, a widow by herself with a sleeping child.

"Try me," he said, his grin growing even broader. Damn, but he was sexy.

And damn her, too, for even noticing. *Widow,* she reminded herself, grinding the word into her mind, as if her overactive emotions were a food processor. *You're a widow.* As in no men, no sex, just loneliness.

For now, that was fine with her. Maybe forever.

And yet, as Gabe shook her hand and held on long

enough to warn her to lock her door behind him, there was a lingering heat in her fingers. The sensation bothered her. A lot.

So did the way he looked at her—a disconcerting combo, in the depths of his eyes, of sympathy, amusement, distance…and lust.

Quickly, she shut the door behind him, trying not to slam it. She leaned on it, closing her eyes.

Gabe McLaren wasn't just a man trying to be kind. He was aware of her as a woman.

She was aware of him as a man.

But that was simply because she was in mourning. Sure, she was lonely—a *widow*—but she wasn't stupid.

Gabe McLaren was a cop. He might remain a part of her life until Thomas's murderer was caught. After that, she'd merely need to convince him that neither Tommy nor she needed his help or any other cop's to survive.

As she dutifully locked the door, though, she realized something: attempting to convince Gabe McLaren of anything he didn't want to believe might be as futile as trying to get the wild waves of the Pacific to settle down for an afternoon nap.

HOLLY COULDN'T sleep that night. Big surprise. She hadn't slept much at all since Thomas's death.

Why? she wondered, lying in the dark with her eyes wide open. It wasn't as if they had been so close that she missed him here, in her bed. Or even out of it.

Still…he had been her husband. He'd been a major part of her life, notwithstanding how distant they had become recently.

She groaned and sat up, flicking on the lamp on her bedside table. Glancing around, she recalled how she had so defiantly made this bedroom her own, decorating it with flowery Laura Ashley sheets and curtains.

One of the quilts she'd sewn was folded carefully at her feet. And a couple of her own favorite stitched creations hung on the walls.

What would Gabe McLaren think of her "silly little crafts," as Thomas had dubbed them?

And why did she even wonder about it? Why hadn't she shown him any when he'd expressed an interest in seeing her artwork?

Forget it. She had much weightier matters to think about. Like her husband. Thomas was gone forever now. He'd been buried today.

No, yesterday. This was a new day, no matter how early it was.

And no matter what Thomas and she had or hadn't been to one another at the end, Holly mourned him.

Maybe it would help to keep busy. But she didn't feel particularly creative right now. Perhaps what she could do was to start going through Thomas's things.

Not his clothes. Not now, in the middle of the night when she felt so sad. But paperwork. That would keep her mind occupied without devastating her.

She rose, put a light cotton robe over her short nylon gown, and went down the stairs to the small room that had been Thomas's office. She flicked on the light and sighed, "Oh, Thomas." He hadn't liked her to come in here, so she hadn't, for months. Thomas hadn't liked to pick up after himself, either, and this room, furnished with desk, chair, small tables for computer and TV, and junk, reflected it. Now, she would have to sort through all the piles, figure out what to save and what to toss.

"Not tonight," she told herself. She nevertheless picked her way through the debris on the floor and sat down on the desk chair. The room smelled musty. She'd air it out tomorrow.

For now, feeling overwhelmed by the magnitude of the task, she decided just to tackle the smallest piles on the desk. One contained mostly magazines. That was easy. Those about police she would donate to the station, if anyone wanted them. The risqué ones she would toss out. The few dealing with investments…well, those were probably disposable, too.

She wondered suddenly if Gabe McLaren read investment magazines, girly magazines or just ones sent to cops. She laughed at herself and went to work on another pile.

This one was more problematic. It contained files, mostly unlabeled. The ones that were labeled were primarily credit card bills—what credit card was this? It referenced a company different from the one that issued their shared card. It had been sent to Thomas at the address of the N.B.P.D. station.

She glanced at the charges: firing range practice, gasoline, a local department store. Nothing unusual. But why were these charges on a separate credit card? She hadn't seen anything recorded in their checkbook indicating payments on this card.

She put that file down and tried another. It contained a list of all the shops along Pacific Way, the traffic-free street perpendicular to the beach where Sheldon, Evangeline and a multitude of other local trendy tourist establishments had their stores. Nothing too exciting about that.

There were a few other files, some with familiar financial information, others with photographs, mostly of Tommy.

Not her, of course. Or of all of them together.

Still, this folder caused tears to flow down Holly's cheeks. No matter what else Thomas had been, no matter how estranged she and he had felt from one another, her husband had loved their child in his own way. And Tommy had certainly adored his daddy.

Who had killed Thomas? Was the money stolen from Sheldon's worth a human life? Or had there been another reason…?

Shuddering, Holly arranged the stacks on the desk into neater piles, then headed back to her bedroom.

"YOU WANTED to see me, Chief?" Al Sharp's posture seemed relaxed, with one hip leaning against Gabe's desk and his arms loosely crossed, but Gabe saw a wariness glinting from eyes too insolent and set a little too close together. He was clad in his police patrol uniform, complete with Sam Browne about his waist containing his .35 Beretta and ammunition, but his hat was nowhere to be seen.

"Yeah. Sit down, Al." Gabe motioned to one of the chairs facing him. It was late morning. He hadn't slept much the night before, thinking about the Thomas Poston murder.

About his cute little son, Tommy.

And about beautiful, sad—sexy—Holly Poston.

Mostly about Holly Poston. About grieving Holly Poston, who was absolutely off-limits.

Still, he was going to get answers. Fast. For her sake and Tommy's, as well as his own.

He'd come into the office full of determination. He'd reviewed the file again. And again.

And now he felt as frustrated as hell.

Al settled in and leaned back. His eyes left Gabe for the first time, taking in the rest of the office.

Gabe had left a lot as it had been when his predecessor, Mal Kensington, was chief of police, but he'd added his own touches to the décor. On the wall now hung a detailed satellite map of the area, some congratulatory plaques and medals Gabe had earned while with the Sacramento Police Department and, for his amusement and the possible discomfiture of those who came to visit, a photograph of himself shaking hands with Evangeline Sevvers, mayor of Naranja Beach—and Aunt Evangeline to him.

He'd also heard that he was a heck of a lot more organized than Mal had ever been. The top of his desk was nearly empty. He was a great believer in keeping things filed for easier access when he needed them.

"What's up?" Al was clearly growing uncomfortable at the delay. With his extra chin and nearly shaved head, he resembled a tall and skinny bulldog. But he'd proven to be much less than a bulldog on the investigation.

"Thomas Poston's murder. You know—"

"Chief. Sharp." Jimmy Hernandez strode into the room and sat in the chair next to Al's.

Detective James Hernandez's Hispanic facial features were broad and sharply geometric, his body lean and trim beneath his khaki shirt and dark slacks. No uniform for him, as a detective. And usually no suit coat, either.

He had been hired by Gabe first thing when Gabe had been hired to run the Naranja Beach P.D. Jimmy had been one of the best damn detectives Gabe had ever met when they'd worked together with the Sacramento Police Department.

He was one of the few people who knew why Gabe had really been hired for this job. He'd come along to assist Gabe—as well as to head the local detective unit.

"Glad you're here, Jimmy. I was just beginning to tell Al that I haven't been happy about the progress we've made on the Poston case."

"Yeah?" Jimmy glared at him. They might be friends

and cohorts, but Jimmy made his own opinions known. *Very* known.

"Yeah," Gabe replied. His cool gaze was on Jimmy, who barely hid a grin. They both knew the criticism was leveled at Al Sharp, not the chief detective. Most likely, Al knew it, too.

Al was a patrolman as his partner Thomas had been, and not a detective. Still, because of the special circumstances of this death, Al had taken a leading role in the investigation. He'd known Thomas well. He knew a lot of the same people Thomas had known. And he, maybe more than anyone else, was motivated to solve his partner's murder.

"I've consulted with Jimmy every step of the way," Al said, "just like you told me, chief. Right, Jimmy?" He glanced over at the detective beside him.

"You tell *me,* Al," Jimmy replied.

"I've talked to everyone you suggested," Al said defensively, "asked the questions you insisted on, and like that."

"I figured," Gabe said. "And 'like that' is why I'm taking a bigger role in the investigation myself. Five days have passed, and we don't even have a suspect. That's too long. *Way* too long."

Gabe rose behind his desk and leaned forward as if he were going to get right in Al's face. The patrolman had insisted on participating in the investigation. Thomas had been his partner. His friend.

But he was going to learn that wanting was not the same as succeeding. And if he took something on while part of Gabe's force, he'd damned well better produce.

Gabe had been attempting to be a good guy since arriving in Naranja Beach and taking over the position as police chief. He'd figured he was more likely to get the information he needed for his covert investigation if he fit in, became part of the furniture. So far that hadn't worked.

And Jimmy hadn't been any more successful than Gabe so far.

Gabe was about to change his strategy. Especially since he believed the two deaths could be related.

"We're going to know who killed Poston and why within the next week, or heads are going to roll. Got it, both of you?"

Jimmy nodded, but Al's tone was curt, his expression surly as he said, "Yeah."

"That's 'yeah, sir,' Sharp."

"Yeah, sir." Al stood and gave a mock salute.

"What's your plan, Jimmy?" Gabe asked. "Al knows people around here. Who do you want him to question?"

"Concentrate on the people who heard little Tommy Poston crying on Pacific Way that morning," Jimmy said. He remained seated, one leg crossed casually over the other as he looked up at the patrol cop. "Did he tell them anything?"

"You know the kid's not talking." Al's attempt to hide his annoyance came across as a sneer he turned into a cough.

"Yes, I know," Jimmy said. "But he might have been then, in his fear and excitement. In any event, talk to those people."

"I have."

"I know," Gabe told him.

Al's glance signaled a hint of relief, as if he believed Gabe was about to support him. Wrong.

"I read your report," Gabe continued. "But there's a lot that isn't in it. Talk to them again. Did they see anything else? Hear anything besides Tommy? I want to know everything from exactly what each of them was eating for breakfast at Naranja Diner that morning when they heard Tommy scream, to how many times it made them belch. How foggy did the marine layer make the air, or could they see anything or anyone along Pacific Way? Got it?''

''Yeah—er, yeah, sir,'' he amended as he met Gabe's eye.

Only then did Gabe let the patrol cop escape his office.

''You figure he'll get those answers?'' Jimmy asked dryly.

''What do you think?''

Jimmy grinned as he stood and walked toward the door. He turned back to Gabe. ''I think I'll do some follow-up myself.''

''You got it,'' Gabe said. ''And while you're at it—''

''Yeah, yeah. If I can be subtle enough, I'll see if anyone knows anything about the other situation.'' Jimmy left the office.

What next? Gabe wondered.

He decided to call Holly, and ask her…what? Something to do with the case, like… Nothing. He was merely looking for an excuse to call her this morning, fool that he was.

Forget the call.

Shaking his head, he went to the file cabinet. Extracting a folder labeled Poston, he thumbed through it.

The physical evidence was minimal and inconclusive. The murder weapon was something sharp, like a knife, but hadn't been found at the scene. Sheldon Sperling had said a decorative letter opener, part of his artsy stock, seemed to be missing. His shop had been dusted for fingerprints, scoured for hairs and other clues, but it was open to the public. Even if everything could be identified, it still might not point to the perpetrator.

Sperling. He'd been hit on the head and didn't remember much. But he was a person Gabe wanted to question himself, a lot more than he'd been able to at Holly's after Poston's funeral.

And if he just happened, in Sperling's shop, to see some of the needlework created by Holly Poston...

He was becoming obsessed with the woman, damn it, and he'd only just met her.

No. He was obsessed with the case. She was an integral part of it. Thomas Poston's murder was his first big challenge as the head of the N.B.P.D.—his first big *official* challenge. He would solve it, and quickly. And, hopefully, the unofficial assignment, too.

But as soon as the Poston case was solved, he would let the others on his force play guardian angel to the Postons.

GABE DIDN'T MAKE it to Sheldon's shop as anticipated. While driving his department-issued brown sedan along Naranja Avenue toward Pacific Way, he saw a familiar vehicle. Holly Poston's bright red minivan was parked at a meter along the street.

Where was she? He pulled over at a yellow line—one of the perks of his job—and looked around. City Hall, where the N.B.P.D. offices were located, was a mile behind him. In this area, Naranja Avenue contained rows of low-rise stucco office buildings and a few retail shops— much less trendy than those along Pacific Way. Two blocks down was Naranja Community Hospital.

Gabe wasn't able to guess where, around here, Holly had gone. But then he spotted her, hand in hand with Tommy, emerging from the nearest building. It contained mostly medical offices.

His insides compressed as if in a vise. Was one of them ill?

He exited his car and approached them.

Holly looked tired. Her lovely dark eyes drooped, and the dark circles beneath them had grown larger.

But somehow the sight of her spurred not only his sympathy but sexual stirrings, too. Again. The heat he felt looking at her wasn't only from the strong California sun that beat down on the avenue on this midsummer afternoon. Not at all.

Holly was dressed in jeans and a form-fitting short-sleeved T-shirt that showed off every soft curve. Curves that just begged to be touched....

Idiot, he berated himself. Or was it *pervert?*

Holly watched her cute little son, who was clinging to her hand but lagging behind. He was in bright red shorts, a navy T-shirt and sandals.

"Holly?"

She looked up quickly, a startled expression on her face.

"Sorry," Gabe said. "Didn't mean to scare you. I was just driving by and saw your van." He glanced behind her toward the medical building. "Is everything okay?"

"Sure," she said, her tone a shade too bright. "We just came to see the doctor." She knelt down beside her son and gave him a hug. But Tommy looked listless and didn't hug back.

Gabe's heart went out to him. To both of them.

"Tommy woke up a couple of hours after you left," Holly continued, "and didn't get back to sleep. He had a bad dream."

Stooping down to their level, Gabe read between the lines. Tommy had awakened, crying, after a nightmare and had kept Holly up all night. She was frightened for him. What caring mother wouldn't be? She had taken him to a doctor. A pediatrician or a psychologist? Poor little Tommy might need both.

"Did Tommy have a tummy ache?" Gabe asked gently, though he suspected what the answer would be.

"No." The frantic expression in Holly's eyes suggested that she had reached her wits' end and didn't know how to help her scared son. "We saw Tommy's new doctor again, a special one who likes to talk to children and likes them to talk to her, too."

"I hope it was a good visit," Gabe said. But he could tell from Holly's demeanor that it hadn't been, that Tommy hadn't opened up even to a specialist.

"It was a fine visit," she said nonetheless, her voice falsely cheerful. "It was so good that we're going back to see the doctor again next week. And maybe then Tommy will take his turn and talk, too."

"Great. How about if I come over tonight and read Tommy another bedtime story. Would that be all right with you, sport?" Gabe held his breath. Tommy obviously had something he was keeping inside. Gabe wasn't an expert like the doctor they'd seen. He wasn't likely to be any more successful at extracting whatever it was from the child. But someone had to, for Tommy's sake, as well as for the investigation. And Gabe was going to try. He'd gotten one word from the boy, at least. Maybe he could get more.

He allowed himself to breathe again when, very slowly and solemnly, the sweet-faced child nodded.

Gabe stood. "Great. You guys like pizza?"

Holly rose, too. "You don't have to do that," she whispered very softly, so only Gabe could hear.

"I know I don't have to," Gabe replied. "I want to." The damned unsettling thing about it was that he did. He wanted to return to that pretty beach community house with its attractive furnishings. He wanted to spend more time with this very sexy woman whose only interest in him, if any, would disappear as time passed and memories of her husband faded.

Any man she became attracted to now, when her emotions were turned upside down by her loss, would be thrown out like yesterday's pizza crusts when she began to heal.

And that wasn't for Gabe. Not again.

But he intended to unravel the threads that had led to her husband's death. As quickly as possible.

Almost subconsciously, his conditioning as a longtime cop kicking in, he heard the sound of someone driving too fast down this busy street. He looked up. At the same time, he heard one bleat from a siren. Good. A patrol officer was on it.

A small, white car pulled over to the side of the street into an empty space right beside where Gabe, Holly and Tommy stood, a patrol car with rotating lights hugging its rear. It was the unit assigned to Bruce Franklin and Dolph Hilo.

Gabe, and all the people on the sidewalk, watched as the two officers did all the right things: taking their time getting out of their vehicle—undoubtedly checking the plates with their onboard computer, then approaching the stopped car.

Dolph Hilo was the officer who got out on the passenger side, nearest where Gabe stood with Holly and Tommy. He smiled and saluted.

And just as at his father's funeral, Tommy Poston began to scream.

Chapter Four

Terrified, wanting to cry herself, Holly dropped to her knees on the hard pavement and hugged her wailing son. "Tommy, honey, it's all right," she soothed. But her voice broke, and she knew she was lying. It *wasn't* all right.

Why did Tommy scream this way? Of course it had something to do with Thomas's death, but why this reaction? *Had* Tommy seen how his daddy was killed? Then why was he still alive?

Thank God he was still alive....

Holly looked up. Gabe—kind, thoughtful Gabe who had been there for her at Thomas's funeral and last evening, too—knelt beside them. Bruce Franklin and Dolph Hilo had joined them. They had been friends of Thomas's, fellow patrol officers, and...

And they were in uniform! Gabe was dressed in a well-tailored suit, befitting an administrator, but the other cops were in patrol uniforms—complete with navy blue military-style shirts with epaulets, badges and emblems, Sam Browne belts, matching dark trousers. Could that be it? There had been many officers in uniform at Thomas's funeral, when Tommy had begun to shriek. Some were dressed more formally, but some looked just like this: the uniform Thomas had usually worn.

"Tommy, honey, are you upset because you see the uniforms like your daddy wore?"

He stopped screaming in her ear, took a breath. When she looked him in his red, blotchy, wet face, he stared at her. He didn't nod, but didn't shake his head no, either.

She looked desperately at Gabe, whose expression was both compassionate and angry, as if he would choke with his bare hands the demons tormenting her son. "Could that be it, do you think?" she asked. "Is this because he misses his father so much that every time he sees someone in uniform he gets upset?"

But how could Gabe know?

"Maybe," he said through gritted teeth. "We'll have to find out. But not now." He took Tommy from her arms. He was sobbing once more, but at least he had stopped screaming. Holly was reluctant to let him go, but Gabe had known instinctively what to do with him before. Maybe he could help now, too.

"You know what?" Despite the ire Holly had seen in his face, Gabe's voice was gentle. "I see these guys every day, and sometimes I feel like crying when they're around, too."

He made a quick sideways motion with his head. The patrol officers must have somehow understood, for Dolph, a short, dark-haired man with a barrel chest and Asian features, said, "Yeah, he does, too, the wimp."

Taking his cue, Bruce agreed, "That's right." He was a pleasant-looking African-American with a lopsided smile, a few inches taller than his partner.

Tommy stopped crying and looked up at them.

"Hey, Tommy, we don't make you cry, do we?" Dolph continued. "We're your pals. Chief McLaren only cries because we don't like him."

Tommy looked skeptically from Dolph to Gabe and back again.

"I know how to get them to like me," Gabe said. "Let's all go get an ice-cream cone."

"We're on duty, chief," Dolph said. "You gonna excuse us?"

"Nope," Gabe said. "You're right. At the risk of your still not liking me, you two get back to work. I'll just get Tommy and his mom some ice cream. That okay with you, sport?"

Tommy stared at Dolph as if he expected *him* to cry, then nodded at Gabe.

"Great," Gabe said. "Let's go."

Only then did he look at Holly. Tommy didn't need any sweets right now. But at least it was a few hours until dinnertime. And the treat sounded appealing to her, too.

"Okay," she said.

They walked the few blocks to Coast Avenue, Tommy between them holding both their hands. In a short while, they reached the ice-cream shop called "Cones." It was decorated in lively colors, and a long list of flavors was posted on the wall.

"Do you know what kind you want, Tommy?" Gabe asked.

The boy shook his head.

"You don't really want me to read the whole list," Gabe said with an exaggeratedly horrified look in eyes that were the shade of green the ocean became when a storm threatened.

Tommy nodded, and Gabe gave a long-suffering sigh. "You stop me when you hear the one you like, okay, sport?" And then he began to read all the flavors by singing them to the tune of the "Alphabet Song." He had a wonderfully rich baritone voice, and he emoted the song as if he were in a musical comedy. Tommy laughed in glee. But he didn't stop Gabe. Holly was glad. She enjoyed the song, too.

Eventually, though, Gabe ran out of flavors. "That's all of them," he sang to Tommy using one drawn-out note. "Which one do you want?"

Tommy crooked a finger at Gabe. Obediently, the police chief bent so his ear was near Tommy's face. Holly watched carefully to see what Tommy would do.

And then Gabe stood up and made a celebratory gesture by pumping his fist into the air. "Yes!"

"What?" Holly asked excitedly.

"Tommy wants rainbow. He told me."

And Holly felt tears rush to her eyes.

SEVERAL HOURS LATER, Gabe knocked with one hand on the door of the well-maintained stucco home that belonged to Holly Poston. He balanced a large pizza box in the other hand.

The door opened quickly. "Gabe, what are you doing here?" Holly sounded surprised. She was dressed in cut-offs and a midriff-hugging T-shirt. Gabe's mouth watered, and it wasn't only from the spice-and-cheese aroma of the food he carried.

He was here on a mission—a dual mission. But he suspected it was better to mention neither to Holly right now.

"I hope you checked through the door who was here," he reprimanded gently.

The soft flush that spread over her lovely face contrasted attractively with the dark tone of her hair. "I will next time," she promised. She looked toward the box in his hands. "I assumed that, after ice cream this afternoon, pizza was off."

"If you already ate, cold leftover pizza is delicious for breakfast," he said.

"Ugh." She wrinkled her small nose in distaste. "Pizza for breakfast, no. But for dinner—it sounds great! I was thinking about soup and sandwiches, but we can do that another time. Come in."

"I hope you like a pizza supreme," he said. "You and Tommy can pick anything off you're not crazy about."

They'd reached the kitchen, and Holly motioned him to put the box on the table. "I like my pizza with everything," Holly told him. "Tommy's more particular, though. Tommy!" she called. "He's watching TV in the living room."

He appeared in the doorway a moment later. He glanced at Gabe and the pizza, then ran toward Gabe and gave him a hug.

"I'm flattered. I assumed it would be pizza first, hugs later."

Tommy smiled, then reached toward one of the plates his mother had gotten from a cabinet.

A short while later, they all sat at the kitchen table nibbling pizza. Tommy had milk to drink, and Holly and Gabe had iced tea.

"So, sport, how about a game of catch when we're done?" Gabe asked Tommy. The little boy, who had tomato sauce at the corner of his mouth and all over his hands, grinned broadly, and Gabe wanted to reach across the table and ruffle his hair.

He liked the kid. He even liked the taste of domesticity. Not that he intended to get used to it. He was just helping another cop's family. It was what cops did.

If he could get Tommy to open up to him, so much the better. He was damn well going to find answers to all the questions remaining about Thomas Poston's death, and he knew this child could help.

He glanced at Holly. She watched him with an expression he didn't understand. There was sorrow in it, and maybe even a touch of suspicion.

He couldn't ask, though. Not with her son right there.

Tommy hopped down and, still blotched with tomato sauce, stood beside Gabe, smiling. He was ready to play ball.

"Let's take a minute and clean up, sport. I've never seen one of the Dodgers or Angels with their faces dirty with pizza, have you?"

Tommy's eyes widened as if in terror. His entire small body began to shake. Gabe grabbed him and held him close. Over his head, he met Holly's irate gaze. She knew what he'd done—reminded Tommy of that morning.

The Angels and the Dodgers. Gabe had previously mentioned to her part of what was in the police report. Sheldon Sperling had told of a friendly argument between Thomas and him about the ball teams just before the suspect broke in. Tommy had obviously heard the discussion, associated the teams with what had happened later.

Good. If he'd heard that, maybe he knew more. And someday soon, he would tell it to Gabe.

"Don't do that again." Holly's voice was quiet but she spoke through gritted teeth as he held her son.

He nodded, understanding her anger. He would do what he had to. But next time, if it was something he knew might upset Tommy, he would discuss it with Holly first.

In a short while, Tommy stopped shivering. Gabe looked down to find him staring at the floor. His face wasn't as dirty now. Some of the tomato sauce was now on Gabe's light blue shirt.

"Let me have your shirt right away," Holly said, a chill remaining in her voice. "I'll get the spot out."

"Don't worry about it," Gabe said. But when Holly insisted, he unbuttoned the shirt and shrugged it off, handing it to her.

He felt self-conscious standing in her kitchen, with only a sleeveless T-shirt covering his torso. But when he noticed her appreciative wide-eyed glance at his chest and biceps, it wasn't self-consciousness that he felt. At least his dress trousers were loose enough that she shouldn't be able to see what was happening at his crotch. He hoped.

Or did he?

He wasn't here to play house with Holly, only to investigate a murder and to see she wasn't lacking for anything—anything platonic that required a man's presence. That was all.

"Hey, Tommy," he said, then cleared his throat to get rid of the gruffness in his voice. "You ready for that game of catch?"

HOLLY WATCHED and listened out the open kitchen window as she used a stain remover to get rid of the tomato sauce on Gabe's shirt. It seemed unsettlingly intimate to be handling his shirt this way. It seemed even more disturbingly intimate to watch his bared biceps ripple and flex as he played catch with Tommy.

"Cut it out," she told herself, glancing down at the shirt. She wasn't some sex-starved vixen. She was a mature woman, a widow with a child.

The stain was gone, thank heavens. She quickly put the shirt down on a chair and began to rinse off the dishes...still staring out the kitchen window.

She liked the way Gabe treated Tommy as they played ball. She liked it a lot.

But she was still angry that he had said something to remind Tommy of the night Thomas was killed. Could it have been inadvertent? She doubted it.

But maybe she was wrong. Maybe the more reminders there were, the quicker Tommy would talk about it and start to heal.

Maybe the fact that Gabe was a cop didn't mean he'd do anything to solve his case, even harm a little boy.

She watched them play with a beach ball large enough for Tommy to grab onto and even catch now and then. When he did, Gabe would cheer. When he didn't, he'd say something encouraging.

Holly tried not to compare this game with the few Thomas had engaged in there in the backyard with Tommy. They'd seldom lasted more than ten minutes. Her husband would grow frustrated at his young son's lack of dexterity and call it an evening.

After nearly forty-five minutes, Gabe led Tommy into the house. "He wore me out," he said, panting. "You have a budding outfielder there, Mrs. Poston."

"Could be," Holly said proudly, ruffling her son's head as he beamed happily up at her. She considered doing the same with Gabe before she felt herself redden. *Fool,* she chided herself.

Later, Gabe not only helped with Tommy's bath, but also read him a bedtime story again. This time, though, Tommy didn't respond to Gabe's good-natured game to try to get him to speak.

Perversely, Holly was glad. Tommy had spoken for Gabe twice but not for her, despite her attempts to convince and cajole him.

"Next time, sport," Gabe said. "Good night now." And he bent down and gave her son a kiss on the cheek.

Holly went into Tommy's room and said good-night,

too. She kept the door partially open behind her when she left.

Tommy didn't like being alone now, but he tolerated it as long as he could see the nightlight across the hall in the bathroom and his door stayed ajar.

Now what? Could she gracefully get Gabe to leave? She didn't want to be alone with him, in her house, with his shirt off.

Nor did she want him to feel obligated to keep coming back, to take care of them.

When she returned to the living room, Gabe had put his shirt back on and was buttoning it. Good. She had no reason to feel so uncomfortable with the man now. But she had to pull her eyes away from his deft fingers as the remaining glimpse of his broad, T-shirt covered chest disappeared below blue fabric.

Holly stood by the door. "Thanks for playing with Tommy tonight. I appreciate it. But we'll be fine, really."

"Tommy's a good kid. And as I told you before, we're all family. Everyone on the force is there for the wife and kid of a downed cop."

"That's sweet, but we'll be fine." Holly repeated louder and more firmly. But instead of taking the hint Gabe sat down on the couch and crossed his legs.

"Tommy needs to talk about what he saw on the morning of the murder," he said.

She couldn't argue with that.

"It'll help him heal," Gabe continued. "And he can help us find the bad guy."

Holly crossed her arms rigidly in front of her. "He needs to heal at his own speed." She heard the chill in her voice. "He won't, if reminders scare him to death— like your transparent reference to what he might have heard. Believe me, I want to know what happened, too, but I won't let you frighten Tommy to solve the case."

Gabe stood. His green eyes were as stony as if they'd turned to granite. "Is that what you think, that I only had solving the case on my mind?"

"Didn't you?"

She tried not to flinch as he took a step toward her. "Your son is hurting, Holly. Unless he talks about what's hurting him, he won't feel any better."

"Yes, but—"

"Turning encouragement into games…well, that's just something I know works."

"How?" she demanded. "From your vast experience as a parent? A child psychologist, maybe?"

"No. From personal experience."

Holly stared. "What do you mean?"

"It doesn't matter. It's time for me to leave." In several strides with his long legs, he reached the door where she stood.

But she didn't get out of his way. "No, it would have been time for you to leave five minutes ago," she said, controlling the anger that simmered within her. "But not now, not after you say something that fills me with a zillion questions." She took a calming breath. "Please, sit down and I'll make us some coffee. Then you can explain."

He was close to her. Very close. He should have intimidated her, standing at his full height, towering over her and glowering that way.

But somehow he didn't. She stood her ground. He stood his.

And then he said, "All right. I could use a cup of coffee. And maybe this is a story you need to hear."

GABE PICKED UP a news magazine from the sleek wooden coffee table by the couch as he waited for Holly's return from the kitchen. He put it down again. He'd come in here because he wanted to organize his thoughts. Thumbing through a magazine wouldn't help.

He was no closer to figuring out how to explain things five minutes later when she returned to the room.

"It's brewing," she said. "I'm making decaf. I don't need caffeine right now. I get too little sleep as it is."

"Fine." He glanced around the now-familiar living room. The off-white paint on the walls was a little dull. Maybe he could offer to redo the room for her. Brighten it up a little.

It'd be a hell of a lot easier than explaining his entire life.

She sat in an upholstered chair, watching him suspiciously. Still, he liked the quizzical quirk to her dark, full eyebrows. The way her soft, moist lips pursed a bit, as if encouraging him to speak. Damn, but she was a pretty lady.

And he was procrastinating…a trait he wouldn't have tolerated among the officers who reported to him.

"Look," he said finally, staring into her deep brown eyes. He prayed she'd stay peeved and wouldn't act sympathetic. He didn't want sympathy. Didn't need it. Not now, after so many years. "It's simple. My father was a cop in Sacramento. My mother died in a car wreck when I was eight. There was a shootout at a convenience store… My dad saved some women, a couple of kids shopping there, but he got hit. He died."

"Oh, Gabe!" He saw the horror in Holly's face.

Damn, there was the sympathy he didn't want. Where had her anger gone? *That* he could deal with.

"How old were you? Did you have any other family?"

"I was ten. An only child. Both my parents had been only children, and my grandparents were gone, too."

"How awful!"

Seeing tears in her eyes, he glanced over her shoulder toward a spot on the wall. "Fortunately," he said, "the assistant chief of police at the time was Lionel Sevvers."

"Sevvers? As in Evangeline?"

"Her older brother. As I told you, all cops on a police force are family. Lionel took me in. He had two kids of his own. And he and his wife Alice were very patient with a scared kid who didn't want to talk to anyone about anything, least of all his fears."

He heard Holly draw in her breath. "Oh," she said very softly. "I see."

She rose and came toward him. He stiffened before glaring up at her. "Do you think that coffee is ready yet?"

"Sure. But—"

He took a deep breath and stood. He smelled her soft scent, like a succulent, ripe fruit that he couldn't identify. He didn't want to smell it, allow it to distract him.

But she reached out. Her hand touched his arm. "Gabe, I'm sorry. I didn't understand. I knew you were trying to help Tommy, in a way. But I didn't realize you know how he feels."

He laid his hand over hers, feeling her soft, warm flesh. His shrug wasn't quite as careless as he'd intended. "I don't, not exactly. I was ten. He's four. I only heard about how my dad died, though it was all over the news for a while. But I wasn't there when it happened."

"Still…"

He looked down into the soft pools of her brimming eyes. "It was a long time ago, Holly. The Sevvers…well, they were great. I eventually started talking about what happened, how miserable I felt about it. How scared I was. After that, things got a hell of a lot better.''

"I know Tommy needs to talk," Holly admitted. ''I've been trying to encourage him, too. But to push him—''

"I have no intention of pushing him," Gabe blazed. She pulled her arm away in obvious alarm at his sudden anger. "Sorry," he said. "The thing is, I want him to talk, for his own sake. For the sake of solving the case, too. As quick as we can get him to, but at as little risk of danger as possible to him.''

"What danger?'' Holly's fury reappeared, a tigress protecting her cub. "Do you think he saw the murder after all?''

Gabe shook his head. "I doubt it, though I wouldn't risk his life on my suppositions. Whatever he saw probably wasn't enough to worry the suspect. But Tommy must have seen something. He's most likely too young to understand its significance. But if the killer's still around and ever feels imperiled—''

"Then he might come after Tommy.''

Gabe nodded. "It's always a possibility. That's the most important reason of all to catch the killer fast. Just in case.''

Holly took an audible breath. "Just in case," she repeated. She looked up fiercely at Gabe. "He hasn't said anything to me or to the psychologist. He responds to you better than anyone. Maybe it wouldn't be a bad idea if you spend a little time around here, encouraging Tommy. You've already said you and your officers will be helping out with chores and things. If you make that public, the killer wouldn't be suspicious. The damn media has been clamoring for an interview, a human interest story, but I've been putting them off.''

"Right. I'll have our public information officer put out

the word. I did notice while Tommy and I were outside that your lawn could stand to be mowed.''

Holly's wry grin showed that her temper had calmed once more. ''True. But Gabe, if Tommy starts talking, it'd be better if no one knew, wouldn't it?''

''We'll make sure it gets out, when he does begin speaking again, that he just won't talk about that morning.''

''That's right!'' Relief lightened Holly's face. She sighed, then tilted her head back to look up at him. ''Thank you, Gabe.''

''You're—''

He didn't finish, for as he gazed into her eyes, he saw the warmth and gratitude there…and something more? Or was that only wishful thinking?

He felt his heart begin to race, even as he reached for her.

She didn't resist as he took her into his arms. His lips touched hers, gently at first. So gently that he felt both unsatisfied and tantalized by the sweet and seductive taste of her. With a soft moan of frustration, he pulled her closer. Tightly against him. Deepened the kiss. Waited for her to resist, to pull away, tell him to get lost.

She didn't. Instead, he heard a soft sound of surrender and need as she pressed herself against him. Her body was slender but nevertheless curvaceous. He wanted to savor those curves even more. He reached between them, touched one soft breast over her tight T-shirt, felt a nipple begin to bud beneath his fingers, rubbed it gently.

His tongue delved farther into her mouth, tasting her. Wanting to taste her more, all over.

His groin tightened almost painfully. He pressed against her, felt her respond with a low moan that made him even crazier. She didn't pull away. Did she need him as much as he desired her?

Only then did the sound he'd been hearing touch his consciousness. A frightened cry. Tommy was having another nightmare.

Holly stepped back. She blinked as if dazed, but in a moment she, too, became cognizant of what had interrupted them. "Tommy!" she said.

In a moment, they were both running up the steps.

Holly turned on the light as she entered the room and picked up the small, sobbing boy.

Gabe stood at the door, watching. Tommy was better off being held by his mother than anything Gabe could do right then. Feeling a little helpless, he glanced around.

On the dresser was a photograph he had noticed before: Holly, Tommy and Thomas Poston. The whole family, in happier times, a posed studio photograph in front of a bright blue background like a brilliant morning sky.

Thomas was holding Tommy, and Holly beamed at them both. Staring lovingly at her husband.

Lovingly. At her lost husband.

Whom she missed. Whom she had probably, in her imagination, just been kissing.

Damn! Gabe thought. Was his sanity being swept away by his sex drive? No way.

He'd been there once before, the second-best substitute for a woman missing another man.

The rebound lover, told to go pound salt when the lady he'd thought he'd loved had decided it was time for her to move on.

"I'll skip the coffee tonight," he called to Holly, whose lovely, shocked face was pressed against her son's. Ignoring the hurt in her eyes, he walked out.

Chapter Five

What had she expected? Holly wondered as she sat on the
bed and rocked the whimpering Tommy in her arms. She
hummed a soothing lullaby, but her own thoughts were
anything but peaceful.

Of course she had felt sorry for Gabe after the story
he'd told. He had lost everyone when he was very young.
At least he hadn't been totally alone. His experience had
been that cops took care of other cops' families. The Sevvers taught him that. Holly realized how special they, and
most particularly Lionel, must be. Gabe's story explained
why he'd once said he was sort of an uncle, but that it was
too complicated to explain. He was part of the whole Sevvers family, though not by blood.

As a result, Gabe felt the sense of duty imparted by his
own background. That was his only connection to Tommy
and her.

She closed her eyes, inhaling the fresh baby shampoo
scent of her son's soft hair, holding him tightly. She
needed soothing, too, for making such a fool of herself.

"Hushabye, hushabye," she sang half-tunelessly, without remembering much of the song or its words.

Cops had an inherent sense of duty that overrode everything else in their lives. Hadn't her father and Thomas proved that over and over?

If Gabe felt his obligation was to take care of Tommy and her, he'd do it. And since that obligation also meant finding Thomas's killer, Gabe would stop at nothing to achieve that, too.

But eventually he'd feel he'd done his duty. Then, he'd be distant. Gone like all cops.

This time, Holly's emotions wouldn't be involved.

Sure, she found Chief Gabe McLaren an outstanding specimen of manhood. What woman in full possession of faculties and female hormones wouldn't?

And the fact that his kiss would have knocked her socks off if she hadn't been in bare feet…? Irrelevant.

He'd stoked her long-dormant desire to near-flame status. She was darned curious what it would be like to make love with that gorgeous, sexy man.

But it wouldn't happen, since she couldn't engage her body without her emotions getting in the way.

No, she'd allow him into their lives just enough to encourage Tommy to talk, to protect them, even to help around the house. But that was all.

Feeling her son's small body relax in her arms, she finished by crooning, "We'll get along, just the two of us." She laid him down gently in his bed and kissed him goodnight once more.

"HEY, JIMMY, how about a little insight from you this morning before I head out?" Gabe asked Detective James Hernandez, whom Gabe had stolen from the Sacramento police. Jimmy was now the highest-ranking detective on the N.B.P.D..

"Where're you off to, Gabe?" Jimmy nearly dwarfed the doorway of Gabe's office, his arms full of files. His stance was firm and planted, as if daring someone to move him.

He was damn good at his job. Gabe respected him. He *liked* him. Other than Aunt Evangeline, Jimmy was Gabe's closest friend here.

Not that he could afford to be friends with anyone else, because of his covert assignment.

Holly Poston's lovely face popped uninvited into his thoughts. *Forget it, McLaren.* Holly wasn't a friend. She wasn't anything to him but a victim, a fellow cop's widow. And yet his thoughts kept turning to her…

"Gabe?" Jimmy interrupted his thoughts. "You want to daydream, or you want my help?"

"Your help. It's about the Poston case."

Jimmy's face registered frustration. "Yeah, damn thing's growing stale already." He stepped farther into the room and continued in a low voice, "Like the other one."

"We won't let it get stale," Gabe asserted.

Any more than he'd permit that other one to die.

Jimmy and he had both put time into the other investigation—their own personal off-duty time. But so far, they'd hit nothing but dead ends.

"I want to throw all the manpower needed into getting it solved," Gabe continued. "Yesterday. There's still a lot of physical evidence to sort through, but it's not going to be easy to figure out which prints, hair or skin samples were left by the bad guy instead of one of Sheldon's customers."

Jimmy nodded. "Yeah. The bad guy could even be one of his customers. And not even a murder weapon yet."

"Right. I'm going to Sheldon's this morning. He's been questioned by Al and you, but not by me, except for a couple of minutes the day of the funeral. I want more of a sense of what he went through. I gather he was cooperative but not particularly useful.''

"A clunk on the head can do that.''

"He told you Poston and he were arguing so they didn't pay attention when someone came in?''

"Yeah, some kind of friendly argument about the Angels versus the Dodgers. They had a running bet. Sheldon was ahead and Thomas wasn't a good loser. But he hastened to tell me it was all good-natured fun. Nothing to lose one's cool and kill a friend over.''

"Got it.'' Gabe had read that in the reports of the interview with Sperling. Had used it around little Tommy and earned Holly's ire… Holly again! She wouldn't leave his thoughts in peace. "I'm off now,'' Gabe told Jimmy a little too gruffly.

The detective frowned. "You want me along?''

"Not unless you want to come.''

Jimmy gave a laugh and held up the stack of files. "There are plenty more that need my attention when I'm done with these.''

"Gotcha. Call on the radio if you think of anything I should ask ol' Sheldon.''

A BELL SOUNDED as Gabe walked in the door. Sheldon Sperling's shop was a clutter of shelves filled with expensive, artistic knickknacks and walls covered with landscape and still-life paintings, colorful decorative primitive masks, plates with pictures of wide-eyed children and leaping sealife…and stitchery. Brightly colored fabrics hung everywhere, supported by long, thick dowels, in scenes representing sunrises and sunsets, palm trees in which plumed birds nested, and more. Gabe found it cheerful and appealing.

He found their creator, Holly, appealing, too….

The place smelled of the sea a couple of blocks away, and something spicy, as if the owner were brewing tea.

"Can I help you?" Sheldon emerged from a doorway at the back of his shop. He still walked slowly, shoulders hunched beneath a Hawaiian print shirt whose faded colors only seemed to emphasize that he, too, seemed faded. His hollow cheeks were so pale that Gabe wondered if he had powdered them. "Oh, it's you, Gabe. What can I do for you?"

"I know you were questioned officially before, Sheldon, but I'd like a personal rundown of what happened the morning you were attacked and Thomas Poston killed."

The ruefulness in his drooping eyes made him appear woebegone. "Sure, Gabe, but like I've told everyone who's asked, there are a lot of gaps in my memory. I suppose the head wound did that. Come into the back. I picked up some scones from Biscuit's Bakery, and I'll brew more tea." The bakery was another shop along Pacific Way. Gabe had noticed it, and the delightfully sweet odors wafting from it, before.

"Don't go to any trouble," Gabe said, but he followed Sheldon.

In a few minutes, the men were seated around the large table dominating the center of the back room. A steaming mug of something that smelled like Oriental spices sat in front of Gabe. One wall was a floor-to-ceiling conglomerate of enclosed cabinets. Along the outer wall was a large sink, and it, too, was set into wood cabinetry.

"Some of my artists give demonstrations and even classes here," Sheldon told Gabe. "Everyone sits around this table and listens, or even tries their hands at creating something. The tourists love it. Usually there's no charge, but they buy a lot of the works of whoever is demonstrating that day. I keep supplies here for the classes."

"I see." Gabe leaned toward Sheldon. "Look, this is probably getting as tedious as hell, but I want your description of what happened that morning. Okay?"

Sheldon nodded, but his expression was grim. "I realize you're doing all you can to find out who did this terrible thing, but you're right. It is getting tedious. And upsetting, since I can't even begin to forget about it. But okay."

Sheldon's story followed the reports. Thomas and Tommy had come in early that morning, as was their habit. They were all planning on heading to the Naranja Diner for breakfast, but Sheldon needed to finish organizing his products for the day, and Thomas agreed to wait. So Tommy wouldn't get bored, they settled him down in the back room with crayons and a coloring book, then Thomas and Sheldon returned to the sales area.

They had talked as Sheldon worked. "Well, yes," Sheldon said with a sheepish expression on his face at Gabe's question. "We were arguing about baseball. It was one of the things we did—all in good fun, you understand. We kept track of bets on paper. Thomas owed me about fifty dollars, I think. We never collected from one another, since sometimes I'd win and sometimes he would."

"I get it." Gabe paused. "And then what happened?"

Sheldon's head drooped. "I wish I knew." Gabe had to strain to hear. "Thomas and I were in the middle of our discussion…well, argument. I half heard the bell on the door ring to indicate someone had entered, but I was so engrossed I didn't even look that way. And then… I felt something hit me, hard. That was all. I didn't see who it was. I don't even know what happened to me, let alone how Thomas was attacked." He shook his head. His recessed, sad eyes met Gabe's. "Sorry. That's all I know. Except that when I was well enough, I verified there was cash missing from my register—about five hundred dollars, what I usually put there to start the day."

"And a letter opener, too?"

"Yes, a very nice one, unique, with a long metal blade and pretty, colorful ceramic handle. I picked it up in the Bahamas. The artist was—"

Gabe interrupted. "I see. Now, I know you weren't aware of it at the time, but could you show me where Thomas's body was, and where you were after the attack?"

"I'll show you what your detectives told me." Sheldon picked up his teacup and preceded Gabe back into the other room. Gabe left his own cup on the table.

Sheldon pointed out the area near the door where Thomas Poston's body had lain. "I know that was correct, since the people I hired to clean up afterward scrubbed blood off the wooden floor there. Not to mention all that black, sticky, fingerprint powder off nearly everything." He glared at Gabe. "Fortunately, they used common sense and mostly checked the register and countertops for prints, rather than ruining any of my artistic pieces."

"And no artwork was missing?"

"No, nothing I'm aware of. Except that letter opener, of course."

"Okay, then. Where did they say you were found?"

Sheldon winced visibly. "Over there." He pointed to the floor behind a set of shelves far to Gabe's right, almost along the wall. "I don't know how I got there, whether I'd been dusting some pieces there or if I was dragged behind the shelves, but that's where I'm told I was when the patrolmen came in."

Gabe walked in that direction and knelt. The wooden floor needed to be waxed, but other than a little dirt where floor met shelves, it was clean. He saw nothing useful. Nothing at all.

"What about little Tommy?" Sheldon asked. "He was in the back room most of the time, but I was told he came out here and probably saw his daddy and maybe me, too, if he walked around. Poor child. Has he said anything helpful yet?"

Gabe rose to his feet again and shook his head. "So far, the little guy isn't talking to anyone about anything."

"Holly told me she's taking him to see a child psychologist to help him get past this terrible thing."

"Yeah," Gabe said. "Anyway, thanks. I appreciate your making the time to talk with me."

"Did talking to me give you any insights?" When Gabe slowly shook his head, Sheldon's look hardened. "Please catch the son of a bitch who did this, Gabe. Not just for me, or for the money I lost. Thomas Poston was a friend."

THE NARANJA BEACH City Hall had always seemed to Holly to resemble one of the missions that had dotted California in the days of Spanish dominance centuries ago. Some missions still stood. City Hall wasn't one of them. It had been constructed in the 1920s. But the charm of its daubed pink adobe walls, center courtyard and tile-lined bell tower was undeniable, especially contrasting with today's bright, cloud-free azure sky.

"This morning, we're visiting Mayor Sevvers, sweetheart," Holly told Tommy as she bent inside the back seat of her minivan to unfasten his seat belt. "Can you help me carry some costumes?"

Her son slid onto the sidewalk and nodded importantly. He looked adorable in his denim cut-offs and orange Naranja Beach T-shirt, his dark hair ruffling in the slight breeze. But there were shadows beneath his bright brown eyes.

"Great!" She gave him a hug, then headed for the rear hatch and opened it.

Glancing in at the heaps of clothing she had been sewing, Holly hoped she had remembered everything. As usual these days, she hadn't slept well the night before. She'd gone to bed shortly after settling Tommy down after his latest nightmare, but had lain there wide-eyed, worrying about her son.

And thinking of Gabe.

He'd suffered childhood trauma as Tommy had. He seemed to have turned out a well-adjusted, self-confident man.

A sexy man...

Oh, yes. She'd considered that damn kiss a lot, too. *Hope you enjoyed it,* she scolded herself. *It won't happen again.*

Since she wasn't sleeping anyway, she'd risen early and done some last-minute stitchery on the costumes she had been commissioned to sew for the Naranja Community Theater.

"Here, Tommy. You take this." She handed him two folded aprons, then smiled at his pleased grin. She filled her own arms but would have to make more trips to the van for the rest.

The lobby of City Hall was even more magnificent than its exterior, with exquisite tilework on floor and walls. As they waited for an elevator, Holly glanced around in alarm. How could she have forgotten that the police station was at the rear of the first floor? What if Tommy saw a cop in uniform? Would he fall apart again?

Tommy had also been to the station with Thomas several times. Would this additional reminder of his daddy upset him?

The elevator arrived quickly—all the more fortunate because Holly recognized a local reporter—one more persistent than the rest who was still, after all her refusals, trying to get her to give an interview.

Holly hustled Tommy inside. "Do you want to push the button?" When he nodded, she told him to touch the number three for the top floor.

The receptionist helped to carry some of the things Holly had toted upstairs into Evangeline Sevvers's inner sanctum. The mayor's office was appropriately subdued, notwithstanding the flamboyance of its current inhabitant, with dark wood paneling, a vast but plain-looking wooden desk, and beige leather chairs.

"Sit down, sit down," Evangeline said, standing immediately upon their entry. As usual, she wore an attractive, feminine suit. Today's was a brilliant lime green that contrasted appealingly with the unusual red of her hair, a cloud of waves about her long, narrow face. Her blouse was tailored, and she wore a multicolor scarf about her neck. This time it was her bright scarlet lipstick that clashed with her hair.

Holly wondered whether her own denim skirt and dark blue blouse were dressy enough for visiting this estimable office. But she wouldn't worry about it. Unlike Evangeline, she didn't need to impress anyone.

"What do we have here?" Evangeline gestured toward the pile of clothing. She regarded Tommy expectantly, as if he would explain.

He held out his arms, proffering the garments he held toward her, but, as Holly anticipated, didn't say a word.

"Can you tell me what these are?" Evangeline persisted.

Tommy's small brow puckered, and his lower lip trembled. "Tommy's still taking a vacation from talking right now," Holly quickly interjected in a bright tone tempered by a warning glance at the mayor. "He'll speak again when he's ready."

"Okay." Evangeline ruffled Tommy's hair as he climbed onto the leather sofa. The mayor was known for political aspirations and for her brashness. But Holly knew her as a kind woman.

After last night, she had more insight into why. Evangeline was a Sevvers, part of the family who had taken in the orphaned Gabe. Holly ached to ask Evangeline about Gabe and his childhood. For Tommy's sake, of course. Maybe she would have some suggestions.

And Holly was curious about the man who had kissed her....

But she couldn't ask in front of Tommy.

Instead, she said, "I think I've brought everything—overalls for sanitation workers, aprons for shopkeepers, T-shirts for lifeguards, yellow vests for crossing guards and polka-dotted pajamas for the actor playing the fire department's dalmatian mascot."

"Great!" Evangeline said. "And right when you'd promised, too. I figured you'd need more time, what with—"

"I'd finished a lot before," Holly told her hurriedly. "And sometimes it's a good thing not to sleep well at night."

"How are you getting along?"

Not wanting to talk about herself, Holly said "okay," then countered with a question of her own. "I've been dying to learn more about your show—a parody of the Olympic Games?"

"Right. We pit government workers against one another

in contests like castle-building. Lifeguards use sand, street workers use concrete and sanitation workers use garbage. Everyone sings and dances—it's a riot! You won't believe how good Sheldon Sperling is.''

Evangeline was right. Holly couldn't picture the usually sedate Sheldon kicking up his heels in a musical farce.

Could he dance now, with his injuries?

"All proceeds will benefit the Naranja Children's Foundation," Evangeline finished.

"Sounds great! But I could have dropped the costumes off at the theater. Now you'll have to drag everything there.''

"The high school orchestra is holding a concert there this evening," Evangeline said. "I didn't want to leave the costumes so a bunch of rowdy teenagers could play with them. We've a few stored other places from our wardrobe stockpiles, too.''

"I understand," Holly said with a grin. "When does the show begin?"

"In ten days. Dress rehearsals start this week, though, so I'm really grateful for your promptness in getting these done.''

"There are still some things in the van. I'll get them, though I might need to make two trips.''

"I'll come and save you some steps." She leaned toward Holly as if about to share a confidence. "Sometimes I go stir-crazy in this office. Too stodgy. I need air.''

Holly laughed.

"Ready, Tommy?" Evangeline asked. She put out her hand. Tommy hesitated before taking it, glancing toward Holly.

Poor child. He'd never been shy before. Holly nodded toward him, then followed the mayor and her son out the door.

In the lobby, Holly turned when she heard her name, praying it wasn't the reporter.

Edie Bryerly hurried toward them from a hallway that led to the Planning Department, where she worked as a secretary. The length of her slender legs seemed exaggerated by the shortness of her skirt. "You weren't going to leave yet, were you, Holly?"

"Not without saying hello." Holly had called Edie earlier to let her know that Tommy and she would be at City Hall. "We're getting the rest of the costumes from the van. Want to help?"

"Sure."

Holly's minivan was parked outside at a meter. She pushed a button on her keychain and the rear latch unlocked. Holly split the remaining costumes up among the four of them, including something small for Tommy.

When they reentered City Hall, Al Sharp was in the lobby with Dolph Hilo. Both cops were in patrol uniforms.

Taking a deep breath, Holly watched Tommy's eyes widen when he noticed them. Steeling herself for his screams, she quickly bent despite the clothing she carried and freed an arm to pull him tightly to her.

To her surprise, though he trembled, he didn't cry out.

"Hey, sport," called a familiar deep voice.

Holly looked around. Gabe McLaren strode toward them. He wore a gray shirt, a tie and dark slacks.

He caught Holly's gaze, then smiled at Tommy. "Looks like you're busy, but when you're done, how would you like to help me decide what kind of candy to keep around the police station for good little kids who come for a visit?"

"Lollipops," Dolph Hilo said. "Please, boss?" He winked at Holly.

"Chocolate's the way to go," Al muttered, but he grinned.

"I'm not sure it's a good idea for us to visit the station right now," Holly interjected quickly.

"What do you think, Tommy?" Gabe asked. "We can settle this candy issue right here, but if you visit my office I can give you samples to help you decide—if it's okay with your mom. Do you want to come in?"

Tommy was clearly torn. He hesitated, looking from Al to Dolph and back again. Or was it only their uniforms he was studying? Holly didn't want to ask.

And then, very slowly, Tommy nodded at Gabe.

FIVE MINUTES LATER, after the rest of the costumes were in Evangeline's office, Holly took Tommy back downstairs. In the lobby, crowded with tourists from a sightseeing bus, Holly held his hand firmly as she asked, "Do you want to go see Gabe now?"

When he hesitated, Holly said, "Would you rather go home?"

Tommy shook his head. He tugged on her hand, heading toward the police station at the rear of the lobby.

Holly was amazed. This seemed a giant improvement. Not only hadn't he screamed at the sight of the uniformed officers, but he voluntarily headed toward the place in Naranja Beach that he was likely to see the most uniforms.

A place that would remind him of missing his daddy.

She might have been wrong about why Tommy screamed. But if not because uniforms reminded him of losing Thomas, what was it?

She held Tommy's hand tightly as they entered.

"Hi, Tommy," said Bruce Franklin, who was, of course, in uniform. "Give me five." He held out his hand.

To Holly's surprise, Tommy let go of her and slapped his small palm against Bruce's larger, darker one.

"There you two are." Gabe approached them. As his eyes caught hers, the rhythm of her heart grew erratic.

Get a grip. He'd only invited them here as part of his campaign to help them. To help Tommy.

"Have you ever sat in the police chief's chair?" Gabe asked Tommy.

He shook his head, and his eyes sparkled.

"Come on then." Gabe held out his hand, and the two headed for the back of the station.

Holly wasn't thrilled. What if her son decided he liked it there, in the chief's chair? What if he decided to follow in his father's footsteps, become a cop?

She shook her head in wry amusement. Tommy was only four years old. He wasn't going to make that decision now, or even later, on the basis of sitting in some symbolic chair.

Holly had known Gabe's predecessor, Mal Kensington. She had even come to the station when he was in charge. But there'd been no reason for her to visit his office. The place looked like a government office. The furniture was clean but utilitarian. The desk was nearly bare.

But Gabe had put his own stamp on the room. On the walls were plaques and photos that spoke of his accomplishments.

Still, the place needed a little color. Holly thought of a wall hanging she'd worked on before her commission to sew the costumes for Evangeline's show. It was a representation of the ocean, with deep blues and greens and occasional brighter colors depicting kelp and tropical fish. It would go well here, in a blank area right behind Gabe's desk.

Not that she'd ever suggest it to him.

She watched with fondness as Gabe gave Tommy small pieces of candy to try, as if his opinion were of utmost importance. She'd planned on getting him straight home for a nap, but this male bonding was important for her son, too.

It might encourage him to talk.

She wondered, though, about allowing him to get too close to Gabe McLaren. It might be a bad idea. A very bad idea.

For both Tommy and her.

Holly's eyes wandered idly over the few papers on Gabe's desk. They settled on a file labeled Poston. It wasn't particularly thick.

Was that what Thomas's life—and death—had come to? A few pieces of paper on the desk of the man who'd briefly been his boss?

Suddenly, Holly needed to get out of there. "Tommy, it's time for us to go home. You can tell Chief McLaren later what kind of candy you think he should keep here."

She watched both sets of eyes widen. Gabe's gaze turned quizzical, then shuttered over. But she owed him no explanation.

"Your mom's right," he said to Tommy. "But I won't make a decision on the candy till I get your opinion, okay?"

Tommy nodded, then shook hands with Gabe.

The ride home was short. Naranja Beach was a small enough town that nothing was too far from City Hall.

Holly parked out front rather than in the garage, for she had some further errands to run later.

After she unstrapped Tommy from his seat belt, she was surprised when he made a beeline for the front porch. He turned back to face her, a box in his arms.

Had the mailman brought something? When she reached

his side on the porch, she noticed the box was addressed to Tommy, and the return address was Edie's. What had Edie sent? And why hadn't she mentioned it before?

"This is for you," she told Tommy. "Let's open it inside."

She saw excitement glimmer in her son's eyes and knew it was all he could do to be patient for even that short amount of time.

In the den, she used scissors to slit the tape at the edges. She rested the box on the coffee table. "Okay, open it."

Using a lot of effort for his small fingers, Tommy pulled the cardboard flaps up. Then he looked inside.

He began to scream.

"Tommy! What is it?" Holly took the box and pulled back the flaps, which had fallen back over the contents.

She suddenly felt like screaming, too.

Inside was a male doll dressed in a police patrol uniform. On its chest were globs of red paint that resembled blood.

Chapter Six

Gabe pounded on Holly's front door again.

He had jumped into his car immediately after her near-hysterical phone call to him at the station. Now, he'd been standing here—what? Two minutes? Three? But no one had yet answered the doorbell or his knocks.

He sized up the door. It appeared thick and solid. It had a deadbolt. And if Holly was taking his advice, she kept the door locked at all times.

Still, if she didn't answer in another minute, he could probably splinter it with one good, solid kick.

He heard a click, and then the door was thrown open.

Holly looked frantic. Her eyes were wide and frightened, her lovely dark hair disarrayed. "Oh, Gabe." Her voice was nearly a wail. To his surprise, she threw herself toward him.

He'd worn his shoulder holster beneath his jacket, and he caught her in his arms at his other side. He doubted that the protection a weapon offered was the kind of comfort she craved as she pressed herself close.

Under other circumstances, the feeling of her slender curves tight against him would have felt good. Damn good.

But these were not other circumstances.

"Let's go inside," he ordered.

"O-okay," Holly stammered. She was trembling so hard he wondered how she remained standing. He led her into the house, then released her to lock the door again behind them.

He faced her. She appeared fragile, almost waiflike, in her long denim skirt and blue blouse.

"How's Tommy?"

She put her head in her hands. For a moment, she didn't reply, and by the way her shoulders shook he knew she was crying.

He put an arm around her, but she pulled back. Her eyes were wet. "I—I'm sorry. I didn't mean to fall apart. Tommy's in bed. I just got him quieted before you arrived. He kept screaming."

"Let me see the package."

Her gaze met his, and in them he saw a mute plea.

"Tell me where it is," he said gently.

She took a deep breath. "I put it in the kitchen." She looked brave standing there, her head high, her tears stanched, her teeth chewing on her full bottom lip.

He wanted to brush his fingers along her chin in encouragement. To touch her lips, rosy from the way she worried at them, with his own mouth, very softly, to show his support.

Instead, he yanked his gaze away. "I'll go take a look," he said gruffly. He was here as a police officer this time, first and foremost. Offering comfort was secondary to this mission.

In the kitchen, he looked around till he found the box. She'd tossed it into the sink. The open end was down, and the contents weren't visible.

He pulled out latex gloves from his pocket and put them on. Touching only edges of the box to avoid damaging latent fingerprints, he turned it over.

"Damn." Holly's frantic description when she'd called hadn't exactly been coherent. But it had been graphic enough. Still, the reality was a lot worse than the disjointed report.

Yeah, it was just a doll. A male doll, dressed to look like a cop. It made Gabe's skin crawl.

He'd seen live cops as bloody as this representation. Dying cops. Dead cops. Brother cops.

Cops like Thomas Poston. And Gabe's own father.

"I'll get you, you son of a bitch," he muttered. Whoever did this had clearly intended the reaction elicited from poor little Tommy. A four-year-old. What kind of filthy crud would do this to a child, remind him of how he had found his own daddy?

Who would do it to that child's mother, a grieving widow?

Gabe would find out. Heaven help him, he would find out.

He left the doll and its box on the kitchen counter. He removed his gloves and stuffed them back into his pocket.

Holly was no longer in the entry. Nor was she in the living room. He didn't want to call out. It might upset Tommy.

He went up the steps. Holly stood in the doorway to Tommy's room. She had obviously heard Gabe's approach, for she glanced toward him. "Tommy's still awake," she said brightly. "I told him you were the person he heard at the door, and he's promised to rest as soon as he's seen you."

He touched Holly's shoulder as he slipped past her into the room. It was late afternoon, and the room was filled with shadows interrupted by slivers of sunlight that slipped through the miniblind slats.

Tommy sat rigidly beneath the covers of his twin-size

bed. His back rested against the wood headboard. He was still dressed in the bright orange T-shirt Gabe had seen him in earlier that promoted Naranja Beach. His face was so grave that he looked like a mini-adult. The room smelled of crayons and baby powder.

"Hey, sport," Gabe said softly. He sat on the edge of the bed and took Tommy's hand. Though the boy was swathed in blankets, his small fingers were frozen.

Gabe considered avoiding the subject of the malicious doll. But when he was a kid, it had helped when people talked about what hurt him instead of pretending it hadn't happened.

"You got a nasty surprise today, didn't you—that package you thought was a present?"

Gabe heard Holly's intake of breath. He turned. She stood beside him, ashen. As their gazes caught, she gave an almost imperceptible shake of her head. She didn't want him to talk about it.

"Just a second," he told Tommy. He led Holly into the hall. "Trust me on this," he said.

"I don't want him to have to think about it." Holly's arms were folded and her eyes glinted in steely determination.

"But it's something else he needs to talk out. Look, just let me tell him one thing, okay? It'll help him."

"You're positive?"

"Sure." He hoped.

Holly continued to stare at him. Then she nodded, very slowly. "I want this piece of crud stopped, Gabe. And I'll do anything to help—anything but hurt Tommy. Is that understood?"

"Of course. That's what I intend, too." Tearing his gaze from her scared but resolute gaze, he returned to stand beside Tommy's bed. "That doll was really awful, wasn't it?'' he said. ''It was dressed to look like a policeman, and it was hurt. Did it remind you of your daddy?''

Gabe felt Holly, who stood beside him, squeeze his arm as if in warning. He continued anyway. ''Sport, your mom thinks we should forget about that doll. Maybe she's right. But first I want you to understand that whoever sent it is a very, very bad person who wanted to scare you. And the best way to pay that person back is not to be scared. I'll make sure whoever hurt your daddy can't hurt you. And we'll be here whenever you're ready to talk about it, okay?''

At first, there was no reaction. Beside him, Holly shifted, her anger and anxiety hovering around him like a cloud of black smoke. Tension squeezed the muscles between his own shoulders. Damn! Had he made a mistake? But then a tear rolled down Tommy's cheeks. His arms slipped from beneath the bedcovers. He reached one small hand in Gabe's direction and the other toward his mother.

''Oh, honey,'' Holly said. Moving around Gabe, she returned to the bed and grasped Tommy with one arm. The other went around Gabe, who knelt, and the three of them held each other tightly in one big, supportive hug.

Gabe liked the feeling. Too much. It imparted sensations he didn't want to feel. He wasn't part of their family.

He gently extricated himself and stood. ''You need to take a nap now, sport. But I'll be around later. I'm really up for a game of catch this evening. How about you?''

Tommy's head appeared from around his mother's side. Gabe's heart turned a somersault of pleasure at the boy's tiny grin.

HOLLY WAS THRILLED.

No, she was furious. With Gabe.

With herself.

But mostly with the horrible person who'd left the doll, who'd most likely killed Thomas and hurt Sheldon.

And terrified Tommy—more than once.

This had to stop. *She* had to stop it. It wasn't only police business when it continued to hurt her family. But what could she do?

Gabe left the room, but she sat on the edge of Tommy's bed. "Rest now, sweetheart."

His eyes began to droop. She stood, but waited in the doorway. And stewed.

She didn't want Gabe to talk to her son about upsetting things. She needed to protect Tommy.

Except… Gabe had been right. Before Gabe had arrived, Tommy's fright had been nearly palpable enough for her to grab it. But Gabe talked to Tommy, and her son had clearly calmed.

Now, Tommy nestled down in the bed, his soft dark hair contrasting with the bright blue pillowcase. His eyes closed. Holly left the room.

She found Gabe in the living room. Tall, with the perfect posture of a man certain of himself, he paced as he talked on his cell phone. At her entrance, he ended his conversation and tucked his phone into his pants pocket. The movement disturbed his jacket, and she glimpsed the strap of a shoulder holster over his gray shirt. She sucked in her breath.

She'd been used to Thomas having guns around. But they had been part of his uniform. Gabe wore a suit like a businessman.

"Is Tommy okay now?" he asked.

"As okay as can be expected." *After being traumatized, then reminded about it. Damn!*

"Good," Gabe said. "Just so you know, Edie Bryerly

is coming here. I called on my way downstairs, and she should arrive any minute.''

"Edie? Why?"

He didn't have a chance to answer. A quiet knock sounded on the front door. "I told her Tommy was napping and that I'd listen for her," Gabe told Holly. He proceeded to answer the door to her house.

Holly wanted to yell at him.

But she had no time. Edie, dressed in the same short red skirt and white blouse she'd worn before, blasted into the entry as if tossed in by a tornado. "What happened?" Her brown eyes were supercharged with emotion. "I was on my way home for the day when Gabe tracked me down. Fortunately, I was nearby."

"Come into the living room." Holly didn't give Gabe an opportunity to take control once more. She fell in line behind Edie, leaving Gabe to follow.

Holly encouraged Edie to take a seat on the sofa, then plumped down, too, and grabbed a gold-and-green throw pillow for support. She began, "Edie, you need to know—"

"Wait!" Gabe interrupted. "Don't say anything. Let me show her." His green eyes asserted command. Holly opened her mouth to oppose him, then shut it again. She had seen that look before, on other cops.

"Oh, my lord!" Edie exclaimed when Gabe returned, that awful box held gingerly in hands clad in translucent gloves. Edie's face paled as she stared at its contents. She turned to Holly beseechingly. "Tell me Tommy didn't see that horrible doll."

Holly felt her eyes water. Edie said, "Oh, no. He did. Holly, how terrible! Is he okay?"

"As well as can be expected," Gabe replied. He maneuvered the box so the bottom was up. Edie's eyes lit on the label.

"That's my return address," she shrilled. She stared at Gabe. "I didn't send it. I wouldn't." She turned mutely toward Holly, pleading for support.

"Of course you didn't, but someone wanted the police to think you did." Holly glared defiantly toward Gabe. "Edie's practically a second mother to Tommy. She wouldn't do this. But why would whoever did it want to implicate her?"

Gabe put the box on top of a pile of magazines on the coffee table. That horrible effigy of a murdered cop—of Thomas—shouted soundlessly at them. Holly wanted to snatch it up and bury it at the bottom of the garbage can beside the house.

No, she didn't. She didn't want to get anywhere near the blasted thing.

"I need to ask you some questions, Ms. Bryerly," Gabe said. He pulled a small notebook from an inside jacket pocket, then crossed one leg over the other. His commanding presence seemed to overpower the chair, the entire room. Or perhaps it was just Holly's sense of inevitability. Gabe McLaren was a cop on a case. He wouldn't quit until it was solved.

This time, she had to applaud. Silently of course. But she had to know all the answers he sought.

"Of course, Chief McLaren," Edie said. "But please call me Edie."

Ah, Holly thought. Her friend must be feeling better, for she was flirting as she did with any male over the age of twenty-one. Holly frowned, then wanted to kick herself. She had no reason to feel jealous of anything between Gabe McLaren and Edie.

She listened to Gabe's friendly but insistent interrogation as he asked Edie where she had been during the past few days, if she had ever bought a doll like that one, if she had any idea who might play such a horrible trick on Tommy, Holly or her. Edie's answers made it clear she was as much in the dark as they were.

When Gabe's questioning was over, he stood. "Thank you, Edie. If I think of anything else, I'll call you."

"Please do." Edie rose and headed for the door, then turned back. "Whether or not your questions have anything to do with police business." She smiled at him, gave a mischievous little wave toward Holly, then left.

For the first time ever, Holly was more than happy to see the last, for now, of her friend's provocatively swaying behind.

BACK AT CITY HALL, Gabe gave the doll to Detective Jimmy Hernandez for analysis and further investigation.

"Miserable stuff, Gabe," Jimmy said, shaking his head as he accepted the box in his own gloved hand.

Gabe agreed. But he didn't have time to talk about it. He'd promised to meet Evangeline that morning on the Poston case—and another matter.

He took the stairs to the third floor. The receptionist asked him to wait while the mayor finished a phone call.

Looking out the waiting area window, he scanned the busy downtown street below with the eyes of a cop. Everything looked in order. In fact, this view was a dream for anyone, whether or not a police officer. Not far in the distance was the curved, sandy shoreline with its pier jutting far into the water—the true beach of the town of Naranja Beach, crowded with tourists and locals and awash with soft ocean waves.

He had wondered what had made Evangeline move with little notice to Southern California while he was away at college, until he'd come for a visit. The temperate weather, the gorgeous beaches, the laid-back lifestyle...they had tempted him, too.

And when Aunt Evangeline had offered him not only the police chief's job, but also the opportunity to pay at least one member of the Sevvers family back for their kindness to an orphaned kid, he'd jumped at it.

Now, he had to perform.

Evangeline opened her office door. "Gabe. Come in."

He waved his thanks to the receptionist and shut the door behind him. "Your Honor. How the hell are you?" Gabe grinned at the woman who had been like an aunt to him.

She grimaced primly, then smiled and hugged him. She was a slender woman, as political in her diet as in everything else. "I'm fine. Have a seat, nephew."

As he'd grown up, Evangeline, now in her forties, hadn't been the closest Sevvers to him, but like the rest, she'd accepted him as if he had always belonged to the family. She'd been a strong-willed young woman prepared to achieve whatever ambition she set her mind to. He had figured it would be something like being her own boss, owning a store.

That was the first thing she'd accomplished at Naranja Beach.

He hadn't figured she'd go into politics. Yet her being mayor, running the whole darn town, seemed a great fit.

But the town hadn't operated as perfectly as she'd anticipated during her tenure. That was why she had hired Gabe.

Now, she joined him on the sofa. Her manicured fingernails tapped a tattoo on the beige leather only a few shades darker than the suit she wore. "So what do you know, Gabe?"

"Not enough." He told her about the butchered doll at the Postons'. The outrage on her face mirrored his own. "Since the Poston murder, I haven't had time for our other matter."

"Poor Holly," Evangeline said. Gabe thought his face was blank, but she must have read something in it for she grinned at him archly. "She's a pretty lady, isn't she?"

"Yeah," Gabe said as Holly's lovely, sad face displayed in his mind as if on a dormant computer screen reactivated by keys that had just been tapped. Or had it ever left his thoughts at all?

She had questioned the way he had handled things with Tommy. But she'd been gracious enough to thank him. She'd begged him again, as he'd taken the doll away, to find out who had sent it.

And he'd made promises he probably had no business making. But how could he resist the plea in those dark eyes, those pools of dark, luminous sorrow and sensuality?

Evangeline shifted on the crackling leather sofa, recapturing Gabe's attention. "It's none of my business, Gabe, but Holly's a friend. She's also a new widow. It's one thing to handle the inquiry into Thomas's death and this new nastiness, but don't expect anything from her, at least not now."

He didn't need Evangeline's warning not to get too attracted to Holly Poston. *As if you can help it, pervert....*

"I don't expect anything except to solve a murder," he said with a scowl, changing the subject decisively. "*Both* murders."

"You don't suppose they're related, do you?"

Gabe shrugged. "Two cops dead? Yeah, I *do* suppose they're related. Though proving it is another matter."

"If anyone can do it, you can. Your reputation says so." She smiled again, but she wasn't completely teasing. His reputation was the main reason Evangeline had wanted him as police chief after his predecessor's death—not only because he was her more-or-less adopted nephew. He had already worked his way up to captain in the Detective Division of the Sacramento P.D. Even at that, Evangeline had only hired him after putting him through a screening that would have crushed a lesser cop.

She'd explained it in advance: there would be accusations of nepotism, and they'd be true. But that didn't bother her.

She'd already weathered claims of conflict of interest during her political campaign, for she had always intended to maintain her own shop. After all, she wouldn't be mayor forever. She'd hit the controversy head-on, put her manager in charge of the store, then described how she would work her tail off for the economy of the whole area. And if that benefited her, too, as one small business owner among others, then so be it.

She had been elected.

The case that Evangeline had needed him for here initially remained a mystery: the murder of his predecessor, Police Chief Mal Kensington. If it even *was* a murder.

Gabe's gut told him it was. But so far, neither Jimmy Hernandez—who knew the story—nor he had unearthed any proof.

"Have you learned anything useful since the last time we talked?" Evangeline asked.

"Only innuendoes. I've had more casual conversations with detectives and beat cops. A lot expressed their surprise that someone as apparently healthy as Mal Kensington keeled over and died. But it happens, even with athletes in top form."

"But that was too facile. I still don't buy it."

Neither did Gabe, though by appearances the conclusions seemed correct. Mal had suffered the symptoms of a heart attack. That was the cause of death according to his autopsy, too. But… "I'd disagree if it weren't for the rest," Gabe said.

Evangeline's brusque nod seemed pleased.

They'd gone through this often. Mal's remains had been cremated quickly and scattered in the ocean. His family left town and settled in Beverly Hills, though his widow had no job. Of course there had been insurance, but not a huge amount.

None of that would have signified much to Gabe, except for what Evangeline had told him was going on when Mal died.

Several months before Mal's death, four shopkeepers along Pacific Way had sold out—cheap. The stores that opened in their places were not of the same high quality as Evangeline's boutique, Orange, or other established shops along the Way.

Worried this was a harbinger of a downturn in the Naranja Beach economy, Evangeline had contacted those who'd left and as tactfully as possible asked why. Three had given no answer but were clearly angry and uncomfortable. The fourth blurted out, "Ask your beloved chief of police," before also clamming up.

Evangeline *had* asked Mal Kensington if he knew what that comment meant. He'd said no, claimed it was merely sour grapes on the part of someone who'd failed in business.

But Evangeline hadn't been satisfied. She'd gone to other shop owners along the Way and asked questions. The answers hadn't satisfied her, so she requested an investigation before city council to ensure that the few sell-outs did not turn into a trend. She'd even asked Mal to appear before council and explain his lack of knowledge about what that storeowner had meant.

There, he had blustered but had seemed more than a little ill at ease, according to Evangeline. Had it been fear?

She would never know, for she couldn't question him further. The next day, he'd had his supposed heart attack and died.

Even if it had been a heart attack, she'd told Gabe, maybe it had been brought on by fear. But fear of what?

Gabe's mission was to conduct a clandestine investigation. But as straightforward as most people had replied to his offhand questions, he sensed there was a lot they weren't telling.

What? Why? And what did it have to do with Mal Kensington's—and now Thomas Poston's—death?

Evangeline stood. She glared at Gabe until he rose, too. "Time's passing, Gabe." Her tone was full of frustration. "If we don't get answers soon, we'll never get them."

"I know." But Gabe wasn't about to fail. Somehow, he would learn what happened—or satisfy both himself and Evangeline that Mal's death had been just a nasty coincidence.

Though Gabe didn't believe in coincidences.

"Can you use Thomas Poston's death as an opportunity?"

Gabe stiffened, surprised at his aunt's insensitivity. She was, after all, a political animal.

She waved her hands as if to erase the comment. "I didn't mean to seem cold-blooded, but it'll give you a reason to ask more questions. If the two deaths were related… What about Holly? Could she know why Thomas was killed?"

Holly's lovely, sorrowful face washed across Gabe's mind. So did her fierce concern for her son. Her sense of humor in moments she wasn't thinking about all that had happened to her.

Her unconscious sex appeal…

She seemed forthright. Eager to solve her husband's murder.

Still, there was always the possibility she knew something she wasn't saying. There were different ways of keeping quiet than the way poor little Tommy was doing it.

"I don't know," Gabe said. "But I've been playing Sevvers to her."

"What do you mean?" Evangeline asked suspiciously.

"Taking care of the bereaved family," he explained. "Helping with what they need around the house. In fact, I'm on my way back there now. It's a good way to get Holly to trust me. And if there's something she knows that she hasn't said yet, she will. I'm definitely going to find it out."

Chapter Seven

Removing the apron from over her blouse and denim skirt, Holly looked out her kitchen window and smiled.

Tommy ran around the compact backyard, laughing as he chased the large ball. His thin legs pumped beneath his shorts. When he reached the ball, he knelt and picked it up in his arms.

Thanks to Gabe, he seemed to be putting the doll incident behind him.

Gabe stood at one side of the yard, clapping his hands in encouragement to Tommy. He was dressed more casually than she had ever seen him. As good-looking as he was while in his regulation suit, he now looked sexier than any man had a right to, in his snug, low jeans and muscle-delineating gray T-shirt.

As promised, he had returned this evening in time to play with Tommy. But something had changed in his attitude toward *her*. Although he had asked if there was anything she needed done around the house, had thanked her profusely for the modest dinner of a tuna-noodle casserole she had prepared, he had seemed more formal. Had acted as if he expected something of her, without saying what.

Holly sighed. Maybe after Tommy was in bed, she could ask him.

The telephone rang.

She went to the extension hanging on the kitchen wall near the door and lifted the receiver. "Hello?"

"Just listen, Mrs. Poston," said a strange, echoing voice. She could not tell if it was male or female or even computer-generated. Probably a telemarketing call, she thought, preparing to hang up. "You know where it is," the voice went on. "What Thomas left for me. You will turn it over to me. Otherwise, you will suffer the consequences, sweet little Tommy and you."

Ice slivered through Holly's veins. "Who are you?" she asked, her tone weak and shaky. "What is it you want?"

"You know what it is."

"I don't," she cried.

"Figure it out. I'll be in touch." There was a click.

"Hello?" For a few long moments, Holly clutched the receiver to her ear. Then, slowly, she hung up. She stared at the wall phone as if it had suddenly morphed into a cobra.

"Tommy!" she whispered. She hurried to the kitchen window and looked out.

The ball game was still in progress. Gabe ran toward Tommy, who held the ball. He grabbed the boy, gently tackling him and laying him on the grass. Tommy, laughing, rolled out from beneath Gabe's grasp and ran. At the end of the small patch of lawn, he plunked the ball down on the patio.

"Touchdown!" Gabe's deep voice resounded.

"Time to come in," Holly called shrilly. "Tommy needs to get ready for bed."

Gabe glanced at his watch, then toward her, puzzlement on his face. He was right. It was early.

But she couldn't stand the thought of her son still being outside, possibly in danger. That damned phone call....

"Okay, sport," Gabe called. "Your mom's the boss. Let's go in."

As they entered the kitchen, she again saw a question in Gabe's eyes. They skimmed down her, as if her distress and fear were inscribed all over her.

Shaking her head, she ushered Tommy toward the stairs—her skin prickling as she felt Gabe's eyes bore into her back.

"OKAY. WHAT IS IT?"

Holly had bathed Tommy and gotten him ready for bed. Gabe had read the boy a story. Now, they stood at the front door. She clearly wanted him to leave.

When she had called Tommy and him inside, he had noticed the pallor of her skin, the anguished, glazed look in her eyes. She looked the same now, almost an hour later. He hated to see her so upset. He wasn't leaving until he knew what was wrong.

She hesitated. "I got a phone call while you were outside."

"Who from?"

"I don't know!" Tears rushed to her eyes. He instinctively pulled her close. She trembled, and he held her even tighter, dipping his head so it rested on her soft and clean-scented hair.

Apricots. She smelled like apricots.

But then she drew back. "Sorry," she whispered. She visibly pulled herself together. "Can you stay while I explain?"

He nodded and followed her back into the kitchen, flexing his hands. They ached. Not with pain. Oh, no. That would have been acceptable.

No, they were stupid enough to want to hold her again.

"Would you like some coffee?" she asked brightly.

The last time she had offered decaf this late. The caffeine jolt of real coffee might knock some sense into him. It didn't matter which he drank, though. He accepted because it would be easier for her to speak if she did something productive. "Thanks. Now tell me about the call."

In an offhand voice, as if she talked about the weather at the beach that day, she described the mechanical voice and what it had said. But her jerky motions as she poured water and scooped grounds for coffee told him how hard this was.

Her anguish fired his fury.

He had wondered earlier if she knew something she wasn't telling. That could still be true. But he didn't doubt she'd received a call that had frightened her. Her terror was real.

When she was done, he went to the phone and slammed in *69, to dial the number from which the last call was received. After ten rings, an irritated, non-mechanical voice answered. He'd reached a pay phone near a bus stop at the edge of Naranja Beach. Gabe forced himself to hang up gently.

Holly sighed at the news. "I didn't imagine it would be that easy."

"What was the person who called referring to?" Gabe demanded. "What did Thomas leave?"

She shook her head slowly. "I don't know." She looked as needy as her small son had when he first woke from his nap.

Was she lying? Gabe didn't think so. He wished whoever made that damned call was right there, so he could practice restraint techniques on the son of a bitch. Hard.

"We'll figure this out," he assured Holly. "Where would Thomas have kept something he didn't want you to know about?"

Her mouth opened as if in protest, then closed again. Did she think her husband would never have kept secrets from her? Her naiveté irritated Gabe—but not as much as the idea she'd been that close to Thomas Poston.

Fool. He was her husband. Her loving *husband.*

"I began going through the things in his study the other night," she told him.

"Let's start there."

Gabe followed her down the hall. She pushed open a door that had been closed each time Gabe had been here.

The small room was clearly a man's study, containing only a scratched desk, a worn leather chair on rollers, a small television on a stand and computer on its own cart with wheels. There were papers everywhere. He followed Holly inside.

When she reached the desk, she cried out, as if in alarm.

"What's wrong?" Gabe demanded.

When she looked at him, her eyes were fearful once more. She gestured toward the messy desktop, which was strewn with papers, folders and magazines. "I—I came in here the other night when I couldn't sleep. I started going through things but realized how monumental a task it was. All I accomplished was to put everything on Thomas's desk in neat piles."

He glanced at the disorganized heap to which she pointed. "Who else has been in here?"

"No one has been alone in the house except Tommy and me, and Tommy learned a long time ago that this room is off-limits. Someone—I'm afraid someone has broken into my house."

HOLLY MADE HERSELF remain calm as Gabe and she went from room to room, making certain nothing had been stolen.

She hadn't much of value to anyone else. The place settings of silver flatware that her parents had given Thomas and her as a wedding present were still in the dining room hutch, and so was her good china. Nothing electronic like TVs or Thomas's computer appeared to have been tampered with.

As far as she could tell, the only thing the intruder had done was to mess up Thomas's desk.

"You didn't leave a window open in here, did you?" Gabe asked when they returned to the office.

She shook her head. "I've kept this room closed up since Thomas's death."

"I'll get an investigative team here right away," he said. "Maybe we'll find prints or other evidence. This and the doll have to be connected to Thomas's murder."

They returned to the kitchen, where she poured them both some coffee. A while later, the doorbell rang, and a crime scene team came in, led by a detective named Jimmy Hernandez, who looked familiar to Holly. After Gabe introduced them, Holly stayed in the office while they went through things, took fingerprints, picked up other small things she couldn't discern in tweezers and placed them in plastic bags—hairs, she supposed.

She made certain they didn't remove any papers. She had to go through things herself later to see if she could figure out what the caller could have been talking about.

Would she even know it if she came across it? How could she, with so little to go on? But she would have to try. Tonight, after Gabe had gone. She wouldn't sleep well anyway. And she had to know. Had to get this terror to stop.

When the crime scene team finished, Gabe stood inside the doorway with her after letting them out. She figured he would say his goodbyes, then leave.

Instead, he dropped a bombshell.

"Holly, I'm staying here tonight."

GABE SAW THE SHOCK register on Holly's face. And then her determination to tell him no.

He forestalled it. "You got a threatening phone call. That person could call again. Do you want to talk to him or her?"

"Of course not, but even if you stay the night, you won't be here forever. And the person might only get angry if I look like I've called in the police."

"You're a police officer's widow. Of course you'd call them in. And I repeat—do you want to talk to that person?"

"No." Holly's slender shoulders sagged. His heart went out to her, but he couldn't let up. He had a case to solve. Two cases. And whether or not she assisted him willingly, he was damn well going to protect Holly Poston and her son.

"Even worse than the phone call, someone has been in this house. Do you know when? How he or she got in?"

"No." This time the word sounded anguished. She took a step away as if he had struck her. But then she asked quietly, "Do you think he'll be back? I'm going to assume it's a man, because—because I just can't imagine a woman so menacing."

Gabe didn't contradict her. "Yes," he said calmly, but with all the brutality that small word implied. "I believe he'll be back. He wants something. He sent Tommy that doll to scare you both. He broke into your house and didn't clean up, wanted you to realize he was here. He threatened you. So, yes, we have to assume he hasn't gone away. That's why I'm staying the night."

"All right," she said finally, very softly.

Perhaps he should have felt triumph at this capitulation. Instead, he felt like the biggest bully on all the state's law enforcement agencies.

HOLLY WATCHED out the front door as Gabe pulled his blue Mustang into her driveway. It had to be his personal car. She had seen him driving a sedate sedan, too, probably N.B.P.D.-issued.

He didn't come right into the house, but seemed to check something in the car.

He glanced up and caught her eye. And scowled. No doubt he didn't like her standing backlighted in the doorway—a target.

But the creep who'd threatened them wasn't likely to shoot her where she stood. He had been more insidious, scaring her son and attempting to intimidate her.

And succeeding.

With a sigh, she withdrew into the house. In a moment, Gabe joined her.

"I've already changed the sheets on the bed in—" She stopped.

He obviously misinterpreted her sudden silence. "If you haven't, that's fine. I can do it myself or else stay on the sofa downstairs."

She nearly laughed. She loved the overstuffed beige sofa in the living room. It was not only attractive, but it was one of the most comfortable pieces of furniture she had ever owned.

But she surveyed Gabe's broad and tall physique, catching the amused look in his eye. She flushed. Obviously, he wasn't reading her mind. She wasn't admiring him— Well, yes she was. But she was also assessing his proportions.

Though her sofa was fair-sized, Gabe's large body

would be excruciatingly uncomfortable on it. And how much good would he do Tommy and her if he awakened with muscles too stiff to move?

But to allow him to sleep in the empty bedroom... That would mean she had to reveal something personal. Very personal.

She steeled herself, noticing the way Gabe's gaze shot unspoken questions. "I've already changed the sheets on the bed in Thomas's room upstairs. It's not very sentimental, I know, but even though I miss him, I'm not a person who subscribes to hanging onto a deceased loved one's old unwashed sheets and towels as if that somehow keeps them closer."

Gabe's suddenly blank expression signaled he'd gotten her unspoken message. *Thomas's room.* Not *their* room. She felt embarrassed, as if she had been describing her total failure as a cop's wife.

Well, she had been. No getting around that.

And Thomas and she hadn't shared a bedroom for over a year. Nor a bed.

"I understand," Gabe said. She chose to interpret that as his acknowledging she was permitted to deal with her grief her own way, eschewing sentimentality if she wanted.

Not as acknowledging that he somehow understood the failure of her marriage in all but its legality. How could he? Not even *she* did.

"I should sleep upstairs. It's smarter for me to stay near the people I'm taking care of." His tone was gentle. Too gentle.

It made Holly consider crying—from mortification about her failure, from grief that her marriage was a farce, and that, even though she was sorry Thomas was dead, she couldn't grieve for him like a good wife should.

"Fine," she said brusquely. "Come upstairs, and I'll show you your room."

He followed at a reasonable distance, yet she felt his presence behind her as if he helped her up the steps.

Thomas's room was the one past Tommy's. Holly's was across the hall. She had the master bedroom, with a bathroom attached.

"This is where you'll stay," she said brightly, opening the door to Thomas's room. As Gabe looked inside, she reached into the linen closet along the hallway and extracted a set of bright yellow towels and a washcloth. "That's the bathroom you'll use. I'll leave these on the counter." She set the towels on the brown and gold tile. "If you need anything else, just ask."

"I will. Thank you, Holly."

She turned to head across the hall to her own bedroom, but she felt his touch on her arm.

"You'll be fine, I promise. Both Tommy and you." His deep green eyes regarded her with such frank assurance that they made her feel safe.

No, not safe. Anything but safe, with this large, handsome cop standing so near her bedroom door, after she had been so lonely for so long....

She tried to tear her stare away. He smiled. His even, angular features softened just a little. Lord, but he looked irresistible.

Except to her.

She noticed how much his broad jaw and sculptured cheeks were shadowed, this late at night, with the unremitting growth of his dark beard. She wondered what he would do in the morning—go home to shave?

"Good night, Holly." There was a huskiness to his tone. No wonder; she saw a flicker of desire in his eyes.

It ignited an answering flame inside her. No, this was wrong.

"Good night," she said firmly. But his touch was still on her arm, and he tightened it ever so slightly.

How did she get wrapped in his arms? Had she moved? Had he?

It didn't matter. She tipped her chin up to receive his kiss.

His lips moved very gently over hers, as if all he intended was the most detached of good-night kisses. But her own mouth wasn't as restrained. She kissed him back, using her hand at the back of his head to hold his head down to hers.

This was their second kiss. Heavens, how seductive it was! His lips ground down on hers. She tasted him, let her tongue enter his mouth as he drew it in and touched it with his own.

She pressed the lower part of her body against his, tightly. Hard. He was hard—there, down below. She moaned—until she realized that there were *two* places of hardness: one very natural. One very unnerving.

A gun. That must have been what he was doing in his car. He wasn't wearing the shoulder holster she'd seen on him before, but he must have retrieved his gun. Cops always carried guns.

And she knew better than to kiss a cop.

Quickly, she pulled away. She let her gaze rove down his shirt to his snug jeans and the two bulges—one not in front but at the side.

And then she looked back up at him.

He was breathing heavily, and his smile was rueful. "Sorry, Holly," he said. "I'll make sure nothing happens to you."

She heard a dual meaning in his words: no one outside would hurt Tommy or her.

And he would not touch her again.

''Good night, Gabe,'' she managed to say, and then she fled into the safety of her own room.

GABE WOKE AT DAWN the next morning and sat up in the bed that had once belonged to Thomas Poston.

Had Holly and Thomas ever made love in it?

Why had they had separate bedrooms? Not that it was his business.

The glow of morning streamed in between the mini-blinds at the windows, and Gabe studied the room. With its austere wooden furniture and little to show it had been occupied, the small bedroom lacked the hominess of the rest of the house. Lacked what Gabe assumed to be Holly's touch.

Maybe she hadn't spent much time here. But that didn't mean Thomas hadn't spent a lot of time in Holly's room.

With a growl, Gabe threw off the sheet and got out of bed. He had slept well, considering that he'd kept his ears alert for anything other than sounds that were normal to this house: a breeze blowing through open upstairs windows, the electrical hum of the clock radio and refrigerator, distant freeway traffic. This street was too far from the ocean to hear the waves—unlike Gabe's own overpriced apartment just a couple of blocks from the beach.

He'd heard none of the noises he had been prepared to deal with: no intruders. Not even a ringing phone.

There had, though, been an occasional moan from Tommy's room. Once, he rose from bed to check on the boy. But Tommy seemed to be sound asleep, peaceful, and nightmare free.

He had heard Holly get up three times and pad softly

down the hall to her son's room. He had considered joining her, but discretion had won out over desire. He didn't want to face that sexy, beautiful woman in the middle of the night. A woman he had foolishly kissed…again. A woman who had responded to him—but whose emotions were strung out to the limits with fear for her son and mourning her husband.

A woman who, if she noticed Gabe at all, saw him as a convenience, a protector, a cop…but not, damn it, as a man.

Gabe had slept in his boxers. He threw his shirt on, though left it unbuttoned, and went across the hall to the bathroom. Tommy was there, pulling up his pajama pants. "Hi, sport," Gabe said softly. "You're up early. Let's let your mama sleep in, okay?"

Tommy nodded.

Gabe wasn't sure what to do with the boy, but Tommy showed him. He helped him wash his face, brush his teeth and comb his hair. They returned to his bedroom and Tommy picked out the clothes he wanted to wear that day. After helping him dress, Gabe told Tommy they were going to play a game that required him to stay upstairs till Gabe came back for him.

He took a quick look around downstairs to assure himself the house was secure. He went back for Tommy and settled him at the kitchen table with a glass of milk and a bowl of dry kids' cereal while he went upstairs to shower. His shave would have to wait.

He dressed in the clothes he'd worn the day before, thrust the gun that had been in easy reach all night back into his pocket. Of course he'd needed to carry it. But if Holly hadn't felt it…

No use thinking about that. He suspected it wouldn't be

the last time his body would crave more from Holly Poston than his intellect would allow.

When he returned downstairs, Holly was seated with Tommy at the wooden table. Her robe was a bright green that contrasted becomingly with her brunette hair and light complexion. When she saw him, the smile on her full lips lit the room brighter than the daylight cascading through the kitchen windows. "Thanks for taking care of Tommy," she said. She appeared well-rested despite her nighttime forays to check on her son, and the dark circles he'd noticed before beneath her sparkling brown eyes had nearly evaporated.

"He took care of *me*," Gabe protested good-naturedly. "Showed me where everything was. He's a great kid."

Tommy, holding a spoon of colorful sugar-coated cereal nearly at his mouth, grinned up at him with a milk mustache.

"Glad you're awake, Holly," Gabe continued. "I need to get on my way. I have to stop at my place before I head for the office." He rubbed his stubbled chin. "What are your plans for the day?"

He caught her flash of annoyance at his intrusive question. This *was* his business, even if she didn't want it to be.

"I'm coordinating schedules," he said mildly. "Some of my officers will be patrolling the street all day. They may stop in to see if you need anything, and if you go out they'll join you."

"Oh," Holly said softly. The widening of her eyes told him she'd gotten the message he hadn't wanted to state in front of Tommy. He was tightening police security around this small family. "Well, I have plenty of work to do to keep Tommy and me home for today. I've been planning a new sewing project."

"Fine. Give me a call if you need to go out, okay?"

Her nod appeared dejected. He wanted to cheer her but couldn't think of anything appropriate to say with Tommy sitting there, his gaze ping-ponging from Gabe to his mom and back again as they spoke.

Cute kid, Gabe thought not for the first time.

A kid he intended to make sure stayed safe.

His beautiful, sexy mother, too.

No one was going to harm them. Or terrorize them.

Not on Gabe's watch.

Chapter Eight

Sitting in her sewing room, Holly felt like a prisoner in her own house. One being watched every moment by a cop.

She had finally gotten Tommy down for a nap mid-afternoon. All morning, he had been restless, unwilling to settle down in front of his usual educational TV shows, unwilling even to play a favorite board game with her.

Unwilling to talk to her, no matter how much she teased or pretended it was a game.

Each time a car passed, he'd hurried to the door as if expecting Gabe that soon.

He had promised, after all, to return later in the day. That gave Tommy something to look forward to.

And gave Holly something to feel ambivalent about.

As soon as Tommy lay down, she started hunting through Thomas's bedroom for…what? She didn't know. But that horrible caller seemed to think Thomas left something important.

She hadn't been able to search with Gabe in the house last night. And she'd had to do something.

After an hour, still empty-handed, she'd given up. Temporarily.

Now, she used her five-year-old sewing machine to

stitch a seam in a new costume Evangeline commissioned by a phone call. Sighing, she looked at the bright orange jumpsuit resembling those worn by local street maintenance workers. Once more she had set aside an artistic wall hanging. It would require more creativity than this less imaginative outfit. And right now, with her mind whirling, she hadn't much imagination to spare.

She pushed the pedal and the sewing machine began stitching with a low grumble.

"That's just how I feel," she said aloud.

The phone rang, startling her. She lifted the receiver on the sewing room extension, ignoring the little jolt her heart made. What if it was the person who'd called before?

"Holly, it's Al Sharp. How are ya?"

She smiled. She had always liked Thomas's partner. "Fine, Al, and you?"

"Okay. Listen, I just got done with my patrol. Did you know we were assigned to cruise your neighborhood?"

"'We'?" Had Al been assigned a new partner already? Of course. Despite death and tragedy, life, and the N.B.P.D., went on.

Al sounded embarrassed. "Yeah, me and...well, my new partner, George." He went on hastily, "Another shift's just begun and another unit'll be patrolling. You're on twenty-four hour surveillance right now."

Holly knew. She'd seen the police units cruise her street often that day. It was one reason she'd felt imprisoned, despite the sense of security it also provided.

"Anyhow," Al continued, "before I go home, I want to come by, maybe mow your lawn or trim that hedge along the driveway that's always hanging over. All right?"

"You don't have to, Al."

"Sure. We're still family, you know."

Family. That sounded familiar. Had Gabe McLaren put Al up to this? Pushed him, at the risk of his job?

If so, Holly would set Gabe straight.

"I know this wasn't your idea, Al," she said, "and you don't—"

"Hey, you know me, Holly. I don't always come up with good ideas like Thomas did, but there's no one better on the follow-through. Right?"

"Right. Thanks, Al."

"See you soon."

Al arrived half an hour later. Thin and with a nearly shaved head, he was in torn jeans and a grass-stained white T-shirt. "Can you let me into the garage for the clippers and lawnmower?"

"Sure."

Al was divorced and childless and lived in an apartment. He probably didn't do much mowing and trimming these days. Still, he was done in less than an hour. Somehow, the loud sound of the mower didn't waken Tommy. Al rapped at the front door.

"All through?" Holly asked.

He nodded. His face and scalp were damp with perspiration. "Yeah. Anything else you need right now?"

"Yes, I need to give you a glass of water. Or would you prefer lemonade or iced tea? In any event, come in."

He followed her into the kitchen. She sat with him at the table, and he accepted the drink of ice water. He smelled of antiperspirant and newly mown grass.

"You and Tommy doing okay?" he asked. Al had always resembled a lovable mutt to Holly, with his extra chin and perennially sad eyes. "McLaren—the chief—told us that you're being harassed. Phone calls, a break-in. I saw the report. It said nothing was taken." He regarded her quizzically.

"That's right." Holly sighed. "I suspect from the phone call that the person was looking for something he didn't find." She shivered.

"Do you know what it is?"

"I wish I did." She didn't mention that she had searched for *something*. "I might give it to the creep so we wouldn't have to worry anymore."

Al reached across the table and laid his hand on hers. His was cold and damp from holding the glass. His grin held no humor. "You didn't hear this from me, Holly, since it's against policy, but you got the right idea. Depending on what the guy wants, I mean. If it's not something valuable Thomas left to Tommy and you, just get rid of it. Tell you what. If you figure out what it is, call me. We'll talk about it, see if there's a good way for you to get rid of it without pissing off—er, making Chief McLaren mad, okay?"

"Maybe," Holly said. "But what if it's the person who killed Thomas who wants something? I want him caught."

"Hey, all the more reason to give it to me," Al said. "Maybe we can avenge Thomas's murder. I'd like to be the one to finger the suspect. What do you say to that?"

"I'd say that's fine," Holly said, "as long as no one else gets hurt."

SITTING AT HIS DESK, Gabe lifted the phone and punched in a number. He smiled when Holly's melodic voice answered, "Hello?" There was a hint of hesitation in her tone, as if she expected the jerk who'd threatened her before to be on the line.

Gabe identified himself. "Would you like me to bring another pizza tonight? Or Chinese takeout, or—"

"Take *me* out," Holly interrupted. Then she laughed. "My treat, but I've been going stir-crazy today, not leaving the house, knowing people are watching—even though they're the good guys. And Al Sharp doing chores, and…I need to get out, especially since Tommy woke up from his nap with a huge streak of mischief in him. I've been chasing him around the house.''

''I feel another game of catch coming on,'' Gabe said, grinning. He had a good time playing with the little tyke. ''I'll come by and we'll let Tommy pick the place for dinner.''

He performed his usual routine for leaving the office in record time: organizing his desk, shutting down his computer, grabbing gun and cell phone. He took his Mustang and headed to his nearby condo, where he packed a few things. Then he drove to Holly's house. He pulled into the driveway to make it obvious to anyone watching that Holly and Tommy were not alone.

When Holly answered the door, she was wearing a form-hugging pair of olive green slacks and a brightly colored floral shirt. Her smile was sheepish. ''You don't really mind going out for dinner tonight, do you?''

Tommy stood beside her, grinning up at Gabe.

''How about it, sport?'' he asked the boy, kneeling to give him a hug. ''Do you want to grab dinner at your favorite restaurant? I bet it's Frank's Fish Food.''

Tommy pulled back and shook his head.

''How about Slithering Sammy's Fried Snakes?''

Tommy laughed and shook his head again so hard that his neatly combed dark hair flew.

''I know. Ollie's Octopus House.''

''No,'' Tommy said.

Gabe drew in his breath, only daring the slightest glance up at Holly, whose hand was pressed to her mouth.

''Well, then,'' Gabe said, as if nothing monumental had just occurred. ''What is your favorite restaurant?''

He waited, watching the boy. Tommy blinked rapidly, as if he only just realized he had spoken aloud. He shook his head.

"Tell you what," Gabe said. "You can just whisper it in my ear. Okay?"

Tommy looked dubious. Gabe stood and said to Holly, "You know, maybe we should go to Sandy's Spider House."

He felt an urgent tug on his sleeve. He bent—and grinned as broadly as his face would allow when Tommy whispered the name of a nearby fast-food chain in his ear.

"Oh, that's your favorite restaurant!" He stood, taking both Tommy's hand and Holly's. "I like it, too. Let's go."

HOLLY SAT with Gabe at an outside table at the fast-food restaurant, keeping a close watch on Tommy, who gleefully used the equipment in the fenced-in play area.

Other than his continued refusal to talk regularly, he was beginning to act like a normal kid again. Even his nightmares seemed to have slowed down.

Holly realized that his improvement was at least partly due to the attention and the patience of the man keeping her company. He hadn't even allowed her to pay for their dinner of hamburgers, fries and shakes.

Despite all her misgivings, she was enjoying Gabe's company. She was beginning to rely on him. To look forward to the times he joined them.

And that was an enormous mistake. She had to tell him to leave them alone, but in the nicest way possible.

"I really appreciate this, Gabe," she began.

Damn! He made it awfully hard to brush him off when he smiled at her so sexily. He had removed his jacket and tie. He looked great with rolled up sleeves that revealed his sinewy arms, and with his top three buttons undone, exposing his very masculine throat.

"I'll join you for fast food any time," he replied to her comment. "I enjoy being with Tommy." He didn't say *and you* out loud, but the lift of one thick, straight brow spoke volumes. "And I'm glad he's opening up, if only a little. I'll spend more time with him, and maybe he'll really start talking to us."

Double damn! Of course he was right. Tommy was opening up not to her, but to him, no matter how much she encouraged her son to talk.

She could resent it all she wanted, but what good would that do? Because of Tommy's progress, she couldn't just ask Gabe to stay away, to instead send Al Sharp or the patrol cops on evening shift to spend the night in her living room for her peace of mind and protection.

"Yes, he's got to start talking again." She hoped she didn't sound as conflicted as she felt.

Gabe told her that the lab report had come back on the doll and on the potential evidence collected in Thomas's office.

Nothing helpful so far.

Yet, fortunately, he still seemed to believe she hadn't imagined the invasion of her home. And he certainly recognized the doll had been sent, the phone call made to scare her.

And then he pulled a cell phone from a pocket and handed it to her. "Carry this with you at all times if you leave your house," he said. "In case I have to reach you. I have the number. And also in case you need to reach me."

In case you need help. Holly heard the unspoken message. She wanted to refuse the phone and therefore what it represented. But she couldn't, for Tommy's sake as much as her own.

They left soon afterward. On reaching her house, Gabe made a quick search of the rooms, then took Tommy outside for a short game of catch.

Holly stayed in the house making lemonade while the guys were in the yard. The kitchen phone rang, startling her. She nearly knocked over the pitcher.

The threatening call had come during a game of catch between Gabe and Tommy.

She took a deep breath before lifting the receiver from the kitchen wall.

"Holly? It's Edie. I wanted to check on Tommy and you."

"We're okay."

Her relief must have been obvious in her voice, for Edie said, "Right. Of course you are. What's wrong besides that damnable doll?"

Holly laughed uneasily. "I should know better than to try to fool you." She quickly enumerated all the things that bothered her, including, on top of the harassment, the police surveillance, and the personal attention being given this situation by the chief of police.

That was enough. She wouldn't tell Edie how attracted to this man she was getting. Edie, who knew her opinion of cops, would rib her unmercifully. And she'd be right. Holly was definitely acting irrational.

"Sounds grim," Edie acknowledged when Holly was done. "And Tommy's still not talking?"

"No." He wasn't, not really. And Holly's dear friend Edie wasn't always as discreet as she should be. If she happened to mention Tommy's few words to someone who knew someone who knew someone—

"Well, I know you don't want to hear it, since he's a

cop and all, but I can't help feeling a little jealous that the hunk Gabe McLaren has taken you on as his personal project.''

Holly hadn't expected that reaction from Edie. Why not? Edie had already made it plain she was interested in Gabe. "You can have him," she said quickly, then realized she'd consider kicking her friend in the shins if she dared to try to steal Gabe's attention away from Tommy and her.

Not that she wanted him. Only his protection.

But she was glad Edie couldn't see her self-mocking smile.

"What's so funny?" asked Gabe. He and Tommy had just entered the kitchen door.

Feeling her face redden, Holly pointed to the phone, as if she were smiling about what the person on the other end had said. In a way, she was—or at least about her own reaction to it.

"Since you're busy, we men will go upstairs and get Tommy ready for bed. Okay, sport?"

Her son beamed up at Gabe and gave him his hand.

"What's going on?" demanded Edie at the other end of the phone.

"Nothing a nice, long bath won't help," Holly replied. *The colder the better.* "Gabe and Tommy just came in from their game of catch, and my son is filthy."

"Anyway, I called to see if you two wanted to grab dinner together tomorrow. But it sounds as if you might be busy."

"Maybe," Holly said. A night out with her friend might be just the ticket to cool it with Gabe McLaren. But she hesitated to make any plans just then. "How about next week some time?"

"Fine. I'll be in touch."

After Holly hung up, she realized she'd forgotten to offer the guys some lemonade. She poured drinks into colorful plastic tumblers and brought them upstairs.

Tommy was already in the tub, and Gabe and he were playing with boats and sponges. It was a delightfully domestic scene. They both seemed pleased about the lemonade. Holly went downstairs again till she heard them in Tommy's bedroom. She returned in time to listen to Gabe reading a story.

When he was done, Gabe said, "It's time for the big decision, sport. Which kind of candy should I keep for kids at my office?"

Without hesitation, Tommy said, "Chocolate," and grinned.

Holly laughed aloud as Gabe said, "Chocolate it is."

Elated, Holly gave her son a good-night kiss. Gabe and she went downstairs together.

As they sat in the living room, Holly on the sofa and Gabe in the reclining chair, she realized they were settling into a comfortable routine of sorts. She would have to stop it somehow.

But first, she thanked Gabe—yet again—for getting Tommy to talk, even a little. She forbore from gritting her teeth in annoyance that her son kept talking to him instead of her.

"You're welcome." His masculine grin set her senses reeling. How could a mere smile make her body fizz like newly opened champagne? She shifted uncomfortably in her seat.

It didn't help when Gabe turned serious. She was still aware of his very male presence when he leaned forward in the chair in a familiar position, his hands clasped between his knees. "I'm sorry you felt cooped up today,

Holly. Tommy and you need to be protected. That's a given. But you should be able to lead normal lives.''

"How can we lead normal lives?'' she asked disagreeably. "Thomas is gone, cops are constantly on my doorstep because you send them here and you're inside my home. A lot.''

His dark brows rose. He appeared amused at her irritation. But then his green eyes clouded over, the way the sea did when storm-challenged. "Yeah, I'm inside here a lot. And I'm a cop. I've gotten the impression you don't like cops much, Holly. Care to explain why? You were married to one, after all.''

No, she didn't want to explain. She didn't owe him a reason. Still, he had told her about his own difficult childhood. And maybe he'd simply leave her alone if he understood. But— "I think I need something stronger than lemonade for this,'' she told him.

He joined her in the kitchen and helped her open a bottle of merlot. With filled glasses, they returned to the living room—same places as before, when it had been his turn to make a deep, dark revelation.

This was silly. She didn't want to do it. She wouldn't be able to flee when finished, as he had, since this was her home.

And were they setting some absurd precedent—can you top this? Which of them could reveal the most miserable secret on *this* night?

"So?'' he prompted.

"So, I'm the daughter of a cop.'' Holly took a sip of wine. *Okay. You started it. Your turn to spill all.*

With a sigh from deep inside, she explained about her father who was always on duty, always available for his fellow cops and never there for his daughter. Or his wife, though her mother accepted that he wouldn't be around for

birthdays, anniversaries, skinned knees, car wrecks...
unless they happened to affect fellow officers. He just
wasn't there for his family. Her mother joined a group of
other cops' wives for support—as if that made up for
Holly's absent father.

"I see." Gabe drew the words out.

He put his glass on the coffee table, rose and took the
few steps to bridge the gap between them. Holly scooted
to the far end of the sofa. She didn't want his sympathy.
And she most certainly didn't want him any closer.

"Your childhood experience with police officers was the
opposite of mine." He sat on the sofa but at the far end.

It didn't matter. She was aware of his proximity. Very
aware. "You could say that."

"Then why did you marry a cop?"

"Because he was like every other cop I know," she
spat. "Demanding. Persistent. Persuasive. He promised
me, though, that he was different. But as soon as he got
what he wanted—me—he showed his true colors. He'd
met the challenge and won. That's all I'd been to him—a
challenge, because I said no so many times. After we were
married, he didn't want me much anymore. And after
Tommy was born, he turned into my father!"

To her chagrin, her eyes began to fill. Worse, Gabe was
suddenly beside her. Holding her.

Worst of all, she *wanted* him to.

"Go away," she whispered perversely.

"Soon," he whispered. He kissed her on the cheek, as
gently as if she were her small son.

"You can't do that," she grumbled and turned toward
him. This time his kiss wasn't gentle at all.

She reveled in the feel of his lips on hers. On her cheeks.
Her neck. And lower.

Was this it? Was she going to let him make love to her? Was she going to make love to him?

Yes! something inside her shouted…just as the phone rang.

She pulled away and stood, her breath ragged. Their eyes caught. His were heavy-lidded with desire. They slid down her body in a caress, then back to her lips. And the phone rang again.

They both laughed, and Holly hurried into the kitchen to answer.

"Hello?" she said.

"Hello, Holly." It was the same horrible, echoing voice that had unnerved her before. "Have you found it yet?"

She gasped. "I—I still don't know what you're talking about." She didn't want to stammer. She wanted to come across as cool and forceful. "Tell me what you want, and then I'll—"

"Haven't you guessed? You know I was in your house looking for it. And where did I look?"

Her breathing grew erratic and quick. Someone *had* gotten into her house. She'd known she hadn't imagined it, but she'd almost hoped she had.

Gabe had joined her. He stood beside her, fury narrowing his eyes and setting his jaw. He bent his head so he could hear, but he didn't say a word.

"You were in Thomas's office." Somehow, Gabe's presence lent to Holly some of the strength she'd failed to grasp before. "So you were after some paperwork?"

No reply.

"Hello?" Holly said.

"I'm still here," the voice said. "You're a smart woman. What do you think I want?"

"There are a lot of papers," Holly said. "How should I know—"

"Because you knew Thomas. And I know that he told you. I'll be in touch," the voice said. "We'll make arrangements for me to get it. Because if I don't, I'll do more than just search your house…when you're out." She heard a click.

Gabe grabbed the phone. Again he pressed in *69. Another pay phone, he told her in a minute. He then called the station, ordered whoever answered to send a car to the location where the pay phone was located and to call the phone company to find out how the call was paid for. He had installed a small recorder with Holly's permission, and he checked to make sure the exchange had been taped.

When he was done, he faced Holly. His expression was as resolute as a stone statue's. He didn't even seem to see her.

This was why this cop was here. He had a case to solve. Her presence was secondary to his assignment. His duty reigned over all. As it *should* in this case. She needed answers, too.

"What papers was that guy talking about, Holly? What was Thomas up to? What did he tell you?"

"Nothing. At least nothing that makes any sense. I've tried to figure it out, but I still don't know what that creep means." She tried to speak firmly, but her voice wobbled.

And the skepticism in Gabe's ominous green eyes told her that, this time, he didn't believe her.

Chapter Nine

"Look who's awake, sport," Gabe said the next morning. As before, he had risen earlier than Holly and helped Tommy wash and dress. Planning ahead this time, he had brought a change of clothes: blue shirt, gray trousers. His coat and tie remained in his car. His shoulder holster was at the bottom of his overnight bag and his gun was in his pocket.

Holly had just walked into the kitchen. Tommy jumped down from the chair at the table where he had been finishing his cereal and threw himself into her arms. "Good morning, sweetheart." She hugged him back and smiled. "And thanks," she said, looking directly at Gabe, "for helping Tommy again."

That was good. She had stopped looking directly at him last night right after that second threatening phone call.

Had it been an act, or had he hurt her by asking whether she actually knew what her husband had allegedly hidden from the son of a bitch who kept calling?

Or had she been embarrassed after explaining her antipathy toward cops? With the cops she'd had around, it was no wonder she regarded him sometimes as if he was a carrier of foot-and-mouth disease. But she still had to deal with him and his officers for her protection and Tommy's.

And the reminder that her marriage to Thomas had been thornier than a real bed of roses? *Don't even think about that, McLaren.* He'd given himself that order more than once in bed the night before.

Rebound was rebound.

After he'd questioned Holly about the call, they had spent a little more time in each other's company before she fled upstairs to bed, but not much. Her cordiality had apparently evaporated as a result of his inquisitiveness.

"Thank Tommy this morning, not me," he said now. "He did all the hard work, like combing his teeth and brushing his face."

Tommy laughed, even as he shook his head in the negative.

"No?" Gabe asked. "Oh, that's right. He cleaned his hair with toothpaste and picked the pajamas he wanted to wear today."

"No!" Tommy said aloud, still laughing.

"No?" Gabe said, smiling not only at Tommy but also at the joy on Holly's face. Maybe a kid who started the day by saying one word would continue by talking more.

Tommy shook his head.

"Well, what *did* you do?" Gabe asked as if befuddled.

Tommy looked up at his mother, who had a hand on his shoulder, and then at Gabe. He opened his mouth as if considering what to say.

"Did you brush Gabe's teeth?" Holly asked.

Tommy regarded her with wide eyes, as if surprised at her teasing, then grinned. Slowly, he climbed back into his chair but didn't eat more cereal.

"That's okay, sport," Gabe said. "Maybe tonight, at bedtime, we can eat some lunch together, all right?"

His grin broadened as he shook his head.

Holly walked behind her son's chair and ruffled his hair. She smiled conspiratorially at Gabe.

He raised his eyebrows in silent acknowledgment.

Holly wore a pastel pink shirt and black slacks. Her dark hair was a soft and attractive frame about her face, which was beautiful, as usual, this morning—except for the telltale shadows beneath her tired eyes.

She must not have slept again. Funny thing about that. Neither had he. Partially for the same reasons: mulling over the call and who'd made it. And considering what Holly had said about cops.

Their respective insomnia had also been at least partially for different reasons, though, for Gabe had spent time in Thomas Poston's office. He'd gone over old territory, since Jimmy Hernandez's crew had been through it twice before—once as routine after the Poston murder, and once after the alleged break-in. But as far as Gabe knew, few of Thomas Poston's personal effects had been removed as possible evidence.

He'd found a few things that triggered questions, but nothing that should have merited someone stressing over, let alone being a reason to scare a widow or her child.

Unless Holly had already hidden whatever it was.

He had checked Poston's computer for suspicious files but found only baseball statistics and Internet access. He'd thought it odd to find a credit card statement addressed to Thomas at the station rather than at home, but the charges didn't appear irregular. Still, he'd felt more like a snoop than a trained investigator while going over items involving the Postons' personal finances.

He had also taken advantage of being assigned Thomas's former bedroom. But going through drawers and closets had felt like an ugly intrusion, worse than viewing the Postons' old bills. He'd become a voyeur, not into some anonymous suspect's possessions, but into the life of the former husband of Holly Poston, to whom, despite himself, Gabe was mightily attracted.

It couldn't get much more distasteful than pawing through Thomas's clothes, his uniforms, even his pockets and underwear looking for something he couldn't even identify. He'd found nothing, but the search had bothered him enough, along with everything else, that he'd stayed wide awake far into the night.

At least that gave him more time to plan the next steps in his investigation. Both investigations.

Now, after Tommy had finished eating and settled in front of his favorite public television show, Gabe led Holly back into the kitchen and told her what he had done last night.

"You went through Thomas's things? What gave you the right?" As anticipated, she wasn't pleased. In fact, judging by her incensed expression, she was downright furious.

As he'd noted before, she was particularly sexy when angry.

Pervert. "Common sense gave me the right," he retorted. "You want me to get a warrant, just say so, but you've cooperated so far. You've been threatened because of some alleged paperwork left by your husband. You claim you don't know what the papers are. Assuming you're telling the truth, I looked in some of the most logical places to find those mysterious papers."

"I *am* telling the truth," Holly shouted. "But you wasted your time. The thug who threatened me admitted he'd already gone through Thomas's office." She paced the kitchen. Her slender, lithe body moved sinuously, like a stalking lioness. "Why did you think you'd find whatever he wanted there when not even *he* could find it?"

"Or she," Gabe corrected automatically, his tone cooler than hers. He purposely leaned against the doorway, near the phone where Holly had taken both the threatening calls. "Good question. But I figured it wouldn't hurt to try. And since no one has found anything there, not even our favorite fiend, I tried the bedroom, too."

Her glare deepened as she continued moving. "Looking for something personal? I already searched Thomas's bedroom but haven't cleaned out his drawers yet."

Gabe felt himself redden. He'd done what he had to, but she'd struck a nerve. And she'd already looked? That could be helpful, if she intended to cooperate. And if she didn't... "I didn't find anything helpful there, either," he said. "Where else might Thomas have hidden papers?"

Holly finally stopped stalking and stared at him. Her rage visibly relaxed into realization. "The garage!" she exclaimed. "I doubt whatever it is has anything to do with the car or warranties on our major appliances, but he kept a box out there with receipts and brochures. Maybe it's there."

They checked to make sure Tommy was still engrossed in the TV program. Holly showed Gabe the box in the garage. Rather than leave the child alone in the house, he lifted the heavy carton and carried it into the kitchen. There, he pushed two chairs beside one another at the table.

Page by page, they sorted through the box's contents. Holly sighed more than once and discarded warranty information on some appliance that Thomas and she had replaced.

But nothing in the carton appeared to be enough to trigger the current campaign of terror.

By the time they reached the papers at the bottom, Holly had wilted. Whatever insufficient rest she got the previous night must have drained away with her adrenaline. She threw the last brochure into the grocery bag they used for trash, then looked at Gabe bleakly. "It wasn't there, was it?"

"No," he said gently, "it wasn't." He rose and approached her chair. He gripped her slender and slumping shoulders, intending to be reassuring. A big brother, a family member, trying to make it easier for a cop's widow. But the heat that surged from the palms of his hand to his groin wasn't brotherly. Not at all. And it only became more electric when she rose and put her head on his chest.

"What am I going to do, Gabe?" she whispered brokenly. "I don't know what it is, and if I don't find it, that horrible creature already showed he could break in here. He terrified my son with that damned doll. He's probably the one who killed Thomas and beat up Sheldon. What would he have to lose by hurting us?"

"I won't let anything happen to you, Holly," he whispered against her fragrant hair.

But she pulled back. Her eyes were bright with unshed tears, but her small chin was raised in resignation. "I know, Gabe. You'll try to keep us safe. For now. Until the next big case comes along and you need to direct manpower toward solving it. That's the way it works in a police force. I understand."

"No!" Gabe contradicted. "You don't understand. There's more that I can't tell you about—"

He stopped. He couldn't explain why he'd actually been hired in the first place. Why he thought the murder he'd come here to investigate on his own time was related to her husband's killing, and therefore related to the way her son and she were being terrorized.

And why he would never give up until the cases were solved. Related or not.

He had come to Naranja Beach under partially false pretenses. He did not want to implicate his aunt in potentially scandalous and damaging claims worse than nepotism. And therefore, he couldn't explain. But looking down into Holly's shining, puzzled eyes, he had to do something. And so he kissed her. Again.

It wasn't a brotherly kiss. That was for certain. Not the way it all but blew his briefs off. But it was quick, for he had stayed here much too long this morning already.

"I'll make sure the patrols come by today," he said as he pulled away. His tone was almost conversational, except for the way it was syncopated by his erratic breathing. "I've got to get to work. See you two later."

OF COURSE he had to get to work, Holly thought a short while later as she pinned together some carefully cut pieces of fabric for a wall hanging she had just conceptualized.

All cops had to leave for work the moment someone needed them. It was their duty.

She'd learned not to expect more from her father. Her husband. And Gabe McLaren was no relation at all, not by marriage or otherwise.

Even though he'd claimed all cops were family.

Right.

She would have to be careful for Tommy's sake. Her son had latched onto Gabe as if they were family. Tommy was vulnerable. He would already be hurt when Gabe stopped coming around. But somehow she had to keep him from becoming even more attached.

The quicker the case was solved, the better.

The telephone rang. Holly froze. *Please, not again.*

She went to her bedroom and answered the extension there. "Hello?"

"Holly? Is that you?"

"Yes, Sheldon." She was so relieved to hear it was someone she knew that she felt her legs wobble. She leaned against the bedroom wall.

"Are you okay? You sound ill."

She assured him she was fine. "In fact, I'm doing so well that I've started a new wall hanging. It's full of bright reds, oranges and yellows. The scorching sun burning Naranja Beach in the middle of the hottest summer day."

The colors meant a lot more than summer to Holly—heat and rage and exposure and vulnerability...and unsatisfied, unquenchable desire for Gabe. But she wouldn't explain that to Sheldon. She would simply work out her misery in her art.

"Great. I'll look forward to seeing it. Meantime, are you coming in soon? I want to show you some displays I have in mind, see if you can add something to them."

"Sure," Holly said. "Real soon."

Maybe. But she couldn't go anywhere without Tommy. Was he ready to go with her to Sheldon's?

They had another appointment with the child psychologist early this afternoon. Holly would ask then.

WHEN GABE REACHED the office that morning, a couple of female patrol officers asked if he would see them. They seemed so anxious that he couldn't say no.

They explained how they were concerned about his administrative policies. Both had been striving to make detective under Mal Kensington. In the three months since Gabe's arrival he hadn't clarified what his promotion criteria would be.

He didn't know yet, either, though he didn't admit it to the enthusiastic young cops. "I've been considering that issue," he told them, which was true—though he'd not had time to focus on it. "I'll issue a written policy soon.

Meantime, be assured that I fully intend to reward hard work and dedication with promotions. Okay?''

Their anxiety seemed relieved as they walked, chatting, out his door.

His own state of mind, however, was anything but relieved.

Especially when uniformed patrol officer Dolph Hilo personally dropped a report on a carjacking on his desk. "It happened last night, chief," he said, his features troubled. "To a tourist."

That required Gabe's attention for the next hour. Public relations was a major part of his job, particularly soothing ruffled feathers of visitors who could either go home furious and bad-mouthing the town, or pleased that, though they'd had a bad experience here, they'd been handled with care by the cops.

A normal day in the life of the police chief of Naranja Beach, Gabe thought wryly, when he took a moment to get himself a cup of coffee in the day room. The good thing about it was that he hadn't had time to think of Holly that morning, how it had felt—again—to awaken in her home, to hold her comfortingly in his arms, to kiss her once more....

Well, he hadn't had *much* time to think about it.

He finally had a longer break around one that afternoon, when the support people returned from lunch. He couldn't get away to eat yet, but that was okay. There was something he had to check out, something gnawing at him since last night.

It wasn't anything earthshaking, but Gabe had recognized one of the myriad pieces of paper in Thomas Poston's office.

A list of all the stores on both sides of Pacific Way wasn't anything a bad guy would threaten someone about, of course. But the other place he had seen a list just like it was right here, in his own office.

The office that once had belonged to Mal Kensington, his predecessor. The *late* Mal Kensington, whose death just might not have been from natural causes.

Gabe had reorganized Mal's files, including computer files, when he first arrived, ostensibly to familiarize himself with them. He'd also wanted to see if anything in them provided a clue about what had happened to the former chief. Maybe everything had been sanitized upon Mal's demise. That would imply to Gabe that someone with access to this office was involved. Another cop. He hoped that wasn't so. It could, after all, simply have been over-zealous people getting things ready for the new chief. In any event, he hadn't found anything of great importance in the files. Still…

He walked across the indoor-outdoor carpeting toward the far wall and knelt to open the lowest drawer in the four-drawer file cabinet. That was where he had kept the things of Mal's he either hadn't sent to the main department files or tossed away. On his knees, he thumbed through labeled manila folders.

There. He found the list in a file labeled Naranja Beach Businesses. He took it to his desk and sat down.

Pacific Way was the center of the town's tourist industry. It was only four blocks long, running perpendicularly from Coast Boulevard, which paralleled the beach. Pacific Way was lined with the quaint shops that included Sheldon Sperling's place, Artisans, and Aunt Evangeline's shop, Orange. Gabe estimated that there were fifty stores and restaurants on Pacific Way.

This list had a date on it: about a month before Mal died. As far as Gabe could recall, it was the same date as the one in Thomas Poston's office. It contained street numbers of each of the shops and who owned them. Even if it had been accurate on the date noted, he doubted it was accurate now. From what Evangeline had said, several shops had recently changed hands.

Did this list have any significance? Maybe not, but both Mal Kensington and Thomas Poston had had copies. And both Mal Kensington and Thomas Poston were dead.

If for no other reason than that, Gabe needed to look into the list, the sooner the better. And so, after checking around to make sure no other crises were pending at that moment, he decided to take a pleasant walk along Naranja Beach streets to Pacific Way, only a mile from City Hall.

The air was pleasantly cool. Tourists were out in full force when he reached Pacific Way. The shopping street had been turned into a traffic-free pedestrian mall. Its stucco, brick and frame-facade one and two-story buildings were crammed together shoulder to shoulder on both sides of the palm tree-lined street, on each of the four blocks.

Sheldon's was on the second block from Coast Boulevard. Gabe looked in the display window before going inside. It contained pottery plates, intriguing primitive masks—and hanging on a dowel, as a backdrop for the rest of the display, a very pretty, brightly colored sewn depiction of the multihued blue sea with brown pelicans gliding above it. That work had an artistic touch Gabe was beginning to recognize: Holly's.

The bell sounded as Gabe pushed the door open. Gabe heard some familiar voices inside.

"Gabe, what are you doing here?" Mayor Evangeline Sevvers was at the cashier's counter near Sheldon Sperling. She was dressed in one of her habitual suits, this one a cool off-white linen, which looked comfortable. Her high-heeled sandals didn't.

"What I'm always doing," Gabe told her. "Getting into

trouble. Or maybe getting this town out of trouble. Its mayor should appreciate that.''

Mayor Sevvers grinned. ''I do.''

''Maybe you can help me with something,'' he said as he wended his way through the store. The labyrinth of display cases, clothed mannequins, free-standing vases and statuettes and more somehow managed to look artistic rather than cluttered. That still amazed him.

And then there were more of Holly's attractive fabric creations.

''I came to show this to Sheldon, get his opinion.'' As he approached them, he couldn't help asking, ''By the way, what brings you to this shop, Your Honor?''

Sheldon grinned. ''Business,'' he told Gabe. ''Show business, that is.''

''Your play?'' he asked.

''Yes,'' Evangeline said. ''I came here to discuss the next dress rehearsal with Sheldon. It's in a couple of days. I've brought some of the costumes Holly Poston was sewing for us to add to the ones we've stored here for a few days. We're also considering adding another couple of roles and aren't sure we should bother her anymore.''

''*You're* not sure,'' Sheldon said. ''I talked to her earlier, and she—''

The bell rang, and Gabe pivoted to see who was entering. He'd been somewhat surprised to see his aunt here. He was even more surprised to see two of his patrol officers enter: Bruce Franklin and Dolph Hilo.

''Something wrong?'' Gabe asked. ''Were you looking for me?'' He reached toward the cell phone in his pocket. It was there. They could have called him.

''No, chief,'' Dolph said. ''Not this time. No more carjackings, at least none that I'm aware of.''

''That's good news,'' Gabe said.

Dolph's mouth lifted in a wry grin that mirrored Gabe's. "Yeah. We don't want to lose any more tourists today."

"What?" Evangeline sounded horrified, and Gabe took a moment to explain to the mayor that everything was under control. They even had a suspect in custody for the prior day's crime.

"We're here because of the play," Bruce said. "Didn't the mayor tell you she asked us to take the roles of some of the cops in it, to lend a little authenticity?"

"She didn't get around to it," Gabe said. He sent a humorously chastising glance toward his quasi-aunt.

"Exactly," she agreed.

"I'll leave you all to your acting careers if you'll just take a look at something I brought," Gabe told them. He pulled the paper out of his pocket, unfolded it and placed it on the glass counter.

"What's this?" Sheldon asked. The older man still looked haggard. He moved a little faster now, though, as he walked around to stand beside Gabe, and his limp was less pronounced. He used the arm that had been injured to help smooth the page.

"It's a list of businesses along Pacific Way," Gabe said. For the moment, he didn't say where this list came from or that he had seen another. "It's a few months old, so it's probably obsolete, but as of the date on it, does it appear accurate?"

Evangeline joined them, standing between Gabe and Sheldon. Dolph and Bruce went around the counter to look at it upside down.

"I'd have to study it," Sheldon said after a minute, "but I think it's correct. Do you agree, Evangeline?"

She nodded. Her gaze caught Gabe's, and she looked quizzical. He lifted one edge of his mouth just a little, as a signal to her that this could be significant. Her tiny nod was almost imperceptible, and she erased every indication of question off her face.

"I guess so." She sounded bored, as if this piece of paper didn't interest her in the least. "Why don't you go over it with Gabe, Sheldon? I want to talk to Dolph and Bruce about their roles in the play."

True to her word, she put an arm around each man's shoulder and led them among the narrow, curio-rich aisles to a relatively open area near the side of the store.

"Do you see any obvious discrepancies in this list?" Gabe asked Sheldon.

"I don't think so. Is it important?"

"Not really. But I was curious about it. I found it in Thomas Poston's things." A copy of it at least. This one happened to come from the file of another possible murder victim, though Gabe wasn't about to say so.

The bell rang again. This time, when he looked up, Holly stood in the doorway, clutching little Tommy's hand.

Gabe knew they'd be out and about today. Holly had called to tell him so. He'd assigned Al Sharp and his new partner to follow her at a distance and make sure all appeared well. They were probably patrolling Pacific Way right about now.

Holly smiled at them wanly, then back down at her son. She was obviously worried about him. This was probably his first visit here since the morning his father had died. His eyes were wide, and he stood very still, blinking. Gabe caught Holly's glance again and saw her inhale deeply, as if she needed more oxygen to deal with being here. And bringing her son.

She spoke almost defensively, as if she expected someone to accuse her of harming Tommy. But she kept her tone nearly cheerful. "Tommy and I were just visiting his special doctor. The one who talks to him a lot. She said he was ready to come here for just a little bit, as long as I'm with him and it's daytime with lots of people around, so we can all feel safe. Though if he's really scared, we'll leave right away. Right, Tommy?'' She looked down at him. He hadn't moved anything except his head, which now turned as he looked over the shop.

He wasn't screaming. In fact, except for how wide his deep brown eyes were, he looked relatively calm. And there were even uniformed cops present.

''Hey, sport,'' Gabe said. ''Great to see you. You let us know when you're ready to leave, okay?'' Despite the way he had sometimes pushed the child, he wondered whether the psychologist had been right, allowing him to confront his fears so soon. But so far he seemed to handle it fine. And maybe this would lead the boy to begin really talking again.

''We came here,'' Holly continued brightly, ''because Mayor Sevvers and I talked this morning and she said she'd be discussing play costumes with Mr. Sperling this afternoon.''

''That's right,'' Evangeline agreed.

''I didn't bring any more,'' Holly said, ''but I have sketches and lists of the ones so far. We can go over them and see what else is needed.''

''Great,'' Sheldon said.

Sheldon, Evangeline and the two beat cops crowded around the counter while Holly described the status of the play's costumes. Gabe excused himself, taking his sheet of paper. He would make his own inventory of which shops were still there and which had changed hands. Before he left, he cautioned the cops not to stay long. Even if they were on patrol on Pacific Way this afternoon, they were still on duty. And other officers in the area were assigned to keep an eye on Holly and Tommy.

Gabe returned fifteen minutes later to see how Tommy was getting along. He'd seen officers Al Sharp and George Greer standing across the pedestrian mall. He told Holly he could take the boy with him, if it would be helpful.

"Sure," Holly said, but her tone wasn't enthusiastic.

"Where is he?" Gabe asked.

"Behind that big front display case, where he's out of the way," Holly said. "I sat on the floor with him a minute ago and got out his new crayons. He started to color in his coloring book."

"Where's everyone else?" Neither Evangeline nor Sheldon were in the shop, either. Bruce and Dolph were also gone, but that was as it should be.

"Evangeline went to put money in her meter and Sheldon joined her since they wanted to talk more about the costumes."

As she spoke, Sheldon came back in the door by himself. "Isn't Evangeline here?" he asked. "She stopped to talk to someone. Did she come back for Tommy?"

"No, he's right over there." Holly pointed toward the big glass case with the wooden back and shelves.

Sheldon took a few steps in that direction. "I don't see him."

"But—" Holly had paled visibly. Gabe didn't wait before hurrying to the display case.

The coloring book and crayons were there.

But Tommy wasn't.

Chapter Ten

"Tommy," Holly cried out, bumping against glass cases and other displays like a spinner in a pinball game as she sped about the room seeking her son. As she neared Gabe, who was also looking, he gently caught her arm. "He was right here a minute ago," she moaned.

She couldn't help searching Gabe's eyes for blame. She was a terrible mother. She had allowed her son out of her sight.

Instead, she saw only concern.

"He can't have gone far," Gabe said. She knew his calm tone and neutral expression were meant to be reassuring, but in her frenzy of fear for her son she could have kicked him for not reacting frantically, too.

"How do you know? Tommy!"

"Where should I look?" Sheldon appeared as distraught as Holly felt.

"I—I don't know." Holly tried to think rationally. She stared around the store. Something looked different. But something always looked different. Sheldon was always changing the displays, as some items sold and others didn't. And she hadn't been in the store for a while.

Since before Thomas was killed. Here.

And now Tommy was missing…

Gabe gripped her more firmly as she tried to pull away. "Was anyone else in the shop when you last saw him?"

"Only Sheldon. I think it was just before he went out."

"Could he have followed you?" Gabe asked the older man.

Holly wanted to hug Sheldon. All color had drained from his face again. It looked nearly as white as his hair.

"No. I would have noticed."

"Was anyone else here when you stepped out?"

Sheldon hesitated before shaking his head. "Only Holly and Tommy."

As Gabe released her, Holly sagged against the nearest case, her heart pounding. Gabe strode toward the outer door. He pushed it open and walked outside. She could see through the glass as he stared up and down the street. His navy suit jacket blew in the breeze from the ocean.

How could he find one small boy in that crowd of tourists?

He seemed to wave at someone, then came back in. "He may be out there. I'll get a patrol officer to look. But let's exhaust the other possibilities first. Have you checked the back room?"

"Not yet," Holly said.

Sheldon was closer. He preceded her through the door to the rear of his shop. He stopped so abruptly that Holly bumped into him. "Tommy!" Sheldon exclaimed.

Not caring how rude she appeared, Holly maneuvered around the bony older man. And stopped.

Her son was there. Thank heavens! She'd upset everyone—including herself—for no reason.

And yet...what was wrong with Tommy?

He lay curled in a fetal position on the floor, beneath the large table at the center of the room. When she thrust some chairs aside, bent and picked him up, he screamed.

His eyes were closed, and he began beating at her. His little hands were curled into fists. They hurt as they connected with her face, her chest. She held on tightly. "Tommy." She attempted to sound soothing—all the while feeling terrified for him. "Honey, it's all right. Please, Tommy. Calm down."

Her child's weight was lifted from her. She started to protest but saw that Gabe had enfolded Tommy into a bear hug that restrained his arms. He murmured softly into the child's ear.

She was the one who should take care of Tommy. *She* was the one who'd always be there for him. Not Gabe, who had temporarily inserted himself into their lives. To whom Tommy responded.

But not even Gabe could calm her son now.

Soon, though, Tommy wilted. Sobs racked his body. Gabe put him down on the floor and, kneeling, held him tightly. "It's going to be okay, sport," he murmured.

"What happened to him?" Holly asked, knowing that neither man present could answer her. She crouched on the dusty wooden floor beside Gabe and Tommy, stroking her son's back. Tommy broke away from Gabe and threw himself into her arms.

Her son. Protectively, she picked him up and held him, leaning against the side of the room's floor-to-ceiling storage cabinet. She combed Tommy's sweat-soaked hair with her fingers. His cries subsided in a flurry of hiccups that quickly ceased.

She carried him to the sink in which artists who worked in this room cleaned their brushes. She dampened her fingers under the faucet and used them to cool her son's hot forehead. "You're fine now, Tommy," she said. She rocked him gently, as she had when he was a baby. Then she pulled back to look at his face.

His eyes, usually a similar shade of deep brown to her own, were nearly black, for his pupils were dilated in fear. He trembled all over. Small mewling noises came from his throat.

Holly felt at her wits' end. What had happened to cause him to go to pieces? "Honey," Holly said, "remember what that special doctor told us?"

Gabe and Sheldon drew closer as if in support, but she ignored them.

"She said you would feel better if you talked about what's hurting you. And I really, really want to know what made you so scared. Will you tell me?"

He shook his head so fast that it nearly made Holly dizzy.

"Why?" Holly knew she shouldn't let her frustration overpower her need to calm him, but the word came out as both a plea and a demand. She didn't expect him to respond.

She was shocked when he did.

He wriggled out of her arms but grasped her hand tightly. He pulled her toward the nearest of the stained and gouged wooden work tables that lined a couple of the room's walls.

On it, propped against the wall, was an elongated, primitive mask, one of Sheldon's prize possessions. Only then did Holly realize that her subconscious mind had noted its absence when she'd searched frantically for Tommy before. It had always been out front, on prominent display, a special piece not for sale. Sheldon had brought it back with him years ago with a long story to tell about its origins in Thailand. Or was it Bali?

It was painted vivid green, with enormous, bulging eyes outlined in black. Its frowning mouth was full of garish, stylized white teeth, and an outsized red tongue lolled from between them.

The mask would be frightening to an impressionable child. It wasn't even pleasant for an adult. But what did Tommy's pointing to it now mean?

He raised his arms to be picked up, the way he had as a toddler. She lifted him, but nearly dropped him, he was shaking so hard. He buried his face on her chest.

Gabe joined them. He rubbed Tommy's back. "Tommy, does that mask scare you?"

The small head nodded against Holly.

"Please tell us why," Gabe said firmly.

So violently that it nearly hurt her, Tommy shook his head.

"What's the mask doing back here, Sheldon?" Holly asked. "I thought you always kept it out front."

"I do. But after the police investigation of…er, you know, there were gouges on it. I brought it here to repair it."

Gabe snapped to instant attention. His eyes narrowed beneath his straight, somber brows. Holly felt glad that their intense scrutiny was focused on Sheldon rather than her. "Did one of the crime scene staff tell you it was damaged during their investigation?"

"No, but it *was* damaged, and I assumed that was how—"

Gabe gently took Tommy from her once more. The boy tilted his head way back to look up at Gabe's face.

"Okay, sport, don't say a word, all right? Just nod or shake your head. Did you see this mask that morning when your daddy got hurt?"

Tommy moved so quickly that Gabe all but dropped him. When his feet were on the floor, Tommy ran into the other room. The adults followed.

Tommy stopped in the front room near the door.

Near where Thomas's body had lain...

He looked about feverishly, as if seeking a means of escape. Holly drew close to him. They both had had enough.

Al Sharp pushed the door open, followed by another uniformed officer, George Greer, Al's new partner. Dolph and Bruce were close behind.

"Everything all right, chief?" Al asked. "We saw Bruce and Dolph down the street and got their attention after we saw you motion to us to come."

At the cops' feet, Tommy buried his face against Holly's legs.

"Are you okay, Tommy?" Al asked. He knelt beside the boy, who scooted far from him along the scuffed floor.

He turned to stare at Al, touched his badge, then drew back as if it had burned him. He cried out once more, then struck at Al and Dolph, who stood next to him.

"I'm sorry, Holly," Al said, looking bewildered. "What did I do?"

"I'm taking Tommy home," Holly said firmly. Though she didn't understand his reactions, he'd had enough. So had she.

As she neared the door, her son in her arms, she turned. Gabe mouthed, *See you later.* There was more on his face than she could read, but she saw both distraction and determination.

Tommy had gone into the back room by himself. He'd seemed terrified about the mask. The cops in uniform seemed to have made it worse.

We don't want to see you later, Holly wanted to cry to Gabe. He'd only ask more questions. Insinuate himself more into Tommy's fragile emotions. Make things worse.

But even so, Holly realized as she hurried out the door carrying Tommy, she would wait eagerly for him to arrive.

She would always be there for her son, to take care of him.

But later, *she* would need a strong shoulder to cry on.

"How was Tommy this afternoon?" Gabe asked Holly as he sat at her kitchen table. It was nearly seven in the evening. He'd wanted to get here early, but as usual the reality of his job had interfered.

Which had been damn irritating. Especially because there was something important he hadn't even gotten to. Tommy's reaction at Sheldon's shop hadn't been the only occurrence that afternoon that triggered a need for further investigation.

When Gabe had taken the list of shops on Pacific Way around for verification—and to listen for clues about why both Thomas Poston and Mal Kensington had copies— he'd met some of the new shopkeepers, who of course couldn't help him.

More interesting was the reaction of the storeowners who'd been around when the list was dated. None had been particularly cooperative. A few were downright hostile.

Why? Could their reactions be related to those of the other disgruntled shopowners, those who'd told Evangeline to ask Mal Kensington why they'd sold out?

He hadn't had time to go back and pursue it further.

He had also brought something to show Holly, but that could wait until later.

"Tommy did just fine this afternoon," she said, responding to his inquiry, but she threw a look toward Tommy that told Gabe more than her words. He probably hadn't been okay at all, but she wouldn't explain in front of her fragile son.

"The chicken smells delicious," Gabe said to change the subject. Holly wore jeans and a cropped shirt, and he savored watching each of her lithe movements as she finished cooking as much as he savored the rich aroma. Her shining dark hair was held back from her face by a golden headband.

He'd called earlier to suggest that he bring in chicken dinners that night, but Holly told him that was just what she'd planned to cook for them.

For *them*. All three of them. The concept was domestic, tempting—and absolutely, unequivocally temporary. He had to keep his mind focused on that: *temporary*.

Gabe helped Holly serve the wonderful home-cooked meal, and enjoyed every bite. He had to step up the investigation's pace. He'd catch the devil who'd killed Thomas Poston. And when he did, and when he'd tied up the other loose ends such as the related threatening calls, there'd be no further reason for him to pop over to Holly's house each evening.

But to get to that point, he had to help Tommy.

"So, sport, you ready for another game of catch?" Gabe asked when they were finished and he'd helped Holly with the dishes.

The kid nodded, but his heart didn't seem in it.

"Why don't you show Gabe the pictures you drew this afternoon?" Holly said. She sounded troubled. Her luscious, full lips smiled at her son, but her eyes didn't.

A frown marred Tommy's face before he slid off his chair and headed for the kitchen door.

Waiting a moment, to make sure he was out of earshot, Gabe said, "Did he tell you any more about this morning?"

Holly sank into her chair. She rested her elbows on the table and propped her chin on her palms, as if it was too much effort for her neck to hold up her head. "What an afternoon. No, he didn't tell me anything. Wouldn't even answer questions by shaking his head or nodding. He was exhausted after what happened, but do you think he would settle down for a nap?"

The question was rhetorical, so Gabe didn't answer. Instead, he put his hand encouragingly on her bare arm. It was warm and creamy smooth. The stimulating sensation of touching her would have distracted him utterly from her story, if he'd let it. He didn't.

"I tried to bribe him to rest by offering to color beside him at the kitchen table. He seemed happy with the idea at first, then ran upstairs and upended nearly everything in his bedroom."

"Was he crying or—?"

Holly interrupted Gabe with a shrug of exasperation. "No. Not a sound. I wondered if he was looking for something, but of course he didn't explain. I got desperate and offered to take him out and buy him a brand-new coloring book. That did the trick, thank heavens. He asked for a blank pad of paper, too, by pointing, and when we got home he drew some pictures of his own on it."

Before Gabe could ask more, Tommy returned. His hands were full of tablets and coloring books and a big box of crayons. "Let me help before you drop something." Gabe put everything on the clean kitchen table.

Tommy crawled up onto his chair beside Gabe. He tilted his head as if asking Gabe something. "What is it?" Gabe asked.

Tommy pointed toward the coloring book.

"Is there a special picture you'd like to show me?"

Tommy nodded. He opened it to a picture of flowers

and butterflies that he had colored in, nearly within the lines. The butterflies were shades of yellow and gold. "Are these monarch butterflies, the ones I told you about the other day?" Gabe asked in delight.

Tommy nodded, grinning.

"Hey, that's great." Gabe leaned over and hugged him. And then he had an idea. "You know what I'd really like?" He didn't look at Holly. If she didn't go along with it, though, he would hear from her quickly enough.

Tommy looked at him with quizzical eyes the same dark brown as his mother's.

"I think something scared you this morning, didn't it, Tommy? At Mr. Sperling's shop?"

He heard Holly's intake of breath, saw her hands move jerkily over the table from the corner of his eye, but when he looked at her, she, too, was just watching him, her eyes wider than Tommy's. She looked upset, but she didn't stop him.

"What I would like is for you to draw me a picture of what scared you, okay?"

Tommy shook his head vehemently. He kicked his feet against his chair. Maybe this idea wasn't going to work.

"If you're not going to draw it, tell me what scared you."

His little head shook in the negative so hard that Gabe wondered if he was getting dizzy. He rose and picked Tommy up.

"If you talk about something, it gets less scary," Gabe said.

Tommy's body stiffened, as if he wanted to get out of Gabe's arms. Gabe put him down gently. Tommy gave him a defiant look, his small bottom lip jutting. And then he sat back at the table. He opened his tablet to a blank page and began drawing something with his crayons.

Gabe wasn't sure how artistic four-year-olds were, but he found Tommy's creation colorful and full of irregular shapes that, taken together, resembled a person.

A person with a green face and red tongue. Like the mask in Sheldon's shop. Its body was blue.

"Is that what scared you, honey?" Holly said. She had been utterly quiet, watching her son work. "The mask?"

Tommy looked up at her from where he sat, eyes troubled. He shook his head slowly at first, then nodded affirmatively.

"Honey, we don't understand. Was it the mask?"

Tommy blinked. He opened his mouth, then shut it again. And then he turned his head toward Gabe.

"Would you like to tell me, sport?" Gabe kept his tone very soft, very soothing and, he hoped, very encouraging.

Tommy hopped down from the chair once more and tugged at Gabe until his ear was near Tommy's mouth.

And then Tommy said one word, very distinctly: "Monster."

"WHAT WAS he talking about?" Holly asked an hour later, after Tommy was in bed. "Did he think the mask was a monster?"

Gabe shrugged. He sat beside her on the sofa in her living room. She had made hazelnut-flavored decaf—wimpy stuff but it tasted good. They had sat down to relax. He was glad Holly spoke to him about her son as if Gabe were part of his life.

Yeah, and it was damn disconcerting, too.

"He needs to tell us what he's thinking," he grumbled. "A word now and then was enough at first, but now I want him really to talk."

"Me, too." Holly looked at him over the rim of her

raised mug of coffee. Her eyes were sad, almost despairing.

He sat—hard—on his urge to hold her.

"I just wish…" Her voice trailed off.

"Should I fill in the blanks? You wish nothing had happened, that your husband was alive and your son was talking and—"

"Yes!" The loudness of her tone underscored her frustration. She punctuated the word further by thumping her mug down on the coffee table.

"I wish it for you, too, Holly." The hell of it was, he really did.

He was startled by her scornful expression. "That's kind of you to say, though you don't mean it. Isn't this the biggest case you've had since you arrived here? If it hadn't happened, where would your challenge be?"

Gabe's fists clenched, but he made himself relax before he snapped the handle off his mug. It wasn't necessarily his biggest case, just his most obvious. "I'd find something to do." Gabe made himself smile, then grew serious. "Holly, I'm a cop. It's what I always wanted to be, and I admit I love its challenges. But whether or not you believe it, I'm still a human being, more or less. And I hate what's going on with you and Tommy. If I could make it all go away, I would. Instead, the best I can do is to solve the case as fast as I can."

Holly's head drooped. "I'm sorry, Gabe. I shouldn't take this out on you."

He edged closer to her on the couch and lifted her small chin with his fingertip. Her eyes were luminous, and for a moment he imagined he saw desire there. Her mouth opened, perhaps to say something, but instead he saw the tip of her tongue move, then grow still. Damn, how sexy she was! His crotch tightened, but he quickly pulled away. She probably had no idea how she was affecting him.

"And as to solving the case," he said almost gruffly, "I brought something of Thomas's that arrived at the station."

Holly's eyebrows knit together as if she were confused. He loved those dark eyebrows, how expressive they were. He had an urge to stroke them....

Instead, he stood abruptly and went to the recliner chair, where he'd left his suit jacket. He pulled out an envelope, then handed it to Holly.

"I don't know if Mal Kensington minded whether his officers got personal mail at the station, but I do. I thought I'd made it clear, but Thomas didn't take me seriously. In any event, you should get this credit card company to send future bills here."

"Sure," Holly said, but she sounded distracted as she opened the envelope.

"Is something wrong?"

"It's just that... I didn't learn about this credit card myself till I went through Thomas's office. And this bill has charges on it. The charges I saw before looked normal, but not these. I knew he bought tickets to some Mighty Ducks games, but this says he got expensive box seats, season tickets. It's an extravagance. I'm not sure how he intended to pay for them."

Gabe was instantly on alert. He joined her on the couch once more, edging close to look over her shoulder at the bill. "Are there other extraordinary charges?"

She pointed at a charge. "Sports equipment from a department store...and I don't even know where he put it. I'm going to have to go through this very carefully." She turned her head to look at Gabe. She looked stricken. "I don't know what was going on, Gabe."

"We'll find out," he said soothingly.

"Do you…" She hesitated.

He thought he knew what she was thinking. "Do I think this could have something to do with his death? Or if it's what that caller is after? I don't know, but it could be. That's why we have to figure out what Thomas was up to."

Holly seemed to wilt beside him. One hand went up to her eyes. "Thomas and I had drifted apart," she said, "but I never imagined he was hiding something that someone might kill him over. Could he have done something illegal?"

"Could be, but no need to judge him until we know for sure." He moved closer and put a comforting arm around her, and she leaned into him.

When she turned her head again, his mouth was close to hers. Very close. Her breath was as sweet as hazelnut coffee and honey. He thought about pulling away but didn't. He kissed her.

He only intended it to be a comforting kiss. A brotherly kiss, from a cop who was a surrogate family member.

It started out that way. But she pressed her mouth against his as if she sought the breath of life from him. He gave it, and he was the one who felt suddenly alive. Alert. He felt his erection grow and throb as his lips explored hers, tasted her, felt her hands begin to move over his chest, down his back….

If he didn't stop now, he wouldn't stop at all. He dragged himself off the sofa. He stood in front of Holly, breathing irregularly, wanting her so much that he hurt, right where it mattered.

But he wouldn't do that to her. Or himself.

"Why, Gabe?" she asked softly. Her lips were swollen

from the ardor of his kisses. "I don't believe I'm saying this, but don't you want to make love with me?"

His smile held no humor. "More than I want to solve this case."

She looked as shocked as if he had hit her. "Then why…?"

He ached to take her back into his arms. Ached bad. But he wouldn't. To avoid the temptation, he sat on the reclining chair facing her, not beside her.

"Look, Holly." He hoped his voice was stronger than it sounded. "We've been thrown together in an emotional situation. You've just lost your husband. You're afraid and lonely. I know how that can affect a woman. But when this is all over, you'll be ready for a new life. If we make love now, you'll regret it. I'll regret taking advantage of you."

"Why would you regret it, Gabe? I'm a consenting adult, so you wouldn't be taking advantage of me. Is there more to it than that?"

"Yeah." He tried to sound offhand. He stood just long enough to retrieve his coffee mug, to give his hands something to do. Sure, he didn't have to tell her, but there was a sadness and fragility in her eyes. It wasn't *her* he was rejecting, just the bitter future that making love with her now would bring.

He'd told her his childhood problems—more than he'd ever admitted to a woman before.

Telling her what she asked now would be a piece of cake. Right?

He tried to keep his tone offhand. After all, this stuff didn't matter to him anymore. "A few years ago, there was a woman I liked. A lot. I met her on a case, too. I helped to prove the charges against her husband that sent him to prison for a brutal crime. She'd loved him before she realized what he'd done, who he was. She decided to divorce him. We got close. But when her divorce was final, she didn't want to have anything to do with that part of her life again. Including me. She'd needed someone to help her through the transition. A rebound lover. I fit the profile. The temporary profile. Afterward, I understood where she'd been coming from, but that's not a situation I care to get into again.''

''But Gabe, Thomas and I weren't...'' She stopped. ''That doesn't matter. I wasn't close to Thomas when he died. But I also have no intention of a relationship with you, or any other cop. You're right, Gabe. Thanks for reminding me. This would have been a very bad idea.''

She rose then, very gracefully, her curves showing through her form-hugging jeans and knit top. He throbbed right where his pants constricted him, but he ignored it.

Until she grew close. Damn, didn't she get the message? But before Gabe could pull her back into his arms and forget everything sensible he'd just told himself, she stood on tiptoe and kissed him on the cheek.

''Good night, Gabe,'' she said, and left the room.

Chapter Eleven

Frustration was Gabe's driving force the next day.

He arrived at his office soon after dawn, made phone calls, left messages. He was too early to reach people, but they'd know first thing that he wanted to talk to them. Fast.

He went through correspondence and files that had piled up on his desk, threw out what he could, and organized the rest.

And then he paced his office, barely noticing as daylight outside his window grew brighter.

He felt frustrated about the lack of progress in the investigation into Thomas Poston's murder and the attack on Sheldon Sperling.

He felt frustrated about the fruitlessness, so far, of his investigation into what had happened to Mal Kensington.

He felt frustrated that he had no time to visit more shop-owners along Pacific Way again, see their reactions to his questions and insist on better answers.

To top it all off, he felt—well, frustrated! Hanging around Holly did it to him. Tommy still wasn't talking much. And though attempting to keep things with Holly platonic made all the sense in the world, he wanted her so bad it was driving him nuts.

She'd shown she was interested. In him. In sex. But if

they leaped into bed now, it would complicate things for both of them in the future.

End of story. Wasn't it?

The first person to return his phone call was Sheldon. No surprise. The man used to meet Thomas Poston at daybreak.

"How can I help you, Gabe?" the older man said. Gabe pictured him sitting behind the main counter in his store, maybe with a cup of tea. Did he miss his early morning breakfasts with Thomas Poston and Tommy?

"That mask." Gabe, at his desk, clutched the phone receiver as if it might attempt to leap away before letting someone on the other end disgorge needed information. "I know someone from my department picked it up yesterday and brought it in for further examination. The suspect may have damaged it rather than the investigative team."

The chances of finding something useful on it were slim. Sheldon's attempt to fix its scratches and gouges probably destroyed any potentially useful evidence. And that was why Gabe had to discuss it with him.

"The way Tommy reacted makes me think he associates it with the day of the murder," Gabe continued, "just like he gets upset when he sees police uniforms that remind him of his dad. When you repaired the mask, did anything on it suggest how it got damaged?"

"The best I could tell, it might just have fallen off its stand on the counter near the door. Or—"

"Or what?"

Sheldon hesitated long enough to take a sip of tea. Or a deep breath. "I don't suppose you know yet what the guy used to beat me, do you?"

"The mask?" Interesting possibility. The lab technicians knew their jobs. They'd check the mask for blood and hair without Gabe's direction. Still, he'd call and mention it.

"I don't know," Sheldon said. "And none of us thinks Tommy saw what happened anyway. He's not likely to have seen the killer hit me with the mask, so I really don't know what he's so scared of."

Monster, thought Gabe. The mask certainly was ugly enough, but why would the kid call it a monster? He didn't ask Sheldon.

"If I think of anything useful, I'll let you know," Sheldon continued. "Tommy's seen that mask every time his mother brought him into the shop. It was on display out front till now. And the poor kid still isn't talking, is he? He didn't seem to be yesterday."

"No," said Gabe, "he's not." A word or two here and there wasn't talking. Knowing he was letting himself in for additional frustration, he asked, "And that list of stores along Pacific Way. I started to check yesterday but got sidetracked. Any idea yet whether it was accurate as of its date?" Or why it also appeared in the file of a murder victim or two. Or why some shopowners responded to it so negatively. Those were questions he kept to himself. Sheldon was a shopowner, too, but his reaction to the list had been neutral.

"I don't know," Sheldon replied, "but that copy belonged to Thomas Poston, didn't it? Do you think it's a clue about who killed him and beat me?"

"I can't see how," Gabe responded noncommittally. "Do you?"

"No, but I was considering why he'd have it. The best I could figure was that, around that date, there was a police-backed fundraiser for the Naranja Children's Foundation. Maybe he was assigned this area for canvassing."

Oh. Great. Then there was a valid reason for the same list to be in Mal Kensington's files.

Still, Gabe thought, he hadn't found lists of other areas in Mal's records, places cops besides Thomas might solicit for donations. And storeowners wouldn't be incensed simply because they had been asked to make charitable donations.

"Thanks," he told Sheldon. "You've been helpful." Except that his answers had made some elements of Gabe's investigation even murkier than seawater swirling with sand in a storm.

He had no sooner hung up than someone knocked on his door. Four patrol officers came in, those who had been on Pacific Way yesterday, when Tommy Poston had gotten so upset.

Four *uniformed* patrol officers. Al Sharp and his new partner George Greer, plus Dolph Hilo and Bruce Franklin. Gabe had left them all messages, too, to come see him.

When they left half an hour later, his frustration was stoked even higher. His gut gnawed at him. Why was it that he felt Sharp, Hilo and Franklin all knew more than they said?

George Greer hadn't known anything useful.

Hilo and Franklin were sympathetic but hadn't added much. Before his father's death, Tommy had never shown any fear of them. And, no, they couldn't explain his behavior now, except to agree it had to do with what happened to his daddy. Yet there was something in the way they tried to be helpful that made Gabe wish he could read minds. What were they really thinking?

Al Sharp was his usual sarcastic, unhelpful self. He verified he'd been out of uniform when he'd questioned Tommy after Thomas's murder. Holly had kept the kid nearly in seclusion, so to Al's knowledge the first time he'd seen police in uniform after the morning of the killing was at Thomas's funeral. But that still didn't explain why uniforms upset him the way they did. The way they had yesterday, in Sheldon's shop.

No one knew why Tommy had acted that way except Tommy. And he wasn't telling.

Eventually, Gabe was alone in his office again. Somehow, he vowed, he would figure out a way to get Tommy to say more than one word at a time. A way that would make him feel good, not frighten the tyke even more.

Of course he would.

He'd need to get Holly on board. Lovely, sexy Holly. He would be staying at her house once more… Frustration!

Was that frustration—*all* his frustration—making him paranoid? Why would he think that three cops who used to work with Thomas Poston didn't want Gabe to find out who murdered him?

None of them was the killer—right?

But Tommy was afraid of police uniforms….

The phone rang again. "Gabe? It's Evangeline. Could you come to my office?"

"Sure."

He wished a while later that he'd not been so quick to agree. He sat on a leather chair in Evangeline's office, staring at her across her huge, plain wooden desk, its top as paper-free as his own.

"What do you mean I shouldn't worry about what happened to Mal Kensington anymore?" Gabe demanded incredulously. As miserably as things had gone for him that day, this was the worst kick in the solar plexus yet.

Evangeline's long, narrow face was expressionless. "You're not listening, Gabe. I know how good an investigator you are. I began to wonder, when you didn't find anything in three months, whether I'd simply been mistaken about Mal Kensington's death. Yes, he was cremated quickly and his family left town in a big hurry, but so what? The medical examiner's report showed natural causes. I just reread it to make sure. And now, I don't want you to waste any more time trying to prove something that was a figment of my imagination. It's time for you to stop looking into Mal's death.''

"But Thomas Poston was a cop, and he was definitely murdered.'' Gabe clenched the arms of the chair to prevent himself from getting right in Evangeline's too-composed face.

"Yes.'' She lifted eyebrows that were brown rather than red like her hair. "He was stabbed to death. Mal was simply found dead in his home. No signs of foul play.''

"What about those comments from former shopowners along Pacific Way, telling you to ask Mal why they'd sold out so quickly? The fact he died so soon after dissembling and acting as if he had sand fleas in his shorts before city council?''

He hadn't held back suspicions or clues from Evangeline before in his investigation of Mal's death. But damned if he would mention the shopowners' reaction to his inquiries the day before. Not while she was cutting this investigation—and him—off at the knees. Or trying to.

Evangeline stood. She leaned over her desk, resting her well-manicured hands on it. "Think about it, Gabe. What's more logical? A man was murdered even though there was no indication of foul play and no concrete evidence of anyone having a motive—except that he was chief of police, of course. That job means you're automatically the enemy of lots of people.''

She gave a sharp little grin that showed her perfect, white teeth. Gabe knew her smile was intended to be humorous. He wasn't laughing.

Her expression sobered. "Or," she continued, "the man died of a heart attack after being put under additional stress on his job. Which is more rational, Gabe? You tell me."

"You brought me here from Sacramento." Gabe made a major effort to keep his voice low and controlled, but he knew his anger showed on his face. "Risked your political career being blown because of claims of nepotism. Gave me what information you had and set me loose. I bought your story. It made sense. And now you're telling me it was all a mistake?"

"That's exactly what I'm telling you, Gabe." She returned to her seat, looking more relaxed. "Just drop it."

"And I suppose you want me to drop the investigation into Thomas Poston's murder, too, Your Honor?" No way could Gabe back off from that, no matter who ordered it. "That would be obstruction of justice."

She glared at him. "Of course I don't want to obstruct justice. Murder is police business. You're chief of police."

"Thank you for noticing." He rose. "And thanks for the suggestion, Your Honor. I'll take it under advisement."

He was nearly out the door when he heard her say, "It's not a suggestion, Chief McLaren. It's an order."

HOLLY HAD TRIED all day to be nurturing to her son. But Tommy was making it difficult.

She ached for him so much she wanted to cry. *Talk to me,* she pleaded silently. *Talk to Gabe. Anyone.*

They were in her bright red minivan. She'd taken him back to the psychologist, and the session hadn't gone well. He'd become upset when Holly told the lady doctor what had happened at Mr. Sperling's shop yesterday. He hadn't calmed down since.

First she'd had a hard time getting him even to walk from the office to the small lot at the rear of the medical building where she'd parked. Now, he squirmed behind her in the back seat. He hadn't wanted to be confined in the booster seat, and she'd had to bribe him—something she wasn't proud of, but it had at least gotten him into the van. They were on their way to his favorite toy store in a neighboring community. Time for yet another coloring book.

"So, honey," she said soothingly, "once we get your new coloring book, we'll go home and take a nap."

Her attention was on the local two-lane highway, one that wound a lot thanks to its proximity to the coastline. There wasn't much traffic this time of day, so she was able to go a little over the speed limit, though the curves kept her from going too fast. In the rearview mirror, she saw Tommy shake his head vehemently in the negative.

"We'll see, Tommy," she said, trying not to allow her exasperation to color her tone.

The highway curved to the right…and then it happened. As Holly turned the van, she suddenly couldn't control it! It swerved from one side of the road to the other. She fought the steering wheel, trying to stay on the pavement. Braking slowly did no good. Neither did pumping the brakes.

A car sped toward her—right in the lane she was in! She overcompensated and nearly went off the shoulder on the other side, into a swampy wetlands area.

"Mommy!" cried Tommy, from behind her.

If she'd been able to concentrate on anything but stopping the car, she'd have made a fuss over his talking. But for now…

There. She did it. The right front dipped off the road, but her minivan had finally come to a stop.

Only then did she realize how hard her heart was pounding. Her breathing had accelerated but she felt she needed air.

She put her head down on the steering wheel while she tried to get hold of her soaring, conflicting emotions: terror, elation, fear.

"Mommy, are you okay?" asked Tommy in a small, shaky voice.

"Oh, yes, honey," she said, turning so she could look at him and smile as reassuringly as possible.

A knock sounded on her window. Startled, she found a young man with a pale face staring at her. "Are you all right?" She nodded and tried to roll down the automatic window, but the engine was off. She opened the door.

The young man waved a cell phone. "Can I call someone for you?"

"No, thanks," she said. But she reached toward her purse at Tommy's feet and extracted the cell phone Gabe had insisted she carry. She punched in his phone number.

BY THE TIME Gabe arrived at the location Holly described, two California Highway Patrol officers were with her. So were the N.B.P.D. patrol officers he'd assigned to follow Holly that day.

A lot of good they'd done.

Gabe flashed his credentials, and the older C.H.P. officer asked to see him alone. Gabe wanted to go to Holly and Tommy, who leaned on the hood of the minivan talking to the other officers. He needed to assure himself they were all right. But they were clearly alive and, even if shaken up, relatively unharmed. He stepped behind the vehicle with the C.H.P. officer.

"The left front tire's flat, sir," the officer said. He was lanky and sober-faced, a veteran who obviously took his work seriously.

"A tread problem?" The flurry of reports of defectively manufactured tires had ended a while ago, but that didn't mean there still weren't problem tires on vehicles.

"No, sir. Best I could tell, the valve stem broke off."

"That doesn't necessarily cause a blowout. The air loss could be slow."

"True, but this time it wasn't, Chief. And you should check on the other tires, too."

"Why?" Gabe stared at the patrolman.

"All four tires have loosened valve cores. One's ready to come out just like the one on the flat tire. Maybe all of them. If one didn't go flat, another would. Soon."

HOLLY WAS GRATEFUL to Gabe for taking charge. He had the van towed to a repair shop he designated in Naranja Beach. He would also take care of having anything extracted from the van that could be used as evidence of who had sabotaged it.

He plopped a subdued Tommy into the back seat of his department-issued sedan and fastened his seat belt. Holly sat in the front seat beside him.

"How would you two like a really good hamburger dinner tonight?" he asked. "Way out at the end of the pier."

The Naranja Beach pier extended from the beach, and at its end was a restaurant—a different, competing chain from the similar one in neighboring Seal Beach. Like that one, it specialized in hamburgers.

Fortunately, it was informal, for Holly wore jeans and a snug top striped orange and red.

"Okay, Tommy?"

He didn't answer. When Holly turned, he was nodding happily.

"Honey, you talked to me before, in our car," she said gently. "Won't you talk to us now?"

His head shook solemnly, and Holly's disappointment nearly swamped her. She could hardly get in an accident every day to get her son to say something.

Their dinner cheered her even though she hadn't much appetite. She still hadn't dared to get on a scale since Thomas's murder. Her weight had plummeted.

The restaurant's ambiance exceeded the quality of the food, but she enjoyed seeing the sun set over the heads of the dozen people still fishing off the end of the pier. Demanding gulls sat on weathered wooden pilings begging for baitfish, and flocks of hungry brown pelicans glided over the pulsing Pacific.

Afterward, they walked slowly back along the pier toward the town, watching the few remaining beachgoers along the wide swath of clean sand bathed by the colorful sunset. Everything seemed so peaceful here. But Holly knew it was an illusion.

Someone had tried to hurt Tommy and her today. Even if it had only been intended as a warning, whoever tampered with her tires would have had no way of knowing when they'd go flat—and if it would injure them. Maybe kill them. That had happened notwithstanding the constant police protection. What was she going to do? Waiting for the cops' solution wasn't enough. But she knew nothing about conducting an investigation.

Gabe drove them home and pulled into her driveway. When he got out of the sedan, she asked, "Don't you have to change cars or anything? I mean, I tore you away from your office—"

"Let me worry about that," he said.

He leaned over and kissed her very softly on the lips. He tasted of hamburger and ketchup and Gabe. She was beginning to know his taste. It was headier than the atmosphere at the restaurant at the end of the pier. She would miss that very special flavor when she no longer was able to sample it.

He retrieved Tommy from the back seat and they all went into the house.

"Are you doing all right?" Gabe whispered to her as Tommy headed for the television.

"I think so."

"Good. Things can't go on as they are. We need to find some answers. And I've come up with an idea for getting solutions to at least one question."

"What's that?"

"Trust me." His slow wink told Holly she should do anything but. That teasing, alluring, blatantly masculine flash of his eye was clearly meant to disarm her.

"We'll see." She didn't sound as grumpy as she'd intended.

She stood at the living room door while Gabe sat beside Tommy on the sofa.

"Hey, sport," he said. "How would you like to play a game of ball where the winner gets a prize?"

Tommy's expression perked up. He was such an adorable, angelic child...most of the time. But he was also a *child*. What did Gabe have in mind?

"Here's what we'll do. If you win the game, I'm going to take you and your mom out for ice cream tonight—rainbow, okay?"

Tommy slid off the sofa and nodded exuberantly.

"And if I win, you'll talk to me about the monster."

Her son's face fell. Very slowly, he shook his head.

Gabe seemed to ponder this for a minute, but Holly could tell he'd already anticipated this response.

Should she intervene? No. Tommy was her son, but like

it or not he had only spoken to her during an emergency. He needed to talk for his own sake. And they needed some answers. She had told Gabe that Tommy spoke earlier, when he'd been frightened. And there was no one gentler about encouraging him than Gabe.

"Okay, then," Gabe said. "We'll make it a little easier. You tell me why you *can't* talk about the monster. How's that?"

Very smooth, Holly thought. And very clever. For after a moment of consideration, Tommy nodded.

Of course the outcome of the ball game was preordained. Although Tommy was in the lead early on, he lost.

He looked sad as Gabe led him in. "Tell you what, Tommy," he said. "You give me my prize, and then I'll give you yours anyway. How's that?"

That cheered him.

"Okay, then." Gabe led him into the living room and effortlessly lifted her child onto his lap on the sofa. Holly took a seat on an upholstered chair facing them. "Tell me about the monster, Tommy," he said, "and why you can't talk about him."

"He came to Mr. Sperling's shop and hurt Daddy," Tommy said very softly. "He came after me. He said if I talk anymore or tell about him, he'll get me."

His little face was ashen. Holly could tell he was about to cry. She held herself still despite wanting to run to him.

"I see," Gabe said very gravely. "Well, you know what? We're going to make sure he can't get you. And no one is going to tell my friend Tommy he can't talk and get away with it. I'm the chief of police, and I said so."

Tommy's stare at him seemed, at first, to be incredulous. And then, her son smiled so brightly that Holly wondered if the power in her house had surged. "Yeah, Gabe," he said. "You can tell him, 'cause the monster's a policeman."

GABE KEPT HIS PROMISE and took Tommy and Holly out for ice cream. But his heart wasn't in it. His mind roiled the entire time.

A policeman.

He kept the chatter with Holly light so as not to frighten the boy into silence once more. Tommy didn't say much, but when prompted he asked again for rainbow ice cream, even said "thank you."

But Gabe shared more than one look with Holly. Judging by the distress in her winsome brown eyes, she was upset, too.

When they returned to her house, he helped to get Tommy to bed and read the boy a story. Hugged him goodnight. Waited for Holly to kiss her son and tuck him in.

And then he followed her downstairs.

"What do you think?" Gabe asked Holly when they reached the living room.

He knew what he thought. He had a damn department full of suspects. *The monster was a cop.*

Holly smiled at him. It was a sad smile. But it was a smile nevertheless. "We've made progress," she said. She took his hand. For a disappointed moment, he thought she was merely going to shake it. Instead, she used it to lever herself up on tiptoes and plant a small kiss on his mouth. A grateful kiss, that was all. But it made critical parts of him stand up and take notice.

He nearly groaned as she turned and walked across the room. "Thank you, Gabe," she said from a distance as close as the other end of the sofa and as far from where he wanted her as if she'd jogged to the beach.

"It didn't solve things," he said with a shrug.

"No. I know. It only triggered more questions. But at least Tommy is talking." She sat on the sofa and regarded him somberly. "Maybe he'll tell us more." She sighed. "I can't believe that the person who killed Thomas was probably one of his friends."

"We don't know that for certain."

"No, but Tommy said that the monster was wearing a uniform. Or at least I think that's what he meant."

Gabe nodded. He took a seat on the couch. "That's what I understood, too. But Tommy didn't see Sheldon hit or Thomas stabbed."

"Thank heavens," Holly said fervently.

"And even if someone in uniform put on the monster mask, there are still a heck of a lot of suspects."

"I know." Holly took a deep breath. "We need answers," she finally said. "If only I knew how to get them—"

"*I'll* get them, damn it," Gabe interjected, suddenly angry as his fear for her boiled over like a cauldron of water untended on the stove. "Don't you start trying to play cop. It's dangerous."

"I know," she replied quietly. She was silent for a long moment, then looked toward him with horror contorting the lovely features of her face. "Gabe, the 'monster' is probably the person who's been making those phone calls. And today, he tried to hurt us, and we don't even know why."

He suddenly wanted to dispel her horror at all costs. To erase every one of her fears.

And the only way he knew how to do that was to hold her in his arms. Make her forget everything, if only for a short while.

Make love with her.

He moved toward her, knowing that she might reject him. After all, he had rejected her sweet advances the night before.

He held his breath as he took his place beside her, enveloped her in his embrace. She lay her head on his chest, her hands at his back hugging him close. He inhaled her fragrance of apricot and hamburger and woman.

And then, he used one finger beneath her chin to tilt her head back.

Her luminous eyes were languid and he saw desire there. ''Gabe?'' she whispered. It was a question and a challenge and a plea. And he could no longer hold back.

His mouth lowered to hers. Her lips opened for him. She tasted like the most luscious of delicacies, warm and inviting. Before he could slip his tongue in to sample the heated cavern of her welcoming mouth, hers darted out teasingly. He played her game, but only for a moment.

His hand slipped between them, beneath the clinging fabric of her striped knit top, to touch the silken flesh of her stomach, then upward to the small, ripe curves of her breasts. He heard her soft intake of breath as he cupped her, ran a thumb over one nipple until it peaked, then explored the other one.

''Gabe?'' she said once more.

Did she want him to stop? He would. He still could. But lord almighty, he didn't want to. Not now.

''What, sweetheart?'' he whispered, holding himself still as he throbbed below.

''Let's go upstairs,'' she breathed.

Chapter Twelve

Holly preceded Gabe into her bedroom, but when he reached for her she slipped away. She could have laughed at the heated question, the overt frustration, in his shining, sexy green eyes.

Instead, she maneuvered around him and locked the door. "Tommy," she explained with a shaky smile. "He's probably asleep by now, but—"

"Yeah," Gabe said. The question disappeared, replaced by an all-masculine grin. He stepped toward her, and then she was enveloped in a burning embrace that she couldn't have escaped if she'd wanted to. Which she didn't.

She drew in her breath as, once more, his hands found her breasts. He cupped them gently, one, then the other, then released them. This time she was the one who gazed at him in question, but he reached down and pulled her top over her head, removed her bra.

Her knees wobbled as her desire was piqued by the appreciative way he stared at her. His eyes met hers, and the primitive passion she saw there made her moan.

The sound gravitated Gabe to move, to propel both of them to her bed, where he laid her down upon the colorful coverlet she had sewn herself. His hands stroked her flesh, then moved downward. She raised her hips, and he used the opportunity to strip off her jeans and panties and kiss his way down her body till she gasped at the erotic feeling of heated lips on yearning flesh.

When he replaced his lips with his hands, caressing her where she was most sensitive, she thought she would expire.

"Gabe!" she gasped, forcing herself to roll away from him. "Let me." She knelt on the bed, naked, while she helped him struggle from his shirt, his pants, his briefs. "Oh," she said softly as she viewed his magnificently male body, bared before her. She had already glimpsed the muscularity of his hard biceps, his sculptured chest. But she had only imagined the rest of him—his solid thighs, taut calves, tight buttocks, and the very obvious, very aroused male protrusion that told her he was as turned on as she.

Her hands reached out, grasped him, stroked him until it was he who moaned. His lips met hers again, even as his body covered hers. His hardness and strength and weight made her buck with need. She loved the erotic male scent of him, the incredible sensation of his hard and heated, damp flesh on hers, his hands touching and caressing and massaging.

She thrust her hips up to tell him how very ready she was—and he immediately pulled away.

She wanted to cry out, except that when she managed to open her eyes she saw him grope for his pants and extract a small foil envelope from a pocket.

She smiled in amusement despite her aching need for him. For a man who hadn't, as recently as last night, wanted to make love with her, he had still managed to be prepared.

"Let me," she said. She fumbled with the wrapper, but

enjoyed every moment of torturing him with her deliberately slow way of sheathing him.

When she was done, he was the one who was smiling. He pushed her onto the bed and moved her legs so she was open to him.

When he thrust into her, she cried out, but the sound was swallowed by his kiss. He established the rhythm with his thrusts, and she joined it with her own.

She rode with him until, in a starburst of color that dazzled her eyes, she felt herself explode into ecstasy.

HOLLY LOST COUNT. The first time Gabe and she made love last night was far from the only time, and each one was as compelling and thrilling as the last.

He was insatiable. And inventive. He'd kissed her everywhere, from her polished toenails to her fingertips. And she loved every minute of it.

When she awakened this time, as dawn poked tendrils of light between the window blinds, she was cuddled up to him spoon-fashion, his deliciously hard body pressed against her back. She rolled over, almost purring. And found him awake, too. Looking at her with eyes that shouted of lust as powerful as anything she'd experienced the night before.

"Again?" she whispered teasingly, although she couldn't keep her own renewed desire from turning her voice husky.

"Again," he confirmed in a deep and very proudly male tone. He rolled on top of her and set his weight seductively upon her breasts and stomach as he reached for the bedside table. His erection was already renewed and pressing at her, and she grinned a feline grin.

"Good thing you came well supplied," she said as she

heard yet again the crispness of foil wrapping being disturbed.

"I sure—"

He was interrupted by the ringing of a phone. Holly's insides plummeted. It was too early for anyone she knew to call. Might it be the creep who'd threatened her? Who'd sabotaged her car and tried, just yesterday, to harm Tommy and her.

"I don't want to answer," she said shakily.

Gabe was already out of bed. "You don't have to. It's mine."

She admired the way taut muscles rippled as he stooped and reached inside the pocket of the pants he had shed on the floor last night. He stood facing her, gloriously, unabashedly male, as he flipped the cell phone open and said, "Hello." Lord, but his body could stimulate the hormones of the world's entire female population. Maybe the universe's.

"Yeah, Jimmy," he said. "You have? Can you tell me…? All right. I'll be there right away."

A chill washed over Holly that had nothing to do with no longer having Gabe's body heat to warm her. She noted the faraway look in his eye as he closed the cell phone's flap. Just like that, his mind was already far from here. On duty.

What had she expected? He was a cop.

And she had been an idiot, sleeping with him. She'd told herself she merely wanted comfort from all that had happened to Tommy and her. To celebrate Tommy's talking. To enjoy fulfillment of a few lustful fantasies.

But looking at him, as he silently drew on his clothes, she realized the miserable truth.

She was falling in love with yet another damn police officer.

"Sorry, Holly," Gabe said.

She stared at him. Could he read her mind?

He had finally focused on her once more. She caught his regretful expression as she pulled the coverlet up to her chin. She wanted to draw it over her head and weep at her own folly. But she didn't.

"I have to get to the station," he said. "I don't want to leave you alone after yesterday, so—"

"Don't worry about us," she said very civilly. Maybe too civilly, for his eyes narrowed.

"I'm sorry," he repeated. "I need to go. I'll assign someone to hang out with you till I can get back. Except..."

"Except what?" Holly asked.

"Look, I need to know the officers on the force who were Thomas's closest friends."

"Why?" she asked.

Finished dressing, he stood in the middle of the room in the casual clothes he'd worn last night while playing catch. Was he going to the station that way? "I want to know which ones I can count on. The ones I can trust most to look out for Tommy and you."

"Oh." She realized what he was driving at. Those cops she named as Thomas's friends would be the ones Gabe would *least* trust. Tommy had said the monster was a policeman. That could mean anyone close to Thomas could have killed him.

"Holly?" Gabe prompted. "Who?" He folded his muscular arms.

She slowly drew in a breath, preparing to reply. "Well... Al Sharp, of course. He was Thomas's partner. And Thomas really respected Mal Kensington." She permitted herself the tiniest of wry grins. "That's not to say he didn't respect you."

"Yeah. He really looked up to me." Gabe's sarcasm was showing. "Anyone else?"

"Bruce and Dolph. Al and he hung out with them the most."

"Is that everyone?"

"They were the closest," Holly said with a sigh. "Look, Gabe. They're friends. I'd still trust them to take care of Tommy and me."

"Right. Look, Holly, how fast can you get yourself and Tommy dressed?"

"If you're going to command us to come with you, forget it. We're staying here." She held up her hands against his stubborn expression. "I know. Tommy said the monster was a policeman. *A* policeman. If you feel you have to, send a bunch of your guys over here to watch us. But we're not going anywhere."

"Then I'll stay—"

"No!" She practically shouted as she shifted on the bed, her coverlet pulled up to her chin. She felt foolish, arguing with a fully dressed man while she remained nude. "No," she repeated more quietly. "You have work to do. Go do it."

"You'll let whoever I send in the house later?"

"We don't need anyone here. Especially a cop under suspicion. We'll be fine."

"Like you were fine yesterday?"

She shuddered. "Okay, Gabe," she said quietly. "Thanks." For everything. For the sex. For acting concerned. For…

"Holly, believe me. After last night, I don't want—"

She stood, hauling the coverlet with her. Bravely, she approached him and stood on her toes. She kissed him lightly. "I understand, Gabe," she said.

And she did.

He was a cop. And whether or not he was physically present, he was already gone.

"SO WHAT was this interesting piece of evidence you couldn't tell me over the phone, Jimmy?" Gabe asked Detective James Hernandez. *And it had better be good,* he thought.

It had, after all, taken him away from an amazing night and morning with an amazing woman... An amazingly *stubborn* woman. The incredibly sensuous, delightfully insatiable Holly.

Or had it been his own insatiability that had turned him on and kept him on for hours? It hadn't ever been like that before, not with any other woman....

He felt a flush creep up his neck, and not from embarrassment. Hell, no. But he had other things he needed to concentrate on now.

He'd made a quick trip home to shave and change clothes. He stood now in Jimmy's office at the station, and the slim, sharp-featured homicide detective looked none too pleased about what he had to tell Gabe.

"This." He thrust a folder toward Gabe.

"And this is...?" Gabe said as he opened it.

"The lab report on the mask from Sperling's store."

Gabe lifted his eyes questioningly toward Jimmy's stormy brown ones. "I take it there's something significant here?"

"You could say that."

Gabe sighed. "Stop playing games, Jimmy. Spit it out."

"You won't like it. There were areas on the mask where Sheldon had apparently tried to fix gouges and scratches. The fingerprints there are blurred beyond redemption."

"Go on," Gabe said at his hesitation.

"There were eight good prints. Most belonged to Sheldon."

"Big surprise," Gabe said. "It's his mask." But Jimmy was obviously leading up to something. "And the others?"

"A couple aren't identified yet."

"And those that are?"

Jimmy looked him straight in the face. "The others belong to Mayor Evangeline Sevvers."

THERE WERE a dozen good reasons why Aunt Evangeline's prints could be on the mask. *Two* dozen.

When he returned to his office, Gabe set up patrols of Holly's neighborhood. Overlapping patrols instructed to keep an eye out for anything amiss, no matter what the source. The patrols excluded Al Sharp, Dolph Hilo and Bruce Franklin. They were sent elsewhere so as not to arouse their suspicion.

The patrols included teams of officers like the ambitious female cops aiming for detective, longtime veterans combined with new hires. All were to knock on the door now and then. Holly would love that.

He'd also sent the word out about how Holly's tires had been tampered with the day before. No one had better dare allow anything like that to happen while assigned to her neighborhood.

He couldn't be there with Holly all the time. She didn't want him, or any cop, constantly. This would have to do. No monsters in cop uniform would bother Tommy or her.

Besides, he now had another suspect—though things didn't add up right. Yet.

He pondered Jimmy's report. A cup of coffee sat beside him. He took a sip. It was cold. He slammed it on the desk. A few drops sloshed onto the bare wood. Grumbling, he wiped them off with his fingers.

Evangeline was a friend of Sheldon's. She'd even been in the shop yesterday, talking about their play.

The mask had been at the front of the shop for years, Holly had said. Evangeline could have touched it months ago, and her prints would still be on it.

Gabe had told Holly the murderer didn't have to be a man. Neither, from what she had told him, did the caller. Or the joker with the doll. And a woman as self-sufficient as Evangeline would know how to loosen valve stems on tires....

Damn! He wasn't going to just stomp in and accuse her of being the town's public enemy number one.

Hadn't she hired him, even before Thomas Poston's murder, to check into the suspicious—and possibly related—death of Mal Kensington?

Yeah. And now she'd told him it was all a mistake.

He stared at a picture on his wall. The one with Evangeline and him standing together. Smiling.

What if she'd only hired him to make sure she'd covered her trail? Did she figure her surrogate nephew would protect her, out of love for her family, no matter what she'd done?

At the expense of truth? His own integrity?

But she *was* a Sevvers. And he owed them.

And why would she kill Thomas Poston? Holly was her friend. Evangeline wouldn't have turned her into a widow. She wouldn't terrorize Holly and her sweet little son. Would she?

Damn. He had to find out from Evangeline which, of all the reasons for her prints to be on the mask, was the real one.

He slipped his suit jacket on and, using the reflection of the glass in the framed picture of Evangeline and him as a mirror, straightened his tie. "Explain it, Your Honor," he demanded of the smiling red-headed woman in the photograph.

He ran into Al Sharp outside his office door. Literally. The patrol officer grabbed at Gabe to steady himself. "Sorry, Chief," he muttered and continued toward the department break room.

He was in that much of a hurry for a cup of coffee?

Gabe had felt Al's hand thrust something into the pocket of his jacket. Relying on instinct, Gabe waited until he was alone in the elevator to reach into his pocket. He pulled out a piece of paper—one that hadn't been there that morning. It said, "Chief, meet me right away in the garage."

It was unsigned, though Gabe had no doubt who he was to meet. What he wondered was *why?*

Gabe had reached the third floor. Instead of getting off, he pushed the button for the parking level. Evangeline wasn't expecting him. She wouldn't be happy with their conversation when he did visit her. She could wait.

The door closed. When it opened again, he was one floor below the main level of City Hall. The inside garage was restricted to parking for city employees and police units. It was late enough in the morning that the garage was filled with vehicles and empty of people. Gabe exited the elevator and looked around.

The garage was well lighted. Still, he felt a prickling at the base of his spine. He listened. He heard the distant sounds of traffic from the road outside, courtesy of the nearby ramp to the street. Voices from the sidewalk above. The humming of the elevator. Footsteps…

He pivoted. Al Sharp walked up to a patrol unit twenty feet away. He stared, obviously waiting for Gabe to approach.

Was this a trap? Why?

Gabe started toward Al. He heard the car door open. Al slid into the driver's side. Gabe got the message and took a seat on the other side.

He was surprised when Al turned on the engine. He was even more surprised when he drove down to the next underground level and parked in an area where there were no lights.

The bulbs had either burned out...or been removed. The only illumination was scant, from other areas of the garage.

Al turned off the engine as well as the computer and radio in his unit. If they'd been seen together getting into the unit, this exercise in surreptitiousness was useless. But if they hadn't already been noticed, lurking in darkness could be effective cover.

Gabe looked at Al in the shadows. The man's sad eyes were even more grim than usual, his extra chin blossoming as he kept his head lowered. At first, he didn't look at Gabe. His face was pale enough almost to glow in the darkness.

"What's up?" Gabe asked.

The thin cop faced him and took a deep breath. The crevasses of his face made him appear ghastly in the shadows. "We're not having this conversation. And what I'm going to give you didn't come from me. Okay?"

"We'll see. If it makes sense, I'll keep you out of it."

Al's eyes narrowed, in fury? Or was it fear? After a moment, he said, "Fair enough." And then he dropped his bombshell. "I know why Thomas was killed."

Gabe stared. "Tell me," he urged. "Why, and who."

"Who, I don't know. But some in the department are using their positions to shake down local businesses for money. Protection money."

"What?" Whatever Gabe had anticipated, it wasn't this.

"It started under Mal Kensington. It was innocent

enough at first. Some shopkeepers along Pacific Way had been hit by a string of armed robberies. They requested special protection. Mal saw a way for a few off-duty officers to make extra cash. Then, when those bad guys were caught, the storeowners were told they could still pay to make sure they weren't hit again. Some protested, and their stores were trashed. One guy hung out in his store one night with a gun to keep his place safe. He was beaten. Bad. The others stopped protesting.''

''Who did the trashing?'' Gabe demanded through gritted teeth. Sheldon Sperling had been beaten…and Thomas Poston killed.

Al didn't answer. But Gabe knew. Cops had done it.

''Were you part of this?'' he asked Al.

''Let's just say I knew about it.''

''And Thomas Poston?''

''He knew even more.''

In other words, Gabe thought, he was part of it. How would Holly take it, if she found out her husband was dirty?

She had loved him enough to marry him. But Thomas had let her down. They'd had separate bedrooms.

And now Gabe loved her… No. This wasn't the time for something like that to pop into his fool brain.

''Do you have any evidence?'' he asked Al.

Al shrugged.

''Did it involve all the shops along Pacific Way?'' Gabe thought about the list of stores left by both Thomas Poston and Mal Kensington. He thought about Evangeline and her fingerprints on the mask. She was the head honcho of the city, near enough to being in law enforcement herself. Could she have been involved in this scheme? Or did this clear her?

''I don't know which shops were involved,'' Al replied.

"Was Mal Kensington murdered?" Gabe asked suddenly.

Al half rose in his seat, but the steering wheel stopped him. "You know that? How—" He shut up quickly.

"Tell me more," Gabe demanded. "Which cops are in on it? How many?"

"Not many," Al said. "It only takes a few. And cops weren't— Look, I don't know anything else. Get out of my unit now. I have to roll. In fact, I left ten minutes ago."

Gabe pushed Al harder but got nothing more. But cops weren't what? Dangerous? Alone? Trustworthy? Gabe decided to let it go…for now. Still… "Before you leave, I want to know why you told me." It wasn't because of burgeoning trust or friendship between them. Gabe suspected it was fear. But what had scared Al enough to make him talk?

"This is why." Al reached behind the seat. He extracted a paper shopping bag and handed it to Gabe. "It was planted in this unit, under my seat. Someone's worried about me, and that makes me worried about them."

"About who?" Gabe said more insistently. The bag wasn't heavy. It rustled slightly, as if it contained a plastic bag. He squeezed it gently but couldn't figure out its contents.

"I've said all I'm going to. Except to say again that what you're holding was planted to get me. And to tell you that, if you're smart, you'll keep it damn quiet, get a lab outside Naranja Beach to take a look at it. Get out, Chief. Now."

"All right," Gabe said. "But we'll talk again." He exited the unit, and in moments it was gone, leaving Gabe holding the bag…at least literally.

He itched to know what was inside it. But not here.

He used his radio to let the dispatcher know he was

rolling out of the area on personal business. He drove his
car from the garage toward the nearest school parking lot.
It was summer. The kids were on vacation, so his was the
only vehicle there.

He parked. Very carefully, he opened the paper bag. He
extracted the plastic bag inside that was wrapped around
a wad of rolled newspapers. And then—

"Son of a bitch!" he exclaimed as he made very, very
sure not to touch anything and spoil any evidence.

Inside was a long, ornate letter opener coated in the
brown stains of dried blood.

Gabe had no doubt he was holding the weapon that had
been used to murder Thomas Poston.

GABE CALLED Jimmy Hernandez first.

When the trusted detective and longtime friend joined
Gabe, he told Jimmy to take the letter opener up to Los
Angeles to have its crime lab do the testing.

"You don't think Sharp's guilty?" Jimmy asked skeptically as he gingerly took possession of the plastic bag.

"That's what we have to find out," Gabe said. "Make
sure no one at the L.A. lab reports to anyone but you or
me."

"You got it."

And then Gabe went to Holly's. He didn't like the day's
developments. He had to make sure she was all right.

She didn't seem pleased to see him. That day she wore
a form-hugging white T-shirt and cut-off jeans. Despite the
way her expression remained as chilly as a can of soda
from the fridge, he wanted to pull her into his arms, take
up where they had left off that morning before the phone
call....

The sound of small footsteps padded from the kitchen.
In a moment, Tommy stood beside his mom, grinning up

at Gabe with a milk-rimmed smile. "Hi, Gabe," he said shyly.

At least someone seemed glad to see him. And the boy was still talking. Gabe was happy.

But Tommy was just passing through. He headed up the stairs. Good. Gabe had to talk to Holly. "How would you and Tommy like to spend the day at the station with me today?" he asked.

Holly's lovely face paled, contrasting more starkly with the dark loveliness of her sleek dark hair. "Why?" The distance in her voice didn't reflect the proximity in which they'd spent the night. And she still hadn't budged from the doorway, invited him in. Damn it, didn't she understand…? No, she didn't.

"Because I asked."

"Thanks, but I got a call from Evangeline. They need some more costumes sewn for the dress rehearsal tonight. I need to work on them all day."

"Forget the dress rehearsal," Gabe growled. "I want you to come for your own protection."

"No thanks. I've got plenty of protection, remember? The whole police force shows up on my doorstep every half hour. There are female officers I don't even know sitting outside in a patrol car, and a couple of the guys weeded around my yuccas and in my backyard garden. Which was good. I haven't felt much like gardening lately."

Now wasn't the time for his troops to heed his orders and help out around the Poston house, damn it. "Which guys?" Gabe asked through gritted teeth.

The officers she mentioned were longtime veterans of the force. Family men who obviously felt for the widow of a downed fellow officer. They hadn't been particularly close to Thomas. They were probably okay. Still…

"Look," he said. "We'll compromise. I'll work here today. There's a meeting I need to go to later that I haven't scheduled yet, and when I do, Tommy and you will come with me. All right?"

"Do we need to?" For the first time, Holly seemed worried. She stepped back to allow him into the house.

"It's better if you do. There are new developments. I can't explain, but until I know what they mean I'd rather you not be alone."

She sighed. "All right, come in. Have you had lunch?"

He hadn't even thought about it. "Don't go to any trouble."

She smiled at him finally, and he felt as if a Santa Ana wind had come in and blown away the clouds to reveal a sunny day. "No trouble at all, as long as you like peanut butter and jelly."

Tommy returned back downstairs with some of his ubiquitous crayons in his hands. While he helped his mother get lunch ready, Gabe hid away in Thomas's former office. First, he needed to set up a meeting with Aunt Evangeline.

He'd suspected her of the murder because of her prints on the mask. Had Al's allegations of police corruption cleared her? Hell, he hoped so. The fingerprints on the mask were potentially explainable.

But if Evangeline wasn't part of the plot, why hadn't she mentioned it? She owned a store along Pacific Way. Gabe didn't know how long the protection racket had gone on, but Evangeline had only been mayor for a year. If she weren't part of the scheme, surely she'd been approached to pay off the police.

He was damn well going to ask what she knew. But when he phoned her office, he was told she'd already left for the day. "It's the first dress rehearsal for the show tonight,'' her receptionist told Gabe. She gave him Evangeline's cell phone number, which he already had.

She answered on the first ring. "Hi, Gabe." She sounded exuberant. "Our dress rehearsal starts in a couple of hours but I'm already at the theater getting set up."

"I have to see you," Gabe told her. "I need a few minutes."

"Not now," Evangeline said sternly. "Why don't you bring Holly and Tommy to the dress rehearsal tonight? Afterward, we'll all go celebrate with ice cream."

Gabe knew Evangeline well enough to realize that, if he showed up when she'd told him not to, she'd simply go about her business. "All right," he finally said. "That sounds like fun."

When he told Holly over their sandwiches, she seemed happy about the prospect of going to the dress rehearsal with him.

He was glad, too. She wasn't fighting him now. He'd be with her.

Watching over her. Emotions aside, that was his job.

What emotions? Any feelings for her needed to be crammed down deep inside, like a stomach ache. *Rebound, remember?*

Today, she'd definitely reminded him.

"I'll get to see the costumes I sewed in action," she said. "And to find out if I need to make changes. I'll ask Edie to watch Tommy. I can't rely on him to be quiet for the rehearsal."

"We'll bring them both along," Gabe said. "So we can keep an eye on Tommy."

Her hesitation told him she was considering a protest, but finally she simply said, "Good idea."

For the rest of the day, Gabe worked in Thomas's office.

He got a patrol officer going off duty to bring over some files, and he made a lot of phone calls.

Holly worked upstairs in her workroom. He got to see her designs and found them outstanding—cheerful, full of color and creativity and pizzazz. "Great stuff," he told her.

"Really?" She looked at him dubiously. "I didn't think men…" Her voice trailed off.

Cops, she meant. She didn't think cops liked this sort of thing. Maybe Thomas Poston didn't, but Gabe did.

"I'd like to buy one from you," he said.

She smiled. "For your office. I know just the one. It's not finished yet, but I'll give it to you when it is." She pulled out some brilliant blue fabric that reminded Gabe of the sky over Naranja Beach.

"It's great," he said. "But I'll *buy* it." He was rewarded with an even wider smile.

In the afternoon, he went with Holly to pick up her minivan. Its tires had been replaced and the minor repairs completed.

He patrolled the house and grounds often, making certain they remained secure. He was usually accompanied by Tommy, except at naptime. In the office the tyke colored on the floor while Gabe worked.

Late in the day, it was time to go to Evangeline's rehearsal. Holly popped her head into the office to tell him she was ready. She had changed into a white sundress that contrasted becomingly with her dark hair and showed off every luscious curve that he had caressed last night….

Knowing in advance it was a mistake, he didn't resist the urge to draw her into his arms and kiss her. He felt the expected reserve in her response. She obviously regretted their lovemaking. He drew back and looked into her eyes. Though she smiled, she seemed remote. As if he were a new acquaintance, rather than the man she'd loved so passionately the night before.

Damn! Sure, her backing off was for the better. For both of them. But he detested the fist of hurt that rammed his solar plexus.

Tommy was dressed up, too, in a button-down shirt and dressy shorts. "Tommy, we're going to play a game tonight. I'm really, really happy you're talking again, but we're going to pretend you're not, okay? I don't want you to talk to anyone else."

"Even Aunt Edie?" he asked.

Gabe nodded. "Even Aunt Edie."

Pain shadowed Holly's expression, but she reinforced Gabe's words with Tommy. "Okay, honey?"

Tommy grinned silently and nodded. Gabe wondered, though, at the ability of a four-year-old to play this very vital "game."

Gabe drove them all to Edie's apartment. She wore one of the shortest skirts Gabe had ever seen. He appreciated how shapely her legs were, yet the woman who gave him a big, come-hither smile couldn't hold a candle to Holly's slender sexiness.

They headed for the theater. The dress rehearsal had begun.

"Keep Tommy toward the back of the theater," Gabe told Edie. "If he gets restless, walk around a little, but bring him back where there are a lot of people as soon as you can."

"Sure, Gabe."

Holly and he took seats near the front. He didn't see Evangeline at first. And when he did, he had to keep himself in check. He wanted to rise from his seat and shout something at her. Demand some answers.

He heard Holly's small gasp of surprise from beside him at the same time.

For Evangeline's costume was a dark blue police uniform.

Chapter Thirteen

Despite her earlier promise, Evangeline didn't have time to see Gabe right after the rehearsal. The cast was meeting to discuss problem scenes. He wasn't surprised.

They dropped Edie off at her place after she assured them that Tommy had behaved well—relatively—and hadn't done anything unusual. Like talk, though they didn't ask her that.

Then Gabe told Holly, "There's someplace I need to go now."

"Fine," she said in the shadows beside him in the front seat of his Mustang. "But drop Tommy and me off first. It's way past his bedtime."

His vehicle was now permeated with the sweet apricot scent of her. He loved breathing it in….

"Come with me." He wasn't sure what he would do with them while questioning Evangeline, but—

"No thanks," Holly said. "We'll be fine. Especially with all the patrols you have running by our house."

He didn't want to argue. Still, he reasoned with her. She wouldn't give in.

"Fine," he finally said, then gunned the engine. He took Holly and Tommy home. He couldn't be with them twenty-four/seven, he reminded himself. He had a job to do.

He needed to find a killer, for Holly's sake as much as anyone's.

He told her to lock the door and not let anyone in but him. "No one," he underscored. "Not even someone else you trust."

"Who says I trust you?"

He hoped she was teasing. But he knew from the remote look on her face as he said goodbye in her doorway that she was slipping even farther away from him. Rejecting him because he was a police officer whose duty called him away.

So be it. He had no choice.

"I'll be back later," he promised, and once again battled wounded pride when she stepped back as he tried to kiss her. He wanted nothing more than to take her into his arms, make nonstop love with her again as they had the night before.

He wanted nothing more...except solving this case so he could put it behind him. Behind them. Only there was no *them*.

"We'll be fine," she said sweetly. She was so beautiful that evening, in her wispy white sundress. And so far away from him. So far away from what they had shared last night.

Sitting in his car in the driveway, Gabe made a call. "Jimmy? I need your help."

"You don't mean now, do you?" came the groan from the other end of the line. "I had a long day."

"I know."

Jimmy had gone to L.A. with the package Al Sharp had given Gabe. It would be days before the Los Angeles lab had answers, though they'd promised to hurry. In the meantime, Jimmy hadn't ignored his other duties that day.

"But, yeah, I do mean now," Gabe said. He'd been in touch with Jimmy by cell phone, lined him up to keep an eye on Holly's place when Gabe couldn't be there.

"Okay." Jimmy didn't sound enthused, but Gabe knew he could rely on him. "I'll be there in fifteen minutes."

Gabe pulled out of the driveway and into a parking spot on the street. True to his word, Jimmy arrived in fifteen minutes. Gabe exited the space and let his subordinate and friend pull in.

Gabe headed for Evangeline's. He'd told her he would meet her at her house that night as soon as she could get away.

He hadn't told her he was going to let himself in.

But her costume was a police uniform. Her fingerprints were on the mask in Sheldon's store. A "monster" wearing the mask and a uniform had frightened Tommy and was probably the person who murdered Thomas Poston.

Evangeline couldn't be the murderer. And yet…

When he'd moved to Naranja Beach, she had given him a spare key to her trendsetting beachfront condo, and its security code, to use in emergencies. This *was* an emergency, though not the kind she'd meant.

If she had any records of the extortion ring, she'd hardly keep them in the mayor's office. And she hadn't been involved in the day-to-day management of her shop since she took office. As a result, if there was any evidence to find, it was likely to be at her home.

He parked along the driveway to her condo unit. The beach was right across the street, and he inhaled a good, heady whiff of the ocean air. He turned on the lights after he let himself in so Evangeline wouldn't be startled to find him inside.

Angry, perhaps. Startled, no.

He went directly to the extra bedroom upstairs that she used as a study. She kept it as clean as her office in City Hall. He had no trouble finding what he sought. It was right at the bottom of the only pile of mail on her desk.

Convenient.

He heard the door open downstairs but didn't move.

"Gabe!" Evangeline strode into the room a minute later, looking, with her red-tinted hair, like an outraged grizzly bear. "What are you doing?"

As forceful as her voice had been, her face was as pale as sand, her hazel eyes round and wide and fearful.

He lifted the unsigned letters. "Let's talk about these. And about what else I learned today."

GABE LEFT forty-five minutes later. He didn't want to believe Evangeline had been directly involved in the protection scheme or in Thomas Poston's murder—or Mal Kensington's, for that matter. But he couldn't rule anything out.

Evangeline admitted knowing about the protection scheme. She claimed, though, she'd only just learned of it. She'd not been approached before. It was *his* fault now, in a way, or so she'd alleged.

She had been contacted anonymously. She was being threatened but didn't know by whom. And she'd been ordered to control Gabe. Make sure he didn't keep digging into what really happened to Mal Kensington and Thomas Poston. Call him off before he found anything.

Otherwise, not just her mayoral office would be forfeit, but her store, too. Maybe even her life. And Gabe's. Even if she'd take a chance on her life, she didn't want him harmed. Or so she said.

The threats had come in the computer-generated letters

he'd found. She'd been warned not to show them to him, yet she had planned to anyway. Soon. Or so she said. And she also claimed she'd received threatening phone calls.

But the letters could have been manufactured to further throw him off the trail. The phone calls might never have happened.

For all he knew, Evangeline could have been involved from the start. And he'd been brought in as the dupe to protect her.

This woman was like family to him. He owed his life to her real family. She'd brought him to this town, given him this job.

This woman he loved and admired might be guilty of extortion, conspiracy, and worse. Much worse.

Murder.

Arriving back at Holly's, he signaled to Jimmy who started his car and left, but not before tossing a salute to Gabe indicating he'd seen nothing wrong.

Gabe rang the doorbell. Holly didn't answer right away. But when she did, she was shaking and pale, clearly terrified.

"What is it?" he demanded, reaching automatically for his 9mm in the holster beneath his jacket. Was someone inside, menacing her?

Jimmy would have walked the perimeter of the house, but there was only one of him. He could have missed a forced entry.

Holly stared at his gun, then his face, with damp and terrified eyes. Her voice was strong and strangely sardonic, considering her obviously fragile emotional state. "That won't help." She gestured toward the gun. "I got another phone call."

"How long ago?"

"I just hung up."

It could have been Evangeline....

A phone call, though, and not a physical threatening presence. Gabe relaxed, but only a little. He put the safety back on the gun, then stowed it away. "What did the caller say?" Gabe wasn't going to use the masculine gender to refer to the creep who called. Not anymore.

"That time is up. If I don't turn over whatever it is I'm supposed to have gotten from Thomas, the caller's coming after Tommy."

CALMLY, Holly ushered Gabe into the living room. He looked tired. And something in his eyes tonight suggested he'd confronted a particularly maleficent demon that day.

Which case was he working on? What was happening with it?

Not that she expected him to tell her. Or that she really wanted to know, unless it involved Tommy and her.

But she hated, despite everything, to see him hurting like that.

She sat, as she customarily did, on the sofa, and gestured for him to take Thomas's recliner chair. She was dressed in a robe. The call had gotten her out of bed. She felt as cold as if she had been left soaking wet on a wintry ski slope. But she tried hard not to let her shivering show.

Holly ached to have Gabe close to her on the couch. Feel his strong arms around her, warming her, protecting her.

But whatever his business was that had drawn him away so late that night, whatever the case that was troubling him, it had taken precedence over her needs and Tommy's.

Of course it had. It was her own stupidity that she had fallen in love with another cop. But her good sense would, in time, allow her to fall right back out.

In the meantime, she needed him to be a cop, for

Tommy's sake. To focus on *their* case. Her son had been threatened.

He'd been sound asleep, thank heavens, when the phone call had come.

Now, Holly responded as Gabe interrogated her about the call with the patience but firmness of the seasoned police detective he was. He had already listened to the tape, and she hadn't any more information about the caller this time than before. Except that he sounded as if he had reached the end of his restraint. There would be no more threatening phone calls. But the menace hung about her now like a poisonous miasma.

She was to get the mysterious item and leave three pennies on the dashboard of her minivan when she was ready. Then she would be given instructions what to do with it.

A childish signal, she thought. But in a way, its usual benign insignificance made it seem even more ominous.

"But I still don't know what he wants," she finished sadly, then asked Gabe, "Should I leave the pennies on the dashboard anyway? Maybe if I'm contacted again—"

"No," he said sharply. "Not yet. If you pretend you've got something and then don't follow instructions, it could lead to more problems."

Like something happening to Tommy. She knew that. But what could she do? She had to do *something.*

"You're right in a way," Gabe said. "Putting out the pennies would be a great way to trap whoever it is. But first, we need a plan."

She nodded. And smiled, if only a little. He had said "we." At least he wasn't shutting her out totally. "Thank you, Gabe," she said, without explaining exactly why.

"Holly..." He was suddenly beside her on the sofa. As she had wanted before, his arms were around her. He cradled her against him, and his lips were on her forehead, her cheeks, her lips.

She didn't pull away. But neither did she allow herself to respond, although she wanted to very, very much.

She waited till he stopped. Pulled away from her. Looked at her with green, stormy eyes filled with confusion, sorrow and pain.

"There are things I just can't tell you." She heard the bitterness in his voice. Toward her?

She flinched, but she put her head down on the planes of his chest and held on. Tight. "I know, Gabe," she said sadly.

THAT NIGHT, Holly knew she shouldn't have allowed Gabe in her bedroom. But she needed his nearness. And although he held her all night, and she felt the rigidity of his desire for her as they nestled together, he did not try to make love with her.

It was better that way, wasn't it?

He awakened with first light the next morning and made some phone calls. When he returned to her bedroom to say goodbye, he told her he had arranged for different shifts of officers to come over and paint the trim around the windows of her house.

"It doesn't really need it," he explained, "but whoever is threatening you must be watching the house or how would he or she know if you put pennies in the window of your van?"

"Unless he sees it somewhere we park when we're out."

"True. Still, this will show you're not alone. I'm having a detective come over to do some more investigation into Thomas's things. Plus, there'll be patrol cars assigned to cruise your street again to keep an eye on you and the teams of guys painting your house.''

She smiled grimly. ''The fox guarding the henhouse?''

''Something like that.''

She thanked Gabe. She did appreciate all he was doing for her. And maybe it was selfish of her to believe that she should come first with any man.

But weren't there men who put their families first? Men who didn't let their duties override all else?

Right after Gabe left for work, Detective Jimmy Hernandez arrived. He seemed nice enough, but gruff. She didn't know what he'd be looking for but gave him the run of the house.

Soon the first painting shift stopped in: Bruce Franklin and Dolph Hilo, out of uniform and in grungy painting clothes. They let Tommy come out and supervise. Of course her son came back in with paint on nose and cheeks and shorts. She didn't allow him out of her sight all day, especially when he was in the presence of the police officers. Not that she wanted to suspect Bruce and Dolph. But how could she help it?

She knew that Gabe suspected them, too. And that must be why Jimmy Hernandez was conducting further investigation, right in her house, that day.

Later, George Greer and Al Sharp arrived. After Tommy's nap, Holly and he baked cookies and gave some to the police officers, including Jimmy, who was underfoot a lot. He told her he knew of the phone calls and was hunting for what the caller wanted. Not that he seemed any more successful than Gabe and she had been.

Holly decided to take matters into her own hands. She had her own plan. Gabe might not be able to tell her everything. Neither did she need to tell *him* everything.

She called Al Sharp away from his painting. On the path

beside her backyard garden filled with fragrant roses and colorful wildflowers, she told him she had received another phone call. "I'd turn whatever the guy is looking for over to you to deal with, Al, if I knew what it was," she said. Her tearfulness wasn't feigned. "But I don't. I hate hearing from him, but I'm thinking about putting the damn pennies on my minivan dashboard. If he calls again, I'll tell him I wanted to talk to him again. I'll demand that he tell me what he wants and promise to turn it over. Then I'll give whatever it is to you. What do you think?"

Al's gruff face lightened. "I don't know, Holly, but it just might work."

"Do you have any other ideas for figuring out what he's looking for so I don't have to go through that?"

"Let me think about it," Al said.

"All right, but if I don't have any better ideas, I'm liable to stick pennies on my windshield this evening."

"From what you say, the guy seems pretty sure you know what he's after."

"I don't," she said firmly.

"Okay, but… Anyway, lay off the pennies for now."

Holly went back into the house. She hated to think that Al was part of all that had happened, but if she got another phone call again this quickly, and this time the creep told her what he wanted, she would turn the information over to Gabe—including what she'd said to Al. And if she didn't hear from the caller again today, she'd do the same thing with Dolph and Bruce on different days.

In the meantime, she didn't put pennies on the dashboard. Jimmy Hernandez might see them. And if she got the call today without the pennies in place, she'd know Al was involved.

Yes, she was playing with fire. She was going against what Gabe and she talked about, since the plan was *hers*, not *theirs*.

Sure, she could just take Tommy and leave town, but where could they go? Not to her parents, certainly. And Tommy and she had protection here, though she still didn't know just who they needed protection *from.*

No, she didn't want to run. Nor did she want to live in fear. She needed to get this over with—whatever it was.

In the middle of the afternoon, Evangeline called. "Holly, we need some costumes altered and a couple of new things. Can you come to the rehearsal tonight to see about them?"

"Sure." But since she would be preoccupied while she was there, she called Edie at work. "Can you come along and stay close to Tommy for me again?" Holly asked.

"Sure," Edie agreed immediately. "I enjoyed my last sneak preview of the show."

"I doubt you saw much, what with running after Tommy."

"That's okay. He's a show himself," Edie said with a laugh.

Despite her planning—and her trepidation—Holly did not get the anticipated phone call. Maybe Al wasn't involved.

Late in the afternoon, Holly stood in the kitchen, staring at the wall phone as if waiting for it to ring. Tommy sat at the table nibbling at the edges of his third chocolate chip cookie that day, and he had chocolate on his hands and at the corners of his lips. He looked so adorable. So vulnerable…

Damn! She almost wished Al had been the cop gone bad so she could get this over with. Somehow, she had to protect Tommy.

With or without Gabe's help.

HOLLY ROSE from one of the seats in the greenroom, the theater's traditional lounge for cast members when not on stage. It was furnished with shabby but chic hand-me-downs from present and former troupe members, and colorful posters hung on the walls from shows they'd previously performed.

"I'll take these out to my van," she said to two youthful actors, a couple of the street sweepers. One needed a seam taken in. Another was a last-minute replacement and his costume needed to be resized. Holly had also gotten direction earlier from Evangeline: they needed two more firemen's costumes.

It was getting late. She'd kept a close eye on Edie and Tommy but had lost track of them over the last few minutes while fitting costumes. No matter. Edie would take good care of Tommy. But Holly would have to find them, for it was nearly time to take Tommy home and get him ready for bed.

She would also have to call Gabe. She'd spoken to him earlier on her cell phone. He'd planned to meet her here and accompany Tommy and her home but she hadn't seen him yet.

Detective Jimmy Hernandez was in the audience watching the rehearsal. Holly realized Gabe must have assigned the detective to watch over Tommy and her. Gabe was determined to protect her, even from a distance. She appreciated that. But it didn't change the fact that he wasn't there, and he hadn't come on time.

Now, Holly gathered up the two street sweepers' orange costumes and went out the back door into the parking lot behind the theater.

The lot was dimly lit and whispered of eeriness, for the haze of the marine layer had rolled in from the ocean. The sodium lights formed a swirl of percolating illumination above her in the mist.

Because Tommy, Edie and she had arrived late, her van was at the far side of the parking lot. She was alone out here, and her footsteps echoed back at her in the creepily silent fog.

She swallowed, feeling her pulse rise. *You're being ridiculous,* she told herself. There were dozens of people, including Jimmy Hernandez, right inside the theater. And there was no one else out here. She had no reason to feel so nervous....

She could always get Jimmy to accompany her, but she'd only be a minute. And she wanted him to keep watch over Tommy.

She hurried toward her van, using the buttons on her key ring to unlock the door and open the cargo door remotely.

Mist tangoed about her vehicle, whose red color seemed strangely muted in the pulsing light. She walked briskly along the passenger side, ready to heave the costumes she was holding onto the seat—

And tripped over something.

She looked down.

And screamed.

GABE HAD JUST reached the greenroom when he heard a scream. His hand on the gun at his chest, he raced out the door and into the foggy parking lot, followed by Jimmy.

Jimmy had last seen Holly heading for the greenroom. He'd ducked out to look after Tommy, with Edie.

Holly wasn't in the greenroom now. Had *she* screamed?

Gabe stood in the dim, cloudy light. He glared around the small sea of parked cars to orient himself. "You see her?" he demanded of Jimmy, beside him.

And then he saw Holly. Her yellow windbreaker flapped in the breeze as she ran toward them from the van.

"It's Al," she sobbed as she reached Gabe. He grabbed her upper arms. Thrusting her gently against the nearest car, he covered her body with his own for protection. He didn't know what the problem was.

He only knew he had to keep her safe.

"What about Al?" he growled. Had the son of a bitch attacked her? He looked over Holly's head and the automobile behind it, toward the direction from which she'd come.

"Al's lying on the ground. I bent down to see if I could help... Gabe, he's covered in blood. Like—"

She didn't finish, but as he glanced into her horrified face he knew the rest of the sentence: like Thomas.

"I think he's dead," she cried.

"Jimmy, check it out," Gabe said. The detective ran in the direction Holly designated. "Holly, come in here." Holding her tightly against him, shielding her from whatever might be hidden in the haze, he brought her back inside. Only then, as he looked at her in the light, did he see the blood on her hands.

He reached into his pocket, brought out his cell phone, called for backup. "Stay here," he said. "Right here." People had gathered in the greenroom. She would be safe in the crowd.

"I need to find Tommy," she protested.

Almost immediately, Gabe heard the bleep of a nearby siren. Jimmy must already have called for assistance. "Don't move," he told Holly, then went into the parking lot just as a marked cruiser rolled in.

Quickly, he directed the officers toward Jimmy, who was at Holly's van. And then he went back inside.

Of course he didn't find her where he had left her. He

would be too much to ask to imagine she had obeyed this command for her own safety.

Grumbling under his breath, he hustled from the room and into the hallway, where cast and crew were dispersing for the night. He saw Sheldon Sperling. "Have you seen Holly?"

"I think she went down into the auditorium to look for Edie and Tommy. She said their names as she passed. She went fast and she was wringing her hands…. Is something wrong?"

Gabe didn't answer. He had been at the theater before, helping Evangeline move furniture onstage, so he knew how to get into the audience area. When he reached the base of the stage, Holly stood there talking to Edie.

"But I didn't tell her to take Tommy," Holly said to Edie. Her hands were clasped behind her. She was obviously trying to hide the blood on them.

"She said you did." Edie's tone was defensive. Her posture was defensive, too—her shoulders were rounded instead of thrust back to emphasize her bustline, the way Gabe usually saw her.

Gabe gathered the gist of the conversation. *She* had taken Tommy. She *who?* But Gabe had a sinking feeling he knew.

"Where is Tommy?" he demanded.

Holly turned to him. Confusion and fear marred the smoothness of her creamy complexion. "Edie said Evangeline came over to her a few minutes ago. She said I told her she was supposed to take Tommy home. But I didn't, Gabe. Why would Evangeline have said so?"

"I don't know," he said. But he was afraid he did.

Chapter Fourteen

Leaving Jimmy to direct the investigation into Al Sharp's
murder, Gabe drove his Mustang to Holly's house. She sat
beside him in the passenger seat. She had washed her
hands at the theater after providing a brief statement about
finding Al Sharp's body. It was clearly the cop's blood she
had gotten on her. And Al was dead.

Gabe wasn't naive enough to believe Evangeline actually had taken Tommy home, but they had to try. Next
stop would be Evangeline's condo. And after that? There
were plenty of places to look. Too many places for a re-
spectable-looking woman with a little boy to simply disappear.... Assuming she didn't harm the child.

Surely he knew Evangeline well enough to be certain
she wouldn't do that.

But he'd also been certain she'd never taken part in an
extortion scheme. Or murder. He would give her the benefit of the doubt before calling in backup. For now.

"The lights aren't on," Holly said as Gabe pulled into
her driveway. "Tommy knows where I hide an extra set
of keys, under a rock in the garden, so they could have
gotten in."

Gabe swallowed the reprimand that flew automatically
to his lips. She didn't need a lecture on security right now.

"Do you know what her car looks like?" Holly continued.

"A navy-blue luxury sedan." Gabe squinted in the streetlights but didn't see it. The marine layer wasn't as thick here, a little farther inland, but Holly's street still hung beneath a layer of light fog. "Stay here. Let me go check the house before we try someplace else."

But of course Holly didn't listen to this any more than anything else he said. She walked beside him on the yucca-shrouded path to her front door.

"Let's go in," he told her, "in case she left a message on your answering machine."

The machine in Holly's bedroom upstairs glowed with the numeral "1" indicating she had one message. Her expression reflected hope as she pushed the button to retrieve it.

It was probably from a salesperson. But Gabe didn't want to be the one to disappoint her.

To his surprise, Evangeline's voice blared into the room. It sounded strained, upset. "Holly, it's Evangeline. I can't tell you what happened tonight, but I heard something and I couldn't... Look, I can't talk now. Gabe will know what this is about. Don't let anyone else but him know, and erase this message. I'm going to Sheldon's shop with Tommy. We'll meet you there, unless— If we're not there, I'll call you later."

To Gabe, Evangeline sounded distraught, as she would if she'd heard Tommy was in danger and she needed to get him to safety.

But Evangeline was an actress. She'd even been at the theater practicing her performance that night. And why wouldn't she just have contacted him if she'd heard something?

"We've got to go to Sheldon's," Holly said. "Let's

hurry. On the way, you can tell me what she was talking about.''

''Holly, you're not going there. I'll take you to the station, and…'' And what? Other than Jimmy, he wasn't certain which of his own officers could be trusted. At least he had an idea which could *not* be trusted.

''Like hell you will,'' Holly protested.

Gabe looked at her. She hardly ever swore. Maybe that was because, when they were together, Tommy was generally there, too. In any event, he could tell she meant it.

Which was just as well, because damned if he knew how else to assure her safety except to keep her by his side.

''IT'S MY FAULT,'' Holly whispered, glad Gabe was steering his car into a turn. That way, he couldn't look at her—not then.

He did an instant later though, just a glance before he resumed watching the road. ''What do you mean?'' His tone was offhand, but she could tell, even in the dim light from the red lights on the instrument panel, that he was white-knuckled from gripping the steering wheel more tightly.

He hadn't told her much, only that someone had been threatening Evangeline, possibly the same person who'd threatened Tommy and her. Evangeline had informed him that whoever it was had sworn something bad was going to happen soon.

And Holly had precipitated it.

''I… Gabe, I didn't listen to you. Not exactly.'' She told him of her conversation with Al. ''If he was the cop who knew what was going on, I figured he could help. I thought—''

''You thought what?'' All pretense of civility had left

Gabe's tone. "Didn't I tell you not— Never mind. Why, exactly, did you do that?"

"I was trying through process of elimination to figure out which of the cops who were Thomas's friends had gone bad. I figured if I heard from the caller after talking to Al, that Al was the one, though I hated to think so. Maybe he did know something. And that's why he's dead."

"Yeah, he knew something," Gabe snapped. "That was one of the things I couldn't tell you, to protect him and the case."

Holly felt the blood drain from her face. "The case? And Al? You didn't do much of a job protecting him. And if you knew for sure he was involved, how could you let him around my house?"

"Because you weren't alone there. I sent Jimmy."

"But the creep who called threatened Tommy, and he—"

"What if it's a *her?*" Gabe interrupted.

"Who? The creep?" Holly asked in confusion. They had reached the parking lot behind Pacific Way. She reached for the door handle, but Gabe leaned over her, stopping her.

He held onto her for a moment without moving. She felt the strength of his upper body pressing against her, smelled his male scent and his breath close to her face. For a moment, she wondered inanely if he planned to kiss her. But then his head dropped to his chest and he shook it slowly. Then he sat back, pulling away from her.

"Holly, I didn't want to tell you any more than I had to, to protect not only you but... Never mind. You need to know. I can't go into detail, but it's possible that Evangeline either killed Thomas and now Al, or knows who did."

"What!" Holly rose in her seat, grabbing again frantically for the door handle.

Gabe gripped her other arm, stopping her. "Wait. You need to know the rest, too. Or some of it. There was something going on. I still don't know the details, but it involves the police. Some of my officers were apparently involved in an extortion scheme, and I'm not certain which ones, except that Al was the one who told me about it."

"Oh, my lord," Holly whispered, feeling as if someone had reached into her and yanked out her stomach. "Thomas. Was he involved in the scheme? Is that why he was killed?"

He hesitated. "I don't know, but I think so."

She turned toward him in the dim light. His strong features were shrouded in shadow, but she suspected she saw the anguish of the damned there. Anguish because a fellow cop, maybe many fellow cops, had gone bad. And maybe the mayor, his aunt, too.

Holly felt anguish, too. No matter what ill will had developed between Thomas and her, she'd considered him a good father, a good role model for Tommy, even though she didn't want her son to follow in his father's footsteps. But cops were supposed to be strong and brave and self-confident. And they were supposed to have integrity.

She'd been grieving over Thomas, damn it! And now, what was she supposed to do?

Find her son, of course. Keep him safe, no matter where the danger came from.

"We can't do anything about that now," she said to Gabe, not looking at him. "But we need to find Tommy. Al knew I hadn't found whatever they were looking for, but maybe Evangeline is holding Tommy hostage anyway, to encourage me to find it. I'm going to Sheldon's shop right now. Are you?''

"Yeah," he growled. "Let's go."

BECAUSE IT WAS a weeknight, and because it was nearing midnight, Pacific Way was almost deserted. Holly held Gabe's hand as they slipped down a street that led to the storefront pedestrian mall. His left hand.

He held his gun in his right hand. He didn't advertise that fact, but she knew it by the way his arm hung stiff at his side, one controlled weapon gripping another.

He no longer wore his suit jacket, just his short-sleeved blue shirt over dress trousers. He looked all business.

Pacific Way was well-lighted, the better to attract crowds of tourists at night. But there were only a few stragglers tonight, mostly right outside the restaurants.

Sheldon's shop sat on a block with few eateries, none open this late.

Holly tried hard to control the speed and volume of her sporadic breathing. The more she called attention to herself and her fear, the more likely Gabe was to try to plant her someplace safely out of the way.

Someplace she wouldn't be able to help Tommy.

They reached the shop next to Sheldon's. Gabe tightened his grip on her hand and held her back. "Wait here." His voice was no more than a slight deviation of the murmur of the sea breeze.

She obeyed, sort of. She hung back, watching as he stiffened his back against the nearest window and slunk sideways, steadying the elbow of the arm that held his raised gun with his opposite hand.

As he reached the window of Sheldon's darkened shop, he sprang into action, blazing toward the door, which he used his hand to thrust open with as much force as if he'd kicked it. Had it been unlocked, or had he used adrenaline as a key? Holly had no idea.

She held her breath. No shots. No sounds at all.

Using the same technique of snaking along the neighboring storefront, then hurrying into Sheldon's, she followed Gabe.

In the few seconds of delay, Gabe had turned on the lights. He knelt on the floor beside a prone body.

"Evangeline!" Holly cried.

"She's alive but hurt," Gabe said.

"Where's Tommy?" Frantic, Holly looked around. She immediately spied another pair of legs behind the counter—adult legs, a man's. "It's Sheldon," she said. "He's hurt, too."

Gabe rose and joined her, kneeling beside the thin man who lay curled on his side.

Gabe had taken out his cell phone. At that moment, Holly didn't see his gun. But before he was able to call for help, Sheldon sprang to his feet with surprising agility.

Holly gasped. "It's us, Sheldon. Gabe and me."

"I know, Holly, my dear." There was a hint of smug laughter in Sheldon's voice that Holly had never heard before, as if he had told a joke that only he understood.

And he was pointing a very lethal-looking gun right toward her heart.

"WHAT THE HELL are you doing, Sheldon?" Gabe asked. But things were suddenly coming clear to him.

Damn, he'd been played for a fool!

"I think it's obvious, don't you?" Sheldon asked. Gabe wanted to wipe that Cheshire cat grin right off his face, preferably with the butt of his gun.

The gun that he held at his side, rather than pointed where it would do some good. Could he raise it and fire it quickly enough?

Or would Sheldon shoot Holly first?

"Put your gun very gently on the floor, Gabe," Sheldon said, almost as if he had followed Gabe's train of thought. But it must have been obvious. He stood there like some kind of dim-witted fool with his thumb in his ear: cell phone in one hand, 9mm in the other, unable to use either to help Holly or himself.

He hesitated for an instant, waiting for a plan to come to him.

None did.

"Put it down!" Sheldon repeated. This time, Gabe obeyed.

As he crouched on the floor for the moment it took to lay his gun there, he considered ramming Sheldon, butting him off balance. But Sheldon had grabbed hold of Holly. He had his left arm around her throat. His right undoubtedly still held the gun. Pointed right into her spine. The slim khaki slacks she wore, her flimsy beige knit shirt, would provide no protection at all.

Gabe rose slowly, weapon on the floor, his hands in the air.

"Where's Tommy?" Holly asked. She sounded cool. As if she faced this kind of danger every day. Her eyes, though, told the true story. They were huge and dark and as fearful as if she knew the next instant was her last.

As it might be. Damn! He had never felt more helpless in his life.

"Tommy is safe," Sheldon replied to her question. "He'll be released as soon as you turn over to me what Thomas left."

"But I still don't know what it is," Holly protested. "I told Al that."

"Yes, Al said so. But he also said he figured you suspected him so you were lying to protect Tommy and you."

"Then why did you kill him?" Holly cried.

"Because he was getting cold feet. He wanted to keep the kid and you out of it, too. But a lot was riding on keeping you involved."

"Were you the one who kept calling me?" Holly demanded.

Sheldon only smiled.

Gabe ached to rush him. But Sheldon was armed, and for the moment he was not.

"Did you kill Thomas, too?" Gabe asked as conversationally as if he asked the price of one of the art pieces in Sheldon's shop. The primitive masks around the room stared at Gabe with blank eyes. Taunting him. *You stupid fool. We saw it all. Of course he murdered Thomas Poston.*

"He threatened to expose me," Sheldon said, obliquely answering the question.

"And you staged your own injuries," Holly said. She sounded breathless, and no wonder. Sheldon was maneuvering her across the room toward one of his tallest display cases, still hanging onto her throat. Smart move, for with the lights on in here and the darkness outside, someone could peek in and see what was happening.

Gabe prayed someone already had. But he couldn't count on it.

"Yes, I did," Sheldon replied. "It wasn't hard to give myself some bumps and bruises and overstate how much they hurt. I am an actor, you know, in my spare time." He laughed aloud.

Gabe wanted to strangle him for the way he was hurting Holly.

They stood behind the tall cabinet now. Gabe shifted so he could see them better.

If he tried to run out of the store, would Sheldon shoot him in the back? Probably. Worse, he would undoubtedly shoot Holly, too.

How could he chance it?

He leaned against the nearest cabinet, attempting to feign nonchalance. He had to do something. But what?

"You put on the mask to scare Tommy, didn't you?" Holly asked. "But why did he seem so afraid of policemen?"

"Because I put on part of Evangeline's costume for the play, of course. She left it here while the theater was being used by the high school. It came in handy, though it was a bit of a tight fit." His leer exposed large, gleaming teeth that made Gabe think of a great white shark. "All the better to make you think that Evangeline was the killer. Oh, and by the way, I know Tommy's talking now. He spoke to me before, told me all about the monster in the police uniform."

"Where is he?" For the first time, Holly began to struggle. Gabe watched in impotent rage as Sheldon subdued her by tightening his arm about her neck. She gagged and grew still.

"Don't worry about Tommy," Sheldon said. "Right now, it's time to tell where I can find the paperwork Thomas left."

"Why should I?" Her voice, though raspy, sounded indifferent. She was doing a great job of pretending lack of fear. What a damn fine, brave woman!

He would get her out of this.

He looked around for a weapon he could lay his hands on without being obvious.

"Then you do have it? Of course you do. And you must turn it over because I told you to." Sheldon was beginning to sound angry. That wasn't good. A bad guy with a short temper did foolish things. Like hurt people.

"Not good enough," Holly said. "You have to let Gabe, Tommy and me go."

"Now, Holly, you know I can't do that."

"He's got to kill you and me," Gabe told her. "We know enough to cook his scrawny goose but good. And he's going to blame it on Evangeline, aren't you, Sheldon? Isn't that why you got her involved lately? So you'd have someone to pin it on?"

Sheldon didn't deny it.

Gabe saw Holly's chest begin to heave, as if she had finally understood what was happening. "I see," she said. Her tone had risen, but she still seemed to maintain her composure. "You will let Tommy go, at least." She made it a statement, not a question.

"That depends on how quickly you get it to me." Sheldon's patience was waning fast.

"I'm not sure I'll get it to you at all," Holly said. "In fact, I've already put it someplace safe where it'll be found with instructions to open it in the event something happens to me."

Good bluff, Gabe thought. Until Sheldon started asking questions.

Which he did immediately.

"How do I know that you even know what I'm talking about?"

"I told Al I had it earlier today," she replied. "But I told him to say otherwise to you. I wanted to continue to play helpless widow. Only he was playing both of us against the other. Maybe it's better that you did kill him."

Gabe wanted to smile at Holly's ingenuity. Unless she was actually telling the truth…? No. He knew Holly. She'd have told him everything earlier when she explained her discussion with Al.

But Gabe needed to do something. Now. While Sheldon was confused. He focused out of the corner of his eye on one of Holly's sewn creations. It hung on the wall near where Gabe stood. It was a depiction of a scene of where sea met sand, with brilliant orange crawling crabs and scarlet and green fish in the bright blue waves. Pretty piece.

More important, it was hung on the wall by a long, thick dowel. A dowel that could be used as a battering ram, given the right angle and opportunity.

"Yeah, maybe it's better that Al's dead. And maybe I should kill you right now, too." Sheldon tugged on her throat again, and she made a small choking sound.

Gabe forced himself to breathe in and out. To stay perfectly still, when what he wanted to do was commit an act very unprofessional for a cop: murder. After a bout of very painful torture.

"That still doesn't mean you know what I'm looking for," Sheldon continued.

"It's evidence of your extortion scheme," Holly said, every word an effort. But Sheldon must have loosened his grip, for she shook her head and rubbed at her throat near his arm. "Stuff Thomas put together about it before you killed him. It'll implicate you. Is that why you killed him? Did he want out?"

Had she actually found something? Once again Gabe's certainty wavered, but only for a second. No, she had to be relying on educated guesses, based on what Gabe had told her before. Smart, brave woman!

Her words must have hit the mark. "Tell me where it is, you bitch!" Sheldon yelled.

"You're hurting me," Holly said. Her eyes met Gabe's—and then she appeared to faint.

Sheldon lost his balance while trying to hold up the inert weight that Holly had become. He flailed out with his free arm. The hand holding the gun rose into the air. It was no longer pointed at Holly.

Gabe lunged toward the wall, praying that the wires

used to hold the dowel were as flimsy as they looked. Surely, the man wouldn't want things he'd need to take down to show paying customers to stick like permanent fixtures.

He grabbed the hanging off the wall with infinite power born of terror for Holly and fury that this man had created so much chaos in his adopted town. He rammed the end of the dowel hard into Sheldon's gut.

The gun fired.

Chapter Fifteen

"Gabe!" Holly screamed as she saw him fall to the floor. Had he been hit?

She rose quickly and headed toward the two men. Only then did she realize that Gabe had Sheldon in a headlock on the ground. Plus, his legs had wrapped around the older man's, immobilizing him despite his thrashing.

With his teeth gritted savagely, his eyes as wild as the ocean's fury, his brow a dipping geometric line of concentration, his dark hair a mass of unkempt tangles, Gabe looked as primitive as any of the masks around Sheldon's store. This man who had been so kind and gentle to her and to her son was brutal and powerful when he meant business. Police business.

Holly had never been happier to have a cop around when she needed one.

His eyes focused on hers. "Call 9-1-1," he ordered. This was one command she had no trouble following.

DOLPH HILO and Bruce Franklin were the first cops to respond to Holly's call for help.

She watched Dolph, on instructions from Gabe, clamp cuffs on Sheldon's wrists, securing them behind his back. "What the hell happened here, Chief?" he asked.

Sheldon looked wilted. Subdued. Nothing like the monster who'd murdered at least two people.

Tommy's monster. Oh, lord, where was her son? Holly's stomach churned like a bile-filled waterspout as she worried.

"We've caught the head of a damn writhing serpent," Gabe growled. "But I've a feeling that the middle and tail are going to do some real damage to our department. And you two? Do you know what I'm talking about?"

"No, Chief," said Bruce—but Holly thought she saw a lie in his eyes.

"Look, Chief," said Dolph. "Bruce and I...well, we had some suspicions. But that was—"

"I'm calling Jimmy Hernandez and a crime scene team," Gabe interrupted. "We'll sort this all out later."

Sirens blessedly sounded, not far away. Holly heaved a sigh of relief. Even if Bruce and Dolph were involved in the scheme up to the collars of their uniforms, they'd act like model cops now, with fellow officers on the way. Or so Holly prayed.

"Mr. Sperling's under arrest for murder, among other things," Gabe said. "Be sure to read him his rights, in case he feels like talking to us. And I'll be listening whether he names any names." He glared at the two uniformed officers, who didn't meet his eyes.

Gabe had his man in custody. That was a good thing, Holly thought. But he had no time for her now. Or Tommy.

After assuring herself that the shot had gone wild, into the ceiling, Holly bent over Evangeline.

Her Honor was wide awake.

"I played possum for a lot of that little performance," she admitted. "I was trying to figure out a way to use the element of surprise to distract Sheldon, but you beat me to it.''

"Do you know where Tommy is?" Holly asked.

"I think so."

With Holly's help, she stood, obviously stiff. For once, she was dressed in slacks rather than a suit, and it was wrinkled and in less than perfect shape. But no wonder, considering what Her Honor had been through.

"Sorry about the confusion tonight," Evangeline said, "but Sheldon told me he'd just received an anonymous but immediate threat against Tommy. Someone was going to kidnap him from the theater if he wasn't taken out of there right away. Sheldon told me to get Tommy away from Edie and bring him here secretly, for his own safety. In my surprise and stupidity, I listened to him instead of checking with you. Anyway, I think Tommy's in here."

They headed for the back room, where Evangeline turned on the lights. "Tommy, are you here?" she called as she crossed the room.

Holly thought she heard a thumping.

Reaching the sink, Evangeline stooped and pulled open the cabinet beneath it. On the floor, behind the cabinet doors, lay Tommy, tied up and gagged. His eyes were huge and frightened.

Together, Holly and Evangeline pulled him out. Holly extracted the nasty-looking scarf from his mouth. He looked from Evangeline to her, then back again. His small body was shaking, and his mouth opened as if he wanted to speak.

"It's okay to talk in front of Mayor Sevvers now, if you'd like," Holly said softly as she worked at the horrid knots in the rope holding her son's hands together in front of him. Damn Sheldon Sperling! Tommy's wrists were raw. So, when she got to them, were his ankles beneath his socks.

"Mommy?" Tommy's voice was small and scared. Holly hugged him closely to her. She lifted him, in time to see Gabe walk into the back room and grin as he saw them.

"What, sweetheart?" Holly said.

"Mr. Sperling showed me the mask. He put it on. Mommy, is Mr. Sperling the monster?"

"Yes, honey," Holly said as tears of joy ran down her face. Her son was all right. She was all right. And Gabe was all right, too. "Mr. Sperling was definitely the monster."

MUCH LATER, after Sheldon had been taken into custody and the crime scene team was finished, Holly asked Gabe, "Is it all right if we leave now?"

They'd remained in the back room, sitting around the table with Evangeline, who looked pretty pleased with herself.

Of course she would be, Holly thought. She'd been directly involved with catching a criminal—a murderer and extortionist. She could make a huge stack of political hay with what had happened this evening. Maybe she could even run for Congress or governor on an anti-crime platform.

Edie had joined them. She'd said she had called around frantically after leaving the theater, everywhere she could think of, trying to learn if Tommy was all right. Eventually, she'd tried Sheldon's. Evangeline had answered the phone, told her what had happened. She had gotten here as soon as she could and kept them company while the crime scene team worked and they were interrogated individually. Uncharacteristically, she was clad in loose, dark clothes, but said she'd run out of her house in a hurry, throwing on anything she could find.

"I simply can't believe it of Sheldon," she'd said when she'd arrived. "But does anyone know yet what he was looking for?" No one did, not really.

Now, Gabe responded to Holly's question. "You can leave in a minute, but first—" He lifted Tommy from Holly's arms, then sat down again with the boy on his lap, hugging him. "Tommy, are you feeling well enough to tell us exactly what you saw here at Mr. Sperling's shop the morning you saw the monster?"

He nodded with all the solemnity of a four-year-old. He slid out of Gabe's arms. "I was coloring here," he said, pointing at the table. "Oh!" A look of surprise and excitement came over his face. "My stuff!"

"What—?" But Holly didn't finish her question.

Tommy ran over to the huge floor-to-ceiling cabinet along one wall of the room and yanked open one of its lower doors. He pulled something out: a bright red plastic zippered pouch. A familiar portfolio case. It belonged to Tommy.

"Did you leave that here that morning?" Holly asked.

"Yes, Mommy." Carefully, with small, thin fingers, Tommy pulled open the zipper. "See?" He pulled out a coloring book featuring one of his favorite cartoon characters and a box of crayons, and some papers. Typed papers.

Holly looked at Gabe, then back again. "May I have those pieces of paper, honey?" she asked.

"Sure." Tommy's face fell. He looked as if he was going to cry as he brought her the computer-generated pages. "They're Daddy's," he said.

"I'll take those."

Edie had risen. Now, she stood just inside the door. She

was small, far from filling the doorframe. But she looked as threatening as Sheldon had earlier. For she had pulled a gun from the tote bag she had brought. A large and lethal-looking gun. She aimed it toward them.

"What the hell?" Gabe demanded, rising to his feet.

"Sit down, Chief," Edie demanded, pointing the gun at his head. His large hands in the air, Gabe complied with a furious scowl. "Now, very gently, Holly, I want you to give me those papers."

"I don't understand," Holly said, making no move to comply.

"You don't need to," Edie said.

"You were in on the extortion scheme with Sheldon, weren't you?" Gabe asked. He had put his hands down on the table. He sounded so matter-of-fact that Holly could have screamed—if it wouldn't get one of them shot.

She couldn't bear it if Tommy were hurt.

Or Evangeline.

And certainly not Gabe.

"It doesn't matter now," Edie said.

"But I'd like to know," Gabe persisted. "I'd imagine your plan is to kill us all anyway, so at least grant me that."

Holly's dear friend suddenly looked more like a fiend from the fires of deepest hell than a pixie. She was sneering.

"All right. Why not? I was having an affair with Mal Kensington when he and I came up with a way to make money we could use to escape this crummy little town. For it to work, we needed help from some patrol cops. After all, who ever heard of a protection scheme without someone to do the protection? I enlisted Sheldon by doing a little seduction number on him, too, so he'd get his fellow shop owners to cooperate."

"Interesting triangle," Gabe said. "Mal and Sheldon and you. I'll bet that didn't last long."

"You'd win that bet. Problem was, cops are a bunch of prima donnas. First, Mal got nervous and out of control. Good thing Sheldon has a heart problem. We just had to give Mal a good dose of Sheldon's digitalis, and he had a little 'heart attack' of his own. Then we paid off his family not to ask questions. They knew about Mal's affair and his wife just wanted out anyway. She had no problem with a quick cremation and a new life."

"And Thomas?" Holly asked, feeling as if the world had tipped upside down on its axis. Edie, her friend, was a thief and a murderer. "Did you have an affair with him, too?" She felt Gabe's eyes on her. She'd had to ask. Maybe she hadn't felt that close to Thomas, but could she bear it if he'd been having an affair with her best friend?

"Not that one," Edie scoffed, leaning on the doorframe. "He was just in it for the money. Only after dear Mayor Sevvers got suspicious and brought her nephew here to investigate Mal's death, Thomas got a little nervous. He decided to sell out the rest of us to save his own skinny little butt." She nodded toward the papers Holly was holding. "He got all that together, then came to Sheldon that morning, who figured Thomas was trying to do his own little extortion game on all the rest of us. The man said he'd used a code, but he had us and our roles listed for whoever could crack it. I assumed you hadn't figured it out yet or there would be a lot more heat on Sheldon and me, but I thought Thomas left the papers with you for his own protection. I never imagined they were in Sheldon's possession this whole time, and I'm sure he didn't, either. And I don't think Sheldon meant to stab Thomas, but the letter opener was handy, Sheldon got mad, and there it was."

"What about the other cops involved?" Gabe demanded.

Edie shrugged. "We didn't need help before, though Thomas cozied up to Dolph Hilo and Bruce Franklin since they seemed to suspect what was going on. But with Thomas, and now Al, gone, we'd decided to start discussions with them about cutting them in. It would have ensured their silence, if they'd gone along. Or even if they didn't, we'd have made sure they didn't tell anyone...." Her grin was evil, anything but the sexy or pixielike expressions Holly was used to.

Wasn't anyone who she'd thought they were?

Edie looked at Holly again. "Now, hand the papers to me."

Holly shrugged, hoping she appeared a lot braver than she felt. "Come and get them. You're going to kill us all anyway." She looked Edie in the eye. "Sheldon is in custody. You're already sunk."

"Not if there's no evidence to link me to what happened. It'll only be his word against mine."

"Can you shoot us all?" Holly asked. "I doubt it. I mean, do you really think you can point a gun at a child and see him die?" Please, Lord, let her *not* be able to, Holly prayed.

For a moment, Edie looked confused. That was enough for Gabe to roll onto the floor and grab her legs, tackling her. At the same time, he grabbed her arm. The gun went off, but he already had it pointing toward the floor.

"Damn you!" Edie growled, struggling in Gabe's grip.

"No," he said cheerfully as he pulled her arms behind her back, "I think you're the one who's damned here." He looked up at Holly and winked. "We're beginning to make a good team," he told her.

It's all over, Holly thought the next afternoon while Tommy napped. She was in her workroom, finishing the alterations to the costumes for the play. Her mind swirled like honey in a blender as the hum of her sewing machine filled the air.

According to Evangeline, the show must go on—this one, without one of its major cast members: Sheldon Sperling.

Gabe had called earlier. Sheldon and Edie were spending a lot of energy accusing one another of being the mastermind and murderer-in-chief.

Edie had been the one to break into Holly's house searching for Thomas's missing papers. She'd also tampered with Holly's tires when Holly had been parked in an isolated area near Tommy's doctor. According to her, that had been a spontaneous act to warn Holly to cooperate.

The bloody doll had been Sheldon's brainstorm. So had implicating Edie by putting her return address on its package, to make sure no one suspected her.

He had made the threatening calls to Holly. He had shooed little Tommy into the back room of his store where he'd seen the monster mask. As with the doll, he'd wanted to keep Tommy scared and off balance so he wouldn't talk. That way, Sheldon wouldn't have to kill the child.

He had killed Al, though, the night before when his cold feet led him to threaten to expose them all. And Sheldon, of course, had been the one to murder Thomas.

They'd both been equally involved with disposing of Mal Kensington.

The missing papers that had been in Sheldon's shop the entire time had been put together by Thomas before he died, because he'd wanted out. They contained a list of all the shops along Pacific Way, their owners, who contacted them for payoffs, and how many complied. The perpetrators' names were in code, but Jimmy Hernandez had quickly cracked it.

Evangeline Sevvers was not among the perpetrators listed. She was exonerated. She had only tried to get Gabe off the Kensington investigation because her life, and his, had been anonymously threatened.

Edie was implicated, though. Like Sheldon's, her name appeared frequently on the list, in code, as having contacted shop owners for money.

The scheme hadn't stopped with the death of Mal Kensington and Thomas. Al Sharp had been peripherally part of it, and he'd been asked to become more involved. He had cooperated, but only to a point. And he had been murdered.

The roles of Dolph Hilo and Bruce Franklin were not clear yet, but Gabe believed they'd known what was going on. They might even have been contacted to take part—especially once the letter opener that killed Thomas was planted on Al, who'd gotten very nervous. Al's role in the ongoing scheme had been limited from then on. He'd known it. That was why he had gone to Gabe. So far, he was the only cop besides Thomas whom the evidence implicated directly.

The shop owners hadn't been told that no police were involved any longer. The scheme had taken on a life of its own. Until they had stopped it—Holly and Evangeline and Tommy…and Gabe.

The media had been informed. Evangeline was effusive in her praise of her police chief nephew and astonishingly grateful to Holly and her brave little boy. A bigger political career was definitely in her future, Holly thought wryly. But that didn't keep her from continuing to be the consummate businesswoman. She had told Holly she was considering buying Artisans from Sheldon if he would or could sell. If not, she would start her own crafts boutique in the area. Holly would still have someplace to sell her work, thank heavens.

And Evangeline had even suggested that Holly might want to manage it, too, for a small salary and a share of the business.

She hadn't given Evangeline an answer yet, but the idea excited Holly. Tommy was nearly ready for preschool, and she could fix up an area where she could supervise him when he was around. And when the shop wasn't busy, she could work on her creations, too.

The phone rang. "Hello?" Holly said. At least she would never again have to fear the threatening calls.

"Holly, it's Gabe. Look, I wanted to stop by tonight. I know you're not in danger any longer, but I wanted to talk to you. The thing is, the details on this case have me tied up, and there have been a couple of armed robberies in a residential neighborhood that I need to look into. I may not make it by there tonight, but we need to talk as soon as I can break away."

Yes, Holly thought. *We need to say goodbye to one another.*

Gabe was doing just as he should. His duty.

He had put his job before anything else. Before Tommy and her. She understood, for that was who he was. He had taken on the job of chief of police, and he was a really good one.

The best cop she had ever met.

But she had to let him go. For his sake as well as her own.

With Thomas's murder solved, the threats over, they had no need to stay involved with each other anymore.

She cared for him. She loved him. But it was over. And

so she said the thing she knew would keep him from feeling he had to come by and explain.

"It's all right, Gabe," she said. "Whenever you get here will be fine. But I want you to know that, now that it's all over, I want to put everything that happened behind me. I'm still mourning Thomas and who I thought he was. In a way, I always will. But some of my closest friends turned out to want to harm Tommy and me. Everything is topsy-turvy. Right now, I don't want to have anything to do with any of them, or with you. I need to begin a new life, starting now."

The silence at the other end of the line was so loud in what it shouted to her that it nearly broke her eardrum. Had Gabe hung up?

And then she heard him say, "Right. I understand. Have a good life, Holly. Bye."

When she heard the click signaling he had hung up, she began to cry.

"WHERE'S GABE?" grumbled Tommy after they finished their dinner of soup and sandwiches. "I want to play ball."

Holly smiled sadly at her adorable, brave little son, who sat at the kitchen table across from her. She had taken him to the doctor that morning to have his wrists and ankles checked.

She'd taken him to the psychologist, too, for a special appointment. He had been pronounced on the road to healing after his terrible ordeals. He was talking about them now, and that was a major step.

But there was one hurdle they still had to leap over—and it was one that caused Holly's heart to hurt as if she'd been flung from the heights of happiness into the bottomless pit of loneliness.

Maybe she had been. But she had brought it on herself, for falling in love with another cop.

"Gabe is very busy catching bad guys," she explained to her son. "He's still working on everything that happened last night, you know."

Tears flowed into his big, sad eyes. "Is Aunt Edie a bad guy?"

Holly sucked in her breath. But she had to tell him the truth. "Yes, honey, I'm afraid she is."

"And Mr. Sperling, too. He's a monster." Tommy smiled at that, then jumped down from his seat at the table. His resiliency seemed boundless.

Thank heavens, Holly thought.

"But I want to play ball with Gabe." Tommy stopped near the kitchen door, his small arms crossed, his expression adamant. "Now."

"Tommy, I told you—"

The doorbell rang.

"Gabe!" Tommy shouted and ran toward the entry.

"Tommy, wait. Don't open the door. It could be a stranger."

But when Holly got there and looked out the peephole, Gabe stood there. He was dressed in jeans and an orange Naranja Beach T-shirt that looked liked Tommy's.

Where was his suit? His gun?

Holly's mind did flip-flops as she opened the door. Why was he here? Did he have more questions to ask them about the case?

She opened the door. "Hi," she said. She didn't move. Not a smidgen. For if she did, she was liable to fling herself into his arms, and that would undo everything she had said before.

"May I come in?" he asked. He looked relaxed. His wide, masculine smile made the lower parts of her body ignite in recognition, but she reined in her inappropriate thoughts of desire.

"Yeah," Tommy said. "Come in. I was waiting for you to come and play ball with me, but Mommy said you were too busy."

"That's what I wanted to talk to you about, sport." Without waiting for Holly's okay, he swooped down and lifted Tommy into his arms, then filled her small entryway with his broad shoulders and commanding presence.

How was she going to get through this? She'd already said her goodbyes. She didn't want to have to do it again. In person.

"Let's go into the living room, okay?"

Why ask me? Holly thought ungraciously. *I only own this house.* But she followed him down the hall.

She expected him to sit on the reclining chair, remote from anyplace she could sit. Instead, he sat in the middle of the sofa. He kept Tommy on his lap.

"Please, Holly, sit here." He patted the soft beige pillows at his side.

She glanced longingly at the upholstered chair at the other end of the coffee table, but she obeyed him. "Gabe," she began, "I don't want you to think—"

"What I think, sport," he said, addressing Tommy, "was that I made a mistake. I told your mommy that I was too busy to get here early tonight. I do have lots of work to do, you know."

Tommy nodded as if he recognized every bit of responsibility that rested on Gabe's shoulders.

"The thing is, there's nothing more important than people we love. Do you know that?"

Again Tommy nodded. "I love Mommy, and I love Daddy, but he's dead. And I love you, Gabe."

Holly's heart wrenched, as if Tommy had hugged it.

Tears filled her eyes. She looked at her son. "Tommy, honey, Gabe isn't—"

"Gabe *is*," the man of that name contradicted, as if he knew just what she was going to say. "Gabe *is* a person who loves a little boy named Tommy. And Gabe does understand that Tommy's mother needs some space in her life and time to heal. She's been through a lot. But Gabe is also a patient man. Gabe also loves Tommy's mother. He'll wait for as long as it takes for her to feel ready to test a new life. One with him in it."

His words were addressed to Tommy, but he was looking at Holly.

Her breathing had ceased. She couldn't move, couldn't think, couldn't respond.

"In the meantime, I know what's really important. My job is important, sure. I *like* being chief of police. But I *love* Tommy, and Tommy's mother. Whenever they need me, I'll be here. I have people in my department who can help me take care of the city, but I'm the one who wants to be here for you."

"Oh, Gabe!" Holly began breathing again in a rush. Her lips trembled so she couldn't say any more.

"So, Tommy," Gabe said, looking at her son, "I want your permission to ask your mom to marry me. When she's ready, of course. Is that okay with you?"

"Will that make you my daddy?" Tommy looked bewildered.

"I won't replace your real daddy, but I'll be your new daddy. If it's okay with you?"

"Cool!" Tommy said and grinned.

Gabe put him down on the floor, then stood and drew Holly into his arms.

"And what about Tommy's mother? I love you, Holly. I'm willing to take a chance on waiting for you, if you're not ready yet. I know it's on the rebound, and you want a new life, and—"

Holly silenced him with a finger on his mouth. She cupped his strong and angular chin in her hand. His skin was rough with shadow and warm. He turned his head and kissed her palm.

"I love you, Gabe." She smiled. "Even if you are a cop. And I'm ready. Believe me, I'm ready."

"Then will you two marry me?" Gabe asked.

"Yeah!" Tommy yelled up at them.

"Yeah," Holly said, and closed her eyes to await the ecstasy of his kiss and their future together.

* * * * *

Look for Linda's
COLORADO CONFIDENTIAL
title in August 2003,
only from Harlequin Intrigue.

Steeple Hill Books is proud to present
a beautiful and contemporary new look
for Love Inspired!

HEARTWARMING INSPIRATIONAL ROMANCE

Love Inspired®

As always, Love Inspired delivers
endearing romances full of hope, faith and love.

Beginning January 2003
look for these titles
and three more each month
at your favorite retail outlet.

Steeple
Hill®

LINEW03

$ Saving Money $ Has Never Been This Easy!

Just fill out and send in this form from any October, November and December 2002 books and we will send you a coupon booklet worth a total savings of $20.00 off future purchases of Harlequin and Silhouette books in 2003.

Yes! It's that easy!

I accept your incredible offer!
Please send me a coupon booklet:

Name (PLEASE PRINT)

Address _____ Apt. #

City _____ State/Prov. _____ Zip/Postal Code

In a typical month, how many Harlequin and Silhouette novels do you read?

❏ 0-2 ❏ 3+

097KJKDNC7   097KJKDNDP

Please send this form to:
In the U.S.: Harlequin Books, P.O. Box 9071, Buffalo, NY 14269-9071
In Canada: Harlequin Books, P.O. Box 609, Fort Erie, Ontario L2A 5X3

Allow 4-6 weeks for delivery. Limit one coupon booklet per household. Must be postmarked no later than January 15, 2003.

HARLEQUIN®
Makes any time special®

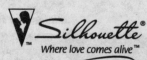
Silhouette®
Where love comes alive™

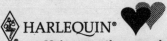